Y0-CAS-465

BARBARIAN SAVIOR

Jarik stared in horror. His blood-smeared sword slipped forgotten from his fingers. Torsy, his un-sister, lay on the sand. She was hurt and bleeding.

He went to her. "Be still," he said. And he began to heal.

"Jarik—"

"Call me not Jarik! I am Oak, the Healer!"

She trembled while his hands traced down her willowy body.

"You—you saved me! You killed them both!"

"No! *He* killed them, the bloody vicious barbarian—Jarik! His second and third human kills! And he enjoyed it! I had nothing to do with it. I am no killer. I heal; I am the healer, Oak."

But he was both, and more . . . and between them they would cling to life with a sword of death.

Ace Science Fiction Books by Andrew J. Offutt

KING DRAGON

War of the Gods on Earth Series

THE IRON LORDS
SHADOWS OUT OF HELL (coming in August)
THE LADY OF THE SNOWMIST

The Cormac mac Art Series

THE MISTS OF DOOM
SIGN OF THE MOONBOW
SWORD OF THE GAEL
THE TOWER OF DEATH
THE UNDYING WIZARD
WHEN DEATH BIRDS FLY

VOLUME ONE OF
WAR OF THE GODS ON EARTH

ANDREW J. OFFUTT

THE IRON LORDS

ACE FANTASY BOOKS
NEW YORK

**to Jodie
until further notice**

THE IRON LORDS

An Ace Fantasy Book / published by arrangement with
the author

PRINTING HISTORY
Jove edition / March 1979
Ace edition / July 1983

All rights reserved.
Copyright © 1979 by Andrew J. Offutt
Illustrations copyright © 1979 by Jove Publications, Inc.
Cover art by Tom Kidd
This book may not be reproduced in whole or in part,
by mimeograph or any other means, without permission.
For information address: Ace Fantasy Books,
200 Madison Avenue, New York, N.Y. 10016

ISBN: 0-441-37363-1

Ace Fantasy Books are published by Charter Communications, Inc.,
200 Madison Avenue, New York, New York 10016.
PRINTED IN THE UNITED STATES OF AMERICA

CONTENTS

There were gods on the earth in those days, and there was strife among them.

It was humankind they fought over, and its future on the earth, and humans fought in that war the gods came to wage among themselves.

First among those warriors of humankind was Chair-ik called Jarik, called too Zhairik and also Iairik; he who was two men and who wielded the black sword of god-metal he had of the Iron Lords.

And this is one of the stories of the war among the gods on the earth, and how Jarik-Who-Was-Two came into it.

The fate of man lies with the gods;
His life's fabric is by their leave.
Let no human misdoubt the odds!
The gods decide; the weavers weave.

The infant pules, and mayhap grows old—
Its life's fabric is by gods' leave.
Changes come, mind and body enfold
The fabric that the weavers weave.

Each hap marks the mind with a scar,
All lead to what he will achieve.
Mayhap each aids; doubtless some mar.
Events befall, while weavers weave.

Chapter One:
Jarik of Oceanside

Beyond the northward bluff the sea glinted in the sunlight so that it was a vast trove of turquoises and sapphires sprinkled with moonstones. In the southward meadowland, the soiled snowballs that moved so slowly and steadily were grazing sheep. Thin-looking and just past the point of ludicrousness since the spring shearing, they pulled at grass as if it would not last out the day. The grass was called sheep-grass. The conscientious herd ram lifted his head to turn tremulous nostrils and pale, pale eyes northward. Nearby a lamb quivered out its throaty cry and butted at the flank of a mother who would no longer interrupt her own feeding to accommodate a toothy three-month-old. The lamb was male; the herd ram made a warning sound. The new looked at the old, and heard the warning, and did not challenge for his time was not yet.

Dogs lazed under a smiling sun that brought twinkles from moving hoes and struck red gold from the brass device on the house of Firstman Stoenik. The tan-splotched dogs ignored the placid snowballs; the sheep ignored the dogs.

Singing filled the air and trembled there, for the people of Tomash-ten sang while they tended their fields; they sang of the crops and of Shrally of the Sun and of Seramik her beloved. The people of the little coastal community were engaged in war, though none thought of it so. Placid as the sheep that gave them clothing and drink and food, they fought the battle against the ancient enemy, weed. Determinedly it invaded, sought esuriently to possess bastions of

9

millet and pulse of three kinds, and leeks and barley and spear-leafed onion.

Derkswife Aquen knelt, tenderly plucking invader shoots from amid her bed of sage and rosemary and scallions. Re-banding a bucket of wood with copper and cord, Derk her man coughed, hawked and spat his phlegm. Farnik Big-ear straightened from his hoeing and stretched. When he arched his broad back in the manner of a dog rousing from its nap, lines of stress shimmered through his dun-hued work smock like wind through tall barley. His bare calves were knotty. So were most everyone's, and dirty.

All this Orrikson Jarik saw. He watched from concealment amid a thicket beneath trees from which foliage hung thick and heavy as a maiden's hair on her wedding day. He looked upon Tomash-ten in its placid sameness, and Jarik sighed. Dull, all dull. Tan-and-pink people with hair ranging from an orangey-tan to brown; dirty-white sheep; houses of stone roofed with tow weighted at the corners by dangling stones and others of wattle and daub; white dogs marked with tan and brown and a little black. Pale earth full of lime and rows of green and yellow-green meadowland. And the sea, sprawling to meet the sky. Jarik sighed.

Jarik was shirking.

Sent with his sister Torsy to the stream in hopes of harvesting fish for supper, he had caught four as fast as he could pull them off the iron hook and throw the line back. Torsy, meanwhile, caught a like number with no more difficulty. The two fishers' eyes shone brighter than the scales of their prodigious catch. Three of the fish were large; eight were enough. Life was incredibly good this day. Bless the Sun Above and the Lords Fog who represented it on the earth!

Orrik's son and Orriksdaughter Torsy had agreed, their heads close and wicked little smiles on their half-formed faces. They would leave the fish in the Trap Place, alive but unable to return among their

10

brethren, and they'd not return into the village. After all, they had done their allotted work. They'd only be put to work at something else. Life was good—so long as everyone retired soon after the sun and rose with it and worked, daily.

Now, in the bosky foliage at forest's edge Torsy and Jarik lay with their heads close together; her hair like overbaked millet cakes and his like new straw; her eyes only slightly darker brown than her hair and his blue as the sky. Both wore fillets of leather; hers was strung with shells. Torsy did like shells. Like two strangers, spies, they watched the others of Tomashten, and they felt deliciously wicked.

Torsy kept pressing close. Jarik kept edging away, trying to be unobtrusive about it. A bit of woevine was pressing uncomfortably into his side.

He watched the maiden Linsy with her hair like new-tanned leather and eyes like old; she was emerging from the women's privy. She returned to the field with her hoe, which was of wood and stone. Jarik noted how for several steps her bone-hued shift clung in the cleft of her backside, which was large. He saw how his stepmother noted Linsy's return, and how she took her large self, heavy with child, to the same little outbuilding.

The wife of Orrik and mother of his children was two years dead; Thanamee was his second wife, and younger, and admired for showing her pregnancy so soon after their wedding.

Jarik looked away. One did not watch women go privy. Especially young boys, and especially one's own mother. Even though she was not his real mother and pronounced his name differently. (His people pronounced the first letter softly, and all their a's were short: Chair-ik, they called him. Orrikswife Thanamee called him "Jairik." He liked the sound of that, and he liked his father's second wife better than Torsy did.)

He watched the slow scritch-scratch hoeing of rheumy Stranik, who was old enough to have seen the father of the lord Baron.

Jarik had never seen the lord Baron, of course. His father had, once. Jarik had heard of that, in detail, five several times. Torsy did like to have Orrik describe that occasion. It made Jarik squirm uncomfortably and wish to be elsewhere during the telling, for he felt that which it should be shame on him to admit: the longing, indeed the envy that was not his meet lot. Not only in the color of his hair and eyes was Jarik different.

Nevertheless he'd had to listen five several times to that story, told glowingly and with pride and some wonder, of How The Baron came to Tomash-ten And Only Two Sevenights After His Accession. The previous baron had died at five-and-thirty, of a disease unknown in Tomash-ten. Jarik and Torsy could not understand how something called syphillis could affect only the distant and lordly, but they were glad.

The name of the seacoastal farming community, in the language of Jarik's people, meant Oceanside. Somewhere far inland was the abode of the King—presumably. Presumably nearer dwelt the lord of the barony of which Tomash-ten, Oceanside, was part. Few of the peasants that were the people of Orrik and his second wife Thanamee had ever seen the baron, and none had set eyes on the distant King. They were obliged to turn over a small tribute each year; this tax was for their protection at the hands of their baron, who paid fealty and a tax to the King, for protection at (from?) his hands.

No one questioned it. It was what they did. It was the Way.

The Way was about to come to an end, in Oceanside.

The people of Tomash-ten did not notice the protection they received, or that which stemmed from the Gods on the Earth they had also never seen: the Fog Lords. The only strife Jarik's people knew

12

emanated from the weather, and occasional beasts and birds of prey. These were enough.

Though they possessed a few fishing boats, most had never seen a ship. Thus Jarik did not know what to call the thing he saw out on the plain of the sea. A winged boat?

It grew steadily larger, he noted. He was fascinated, rather than fearful. He moved a bit, the better to see. Torsy had fallen asleep.

Of enemies Jarik knew nothing. The weather was both best friend and only enemy to his peasantish people. Of sea monsters he had heard nothing for years, since he had ceased to wander down by the water. His mother had frightened him out of that with stories of the monsters that dwelled there. She was gone now, and Jarik was older, past seven, and he had no thought of monsters or danger as he watched the steady growing of the thing on the sea.

It was long and of wood decorated with brass that dully caught the sun. From it sprouted a single great wing, tall and broad and striped in scarlet and orange. Despite that wing, it did not fly. It coasted along over the sea like Pelornik the Fisherman's boat, grown gigantic. Jarik watched it for a long while. It did not fly. It kept growing. After a time, Jarik realized that it had been distant, and was nearing. The boy saw that its high-riding prow bore the head of a bird of some sort. Eyes gleamed.

Two somethings left the ship and came soaring shoreward, black dots moving against the sky.

They grew, nearing, and he saw that they were large black birds from which the sun struck blue highlights. He wondered that he did not see them flap their broad blue-flashing black wings. Nor did they emit any cry, as did birds of the sea. Birds of the sea were white or gray or slate, though, while these were all black, blue-black and shiny as if wet.

Jarik watched them fly past Oceanside, over the woods, and then out over the settlement as though

13

coming from the woods. They were seen, then. Crossing the small expanse above streaking black shadows that seemed to flow over the land, they wheeled short of the meadowland to fly again over the community. People interrupted their work to point and mutter. They called out comments and queries that none could answer. The birds glinted and flashed in the sun. So did other, more familiar black birds, also glossy. Did not ravens gleam in the sun?

Aye, and they flapped their wings, too!

The wingèd boat on the sea was tall and very long. It had reached the sand at the base of the bluff. Torsy napped on. None other had seen the winged boat, save only Jarik. Its prow was carven into the likeness of a hawk's head, with a vicious curved beak and viciously staring eyes: amber, circled by iron. Crimson runes marched along the wingèd boat's side: I S P A R E L A. That was like a combination of the signs for "snow" and "lady," though Jarik's people would have rendered them E S P A R E L L Y.

Orrikson Jarik gazed upon the great wingèd boat called Isparela, though his people did not. They were much taken up with the birds. His people kept no watch. There was no reason. The enemy was the weather, and watching it did not help. Besides, the people of Tomash-ten were distracted by the silent, sun-glinting birds that did not flap their wings.

The huge wingèd boat at the strand disgorged men.

With great interest Jarik saw that they were strange. All their clothing seemed to be of leather or metal! They wore pots of iron or brass on their heads! Their legs were covered! Cloth or leather wrapped them snugly, below short tunics. Some wore iron or bronze on their arms and on the leather covering their chests. Each man carried a thing like a barrel-lid with a gleaming center handle—but Jarik had seen shields and knew that these were round shields of wood made around metal centers called bosses.

Perhaps forty men came off the ship; a few less

14

men than lived here, and perhaps a quarter of the population of Oceanside and its immediate environs.

They carried spears or axes and bore swords and they were coming up from the sea and all Jarik's people were watching the birds while someone exhorted them to return to work and the dogs lazed and the sheep grazed and Jarik wondered if this could be the lord Baron and he recovered somewhat from his fascination so that he was about to leap up and call out to his father when the men from the sea topped the long rise beside the bluff and there was Jennik and one of the men stuck his spear right into him.

Jennik's father screamed and ran at them, brandishing his hoe.

One of the two blue-black birds swooped down from the sky. It slammed into the face of Jennik's father. He fell down and lay still with his face like currant preserves.

The bird leaped back into the sky, and Orrikson Jarik was sure that it did not flap its wings. Rheumy old Stranik struck at it with his hoe, which was one of the four in the community with iron blades. There was a ringing sound and the hoe rebounded! So did the bird, aloft—but it flew on.

The men from the hawk-prowed ship yelled, then, and came running into the field wherein Jarik's people worked. Like flung black spears the birds streaked out over the meadowland.

It had begun. What was to be a wind age, a sword age, a wolf age had come upon the earth.

Never before had terror and true horror appeared in Tomash-ten. The weather was a sweet friend and the animals of the forest timid and gentle, compared to this enemy.

Jarik saw that the yelling men from the sea wore mustaches and beards that were yellow and orangeish and, even though on young faces, sun-white. Their eyes were like his, and he who was different looked upon many like himself, for the first time.

15

They were not as he, though. They were not as anyone. They were armored and armed men from the sea, from the hawk-prowed ship; hawk-men, and their business was pillage and murder.

Jarik saw that the hawk-men had come from the sea to do the inconceivable and incomprehensible: to stab and strike and hack and stomp, to shed blood so that it soaked the soil like red rain; to cleave away stout wooden hoe-handles with their curved axes and long iron swords and to strike men with sword and ax and heavy shield; to ravish women and children. To plunder, to destroy, to burn.

The day was filled with noise and Torsy awoke beside Jarik. Darkness and terror welled in her and she shuddered and gushed forth her breakfast and shuddered. Terror and darkness robbed her of reason and then consciousness so that she lay still again beside Jarik, with her cheek in her vomit.

Jarik lay where he was and stared with eyes that were like marbles. His eyes saw only horror. His ears heard only horror, for amid the shrieks and screams there bubbled and bellowed the laughter of the hawk-men from the sea, and that they laughed as they slew was more horror. The innocent died unprotected by gods or baron or king. The barbarians in their ship with its bird-of-prey prow had come to the land, and they slew, and raped, and burned all that they could not or deigned not carry off. And there was neither king nor baron to protect, and unseen gods slumbered while the weavers wove. And Jarik watched from the bosk with the scent of honeysuckle in his nostrils, mingled with his sister's vomit.

The hawk-men carried off only goods and ale and some animals.

They slew all the people, and the dogs too, and those sheep they did not take were slain by the swooping diving birds.

Nor did they slay for food. Nor was any of the attackers or either bird slain or even sore wounded. The

16

blue-black birds swooped and dived amid screams and they slew along with the men they accompanied. Nor were they slain or hurt, though Derk Alemaker struck one with an iron-bladed hoe before an ax struck into him so hard its wielder had to set a foot against what had been Derk in order to free the big curved blade of blue-grey iron.

Jarik heard them shout out their leader's name again and again; it was *Kiddensok* or *Kiddensahk*. He muttered the word. Kiddensahk. He would remember.

A man fell upon Linnee Anrikswife and sought to use her and she fought so well and viciously that he sliced her open instead. He took his time about mutilating one of Oceanside's most beauteous faces and bosoms.

A white-bearded man with an unlined face and eyes like water in a stone basin sworded open Thanamee's swollen belly so that he took two lives at once.

A man with five big hemispheres of bronze flashing on his tunic of brown leather chopped open the door of the hut into which had fled the wife of Firstman Stoenik and tramped in and soon shrieks and howls came out of the brass-marked house and before the smiling hawk-man emerged smoke, too, was pouring forth.

Orrik struck down the man who was bent on spearing a child and another came at him and Orrik struck with his hoe so that he knocked away the spear-haft. The startled hawk-man snarled and used his spear as a stave to break Orrik's leg and then to brain him. And he stabbed him as well, and Jarik, watching, was still not able to weep or cry out. His body was as if sheathed in ice, though he sweated profusely.

A snarling barking dog—a yearling pup hopefully named Baron—circled and circled so that one hawk-man threw his ax to strike and maim it, and was scratched in retrieving the weapon, which he used to brain the crippled animal. Eight or nine hawk-men used Linsy, who at last left off screaming, and more

17

used Tensy wife of Ramhead, and then both women were butchered for *Kiddensahk* bawled out that they did not want to enrich the blood of these people with theirs, and his butchers laughed.

So Jarik thought he said or rather shouted; he heard them shout and laugh, challenge each other and jest with monstrous callousness, in a language that was like his and that was also different. The hawk-men seemed to have no r's, for one thing, and he heard no sound like the one beginning his own name.

Old Stranik emerged from the grain-barn and ran at Linsy's slayer with the iron-headed scythe Stranik swore was given his father by the baron's father's father. The hawkship-men laughed, attacked by the eldest of Oceanside's citizenry—and the last, to their knowledge. Already flames crackled and smoke rose all about as Stranik swung his scythe. He missed, and fell down with the force of his stroke. A sword clove his skull as a goodwife would use her good long kitchen knife to chop an apple into two pieces. And smoke rose and billowed and flames crackled and blood flowed and flowed and no one screamed the more, and at last Jarik could bear no more.

Sweat-soaked, the boy emerged from his cocoon of ice. A bright light seemed to fill his eyes. That there was nothing he could do other than provide another victim did not occur to him; he had gone mad. He was *morbrin*. He started up to plunge forward through the bushes. He would kill them all.

He was *morbrin*, but he was not ready yet; were he to complete that ridiculous charge, he must surely die. And so his brain protected him: A great thunder sounded in Jarik's ears, seeming to well up and crescendo to sound on and on, and the sun flamed and them went out and Jarik fell down hard, still within the thicket where lay Torsy.

18

"Kiddensahk, monster; butcher, I am Jarik son of Orrik of Oceanside in the barony of Oaktree of the Kingdom, and I am come for vengeance!"

So he cried out, and he saw the thing with the sword. Before him reared a great pocked stone or incredibly massive chunk of iron, just less than half a sphere resting humpbacked on the earth. From its very top, the very outermost uppermost point of its pitted, jagged perimeter, stood a sword. A Sword. It was as if someone—someone tall—had struck into the mighty chunk of stone or iron, sinking the sword's point in, and then left it there. And the sword was black, all black, shining and sleek and smooth, black pommel and hilt and guard and blade shiny as sunlit black water. A black sword, and Jarik looked upon it, and drew it forth, and it was his sword.

"Kiddensahk, butcher, I Jarik am come for vengeance with my terrible sword!"

And Jarik struck into Kiddensahk's sword-arm with his own sword, which was jet black and shining like the wing of a wet raven. "I am Nemesis, come to avenge Orrik of Oceanside in the barony of Oaktree!" And Jarik struck through the brass that covered the chest of Kiddensahk, the sword slicing into the chest of Kiddensahk, who was bearded yellow as the winter sun but whose face was that of a hunting predator; a hawk. "I, Jarik, son of Orrik, true servant of the Lord Baron and the Lords of Fog Themselves; do vengeance for my half-brother, Oak!"

"You have no half-brother or brother either, Baron of Oaktree!" *Kiddensahk* said sneering, and he bled as Stranik had bled and there was a smell of smoke in Jarik's nostrils.

"He was all unborn and died in the belly of my mother Thanamee," Jarik said. "I was glad he was there, growing like a seed in a pod, for I wanted a brother very much. His name would have been Oak. I wanted my brother Oak very much." And Jarik struck

19

off the hand that pointed and the great black sword streaked blood.

"You have no mother Thanamee," *Kiddensahk* told him, jeering even as he bled as Derk had bled, "and no sister Torsy either!"

"My stepmother then, for my true mother was Shalsy who died and I am Orrikson Jarik of the Black Sword!" And Jarik struck away *Kiddensahk's* beard, which bled just as Orrik had bled.

The hawk-man was smiling, laughing, smugly jeering. "Nor have you a mother named Shalsy, nor are you Oddik's son, Baron Jaddik, for you have no mother and no father on this earth, but—"

And Jarik struck off *Kiddensahk's* head to silence him, and Jarik was weeping. For he had been accused of being so different that he must be somebody's bastard, not Orrik's and Shalsy's son, and not to be or to belong was unbearable.

Kiddensahk fell dying, bleeding as Oceanside had bled, and Jarik was a great hero.

Before him stood a weird vision, amid shifting mists; a womanly form, faceless in a mask that matched her garb, which was tight unto the skin and all silvery-sheeny. All in white and silver and grey she was, in her form-fitting armor and the mask that was like frost in the first sun of morning that makes it vanish. Silver was her helm and white were its wings and on each wrist she wore a silver bracer and horripilation made Jarik shiver.

"You are come to slay me, Jarik, poor mystery-man idiot Jarik without parents . . . come to slay *me*, with your reward already in your hand and dripping blood. You cannot slay me, Jarik, poor adopted abandoned exiled brainless people-less *Jarik*. Not *me*! You cannot be suffered even to live! You are less than an ant beneath the world-stamping feet of the gods on the earth, Jarik the ever-Different!"

And Jarik fell down onto his knees before her, so that his knees hurt, and Torsy screamed his name again and again. Yet also she said, "You are not my brother! Father is *dead*! Where is my brother? *Who are you?*"

Jarik did not know. He knew only that he was coughing with the stench of smoke and of blood in his nostrils, and that her voice was very loud, and that his knees hurt, and the odors of blood and death and smoke were overwhelming him, were unbearable. So he awoke.

He was kneeling beside his father. Smoke billowed and Jarik's eyes streamed. The hawk-men were gone. His knees ached and his nostrils stung. His hands were all bloody. The odors of smoke and blood and death were to his nostrils as was a heavy blanket on a warm night. And still Torsy was screaming his name.

Jarik turned his head to look at her.

"I am here," he said. "Be still, Torsy. Stop screaming, Torsy. I am here."

"But you—you—"

Torsy broke off. She stared strangely at him, as though he were strange. It was she who was, though, all huge-eyed and brooding. It was she who was strange. Instinctively or preternaturally, he knew that she would never be the same again, or quite normal. But then neither was Jarik.

He looked about him, without wondering at how he had come here from the woods, and why his knees were sore as if he had held this position long. The bewildered boy looked around. The world was aired with smoke and carpeted with corpses and coagulated blood, brown and gleaming like metal. Oceanside had been destroyed, annihilated, extirpated. (*And Dread; don't forget Dread,* the thought came into his mind, but he did not know why.) He and Torsy alone lived. It was inconceivable and incomprehensible. His mind staggered under a load it could not bear and remain wholly sane.

He looked down.

He knelt over his supine father—who had been *bandaged*!

Yet the man's eyes were wide, and glassy and fixed. He was grey; eerily horribly grey. He was dead. And bandaged. Surely the bandaging—neat, Jarik noticed—had been futile. Besides, who . . . surely not the hawk-men! Surely Orrik had been dead when he fell, or after the sword had struck into him as he lay with the far side of his head caved in.

Jarik looked again about him. Smoke swirled and shivered on the air. He coughed and his eyes streamed. There was no one. No one was there to have bandaged Orrik, save only Torsy. She and Jarik were the only survivors of what had been a community called Oceanside, a community with no enemy and no menace.

Jarik looked at her. She stood staring at nothing. Her eyes were huge and a little glassy, and brooding. She was Torsy, but she was not. She was different. She would never be the same Torsy again, nor wholly normal. But then neither would Jarik.

There was no fathoming the mystery of Orrik's bandaging.

It was a small matter anyhow, amid so much.

Jarik put his hands on Orrik then—and snatched them away. Fire blazed and Jarik was hot and sweaty, with streaming eyes and burning nostrils. He and Torsy must get away from here. Everything was dead or burning. The world was dead and burning. Orrik, though, was cold. Jarik sheathed himself in ice and put both hands on the cold, grey, bandaged face, on Orrik's cold moveless lips.

"I will follow and kill those men. I swear it by the Sun Above and the moon and the gods on the earth. I vow it. I swear it. I will follow and kill those men. Hear the vow of Jarik! I will avenge Orrik, and Thanamee, and him who would have been Oak."

For no reason Jarik knew then, Torsy screamed.

22

Chapter Two:
Orrikson Jarik

Torsy looked back at the smoke of incinerated dreams, the ruins of her shattered life. The calm sea whispered against the boat like the farewells of ghosts. Above, the sun was kind and clouds strung lazily across a sky pale as the blue eyes of an old man.

Torsy accompanied Jarik in his madness because she had to. What else was there to do? He had vowed vengeance. He would have it, and the boy muttered to himself like an oldster in the greyness of his mind's decline while he prepared for a hopeless journey to a destination neither of them could name. The hawk-prowed ship had come from the northeast. Jarik could row. He was strong. He could row. He was strong. He was not yet a man, not yet quite eight years of age much less the twelve of manhood, but now he had to be a man. There was Torsy. Hundreds of wounds in two hundred corpses were red mouths calling out for vengeance. He was Jarik. He was strong and he could row. He would follow the hawk-men to their land, and there, in the names of Orrik and Thanamee, of Stranik and—all the others; in the name of Oceanside, he would slay and slay.

Not all the food of Oceanside had been stolen, or burned. Nor all clothing. Jarik found knives, too, three of them. And Dundrik's big boar spear. It was very heavy, and long for arms not quite eight years old. Jarik put it into the boat. He found cloaks, hooded. Never mind whose they had been. They were the good hooded cloaks of his people, made of the wool of his people's sheep. He put them into the boat.

They were almost ready to go when Torsy reminded him that sea water was not drinkable and that it did not look like rain. Torsy was nearly a year older than he. He was determined to be the man, but Torsy remembered that they must bring water with them. Well, she was a year older.

"Yes, water!" he said. "Water. We must bring lots of water."

And so they brought lots of water, and loaded it too into the fishing boat that had been Othik's; burned with the house from which he'd been unable to save his ravaged wife and bludgeoned child, Othik no longer needed a boat. The boat was about ten feet long, squared at one end and pointed at the other, with two seats and two oars and a deep well for the fish Othik had used to bring forth from the sea. The boat was of stout good wood, covered with leather that Othik had oiled after each excursion asea—along the coast, only. There was even a little house or canopy at the stern end, wicker and oiled leather; Othik had put that there to shade the son he'd used to take out with him. The boy had died last year at five, of the sea-fever, or something. The people of Oceanside had had many babies, and many died. Now all the grownups had died.

Jarik and Torsy entered into the boat and made ready for his great mission of vengeance.

They set forth to sea: two children, one with hair the color of newly tanned leather and eyes like an old belt—and wide, and staring, for Torsy was affected differently from Jarik by what had happened.

He was spurred to action, however silly, irrational; even un-sane. He muttered and he babbled, whether to himself or to Torsy. She was silent. She had retreated far into herself, holed up in the wounds of her mind. After fleeing through all those dark mental corridors to the rearmost one, she seemed to have closed every door behind her. She had spoken once: about the necessity of water. Otherwise she was silent. She had not gone vegetative but rather listless and staring. And, fortunately, malleable. It did not occur to Torsy not to go along with Jarik, though she did know that their putting thus to sea was not sensible, not rational. Perhaps not sane.

Thus they put forth to sea on Jarik's great mission, two children in a rowboat and with no destination. Nor had their people been a seafaring folk.

The sea held them as in an open mouth, ready to swallow them at a gulp. The sun seemed bent on showing them how hot it could be, even north of their land with its several well delineated seasons.

Jarik rowed. He knew nothing else to do, for his people were not a seafaring folk.

He rowed and his hands grew rough and then sore and he rowed. Blisters rose on his hands and he dragged the oars and pushed the oars and dragged them back again and the boat moved asea and one by one the blisters on his hands popped, and he rowed. He moaned and shed tears without weeping, so painful was the salt water in his wounded palms.

Perhaps the brine saved him from infection; he suffered none.

Torsy rowed, too. He told her when it was her turn, and she took it, fighting the oars with frequent splashes. He decided when she should stop, and told her. She stopped. He had rowed much longer than she, and now he would again. He had a mission. Torsy made no comment. Torsy probably did not notice how he favored her. Consumed with his soaring feelings of manhood and his illogical sureness of gaining revenge, Jarik felt very good about himself. His horror and grief were all wrapped up, like a festering wound beneath a yellowing bandage in his brain, in the busy work he had made for them and the purpose he had devised. Nor did he know what brilliant and effective therapy he had devised for himself. The brain of Orrikson Jarik was like few others.

(Indeed, it was like no others at all, but it would be long and long before he knew that, and why.)

Jarik was, however, worried about Torsy.

After all, he was the man.

I am the man. I got to take care of us.

I will!

The gods must have been watching, and smiling, not in maliciousness, on the two children in the small boat on the northward sea. They rowed, they ate, they slept. Neither strong wind nor storm came in the night. A little breeze did rise to caress their sleeping heads. It ruffled their hair like a doting mother. Above those heads stars twinkled like the beaming eyes of a million doting grandparents. No sea monsters came from the sea.

They slept very soundly, for they were exhausted in brain and in body. The gods must have been watching, and smiling their favor. The boat drifted in the current of the sea and in the breeze. It did not matter. The boy did not know where he was going. Northeast; just northeast. His mind was hardly old enough for more specific planning. Had it been, he'd never have left the land, but would have walked inland, with Torsy, hoping to find the manse of the baron for whose protection the people of Tomash-ten had so long paid.

In the morning Jarik awoke and was stiff.

His back hurt and his hands, too, were stiff. In agony and with his face set in determination, he washed his hands over the side of the boat, and then worked them as though it were a religious act, like an archer before the important shot, a warrior before the battle.

Jarik looked about. The world on three sides was a plain of green dotted with patches of white that could have been distant sheep on a meadow of dark grass. It was only the sea. Back there, when he turned and looked, was land. He could just make out some smoke, quivering above the land. He looked away. He had not known that the bluff from Oceanside to sea was whitish. He piddled over the side of the boat and was a little embarrassed to see Torsy awake with her huge-eyed gaze on him.

He dropped his tunic. "We have come far. See how far we have come, Torsy? We are good seamen! Here, time to eat. You're the woman. Fix up something to eat there, woman, while I row."

And irrationally, insanely, in pain of hands and back, he rowed.

Later they saw a fish jump out of the water, and it looked silvery in the sunshine, shedding droplets of sea that also sparkled silver. Jarik remembered his . . . dream?—and the lady in it. The silver lady.

He rowed, thinking.

"Torsy."

He rowed some more, pushing and dragging the big heavy oars, and Torsy continued to stare at the place where the fish had erupted from the water. The blue sky was strewn with streaky clouds like spilled milk. The sea around them was neither turquoise nor sapphire now, but a heavy, dull green. Torsy stared at it.

"Torsy."

She stared on at the sea, and the third time, Jarik shouted.

She turned wide eyes on him. They stared, as if Torsy had gone away and left her eyes behind to pretend that she was alive. Jarik, the heroic vengeance-seeking man, rowed. He was worried about her. He knew he was fine. He was very proud of himself, but Torsy needed to talk.

"Torsy . . . I stood up to run at the men . . . the hawk-men."

She continued staring. Her features did not change. She stared, and it was as if there was a hole back inside her somewhere, and she had crawled into it. Her eyes were light brown agates set into her head, bits of round and polished jasper pretending to be eyes.

"Do you hear me? I watched them and watched them and it was like I couldn't move, Torsy. Then everybody was dead and the . . . the net over me broke. You were asleep. I stood up to run at them and I think I was going to kill them all. That's what I think I thought. All of the hawk-men!"

She stared. Brown agates, round and glittery, with tiny black spots in their centers.

He left off rowing long enough to wave a hand toward her face. Her eyes did not move to follow the gesture. Jarik rowed, and chewed his lower lip, which was rather full. His blond hair stirred like a little pile of thin straws in a gentle breeze.

Orrik's son Jarik, who had never been out in a boat in his entire seven years and nine months, rowed. After awhile his hands began to bleed, and he had to bid Torsy row; the blood made the oars slippery and his hands hurt. He wiped the oars, and she exchanged places with him. She rowed. Catching his lip in his teeth, Jarik closed his eyes and thrust one red-slippery hand into the water.

He could not help it; he cried out. It was surely not what a man would do, he thought miserably, accusing himself. Yet surely he told himself no boy, no mere boy could have been brave enough to thrust his raw and bleeding hand into salt water! *See how brave I am, father? Oak's big brother is a brave men!*

I am strong, he thought, *I'm a man. I have to be. I have to take care of Torsy. I have to be a man. I'll kill them all! After I kill the first one, I'll have a sword or an ax, whichever one he has, and then it will be easier to kill the others.* Kiddensahk, Kiddensahk. *He will be last. I wonder why he called me baron, in my dreams? Was that a dream? Of course it was a dream. I wonder who She was?*

Very carefully he moved to the other side of the seat of his brave pursuit vessel, so that he could stare straight ahead and not look while he prepared himself, took a deep breath, took his lip in between his teeth: all in one movement he shoved his hand straight down into the water, to the wrist. He couldn't

28

help it; he moaned loudly. But this time he did not cry out. He did bite hard into his lip. Torsy rowed.

Kiddensahk, he thought. *Kiddensahk of Isparela. I come, sea monster Kiddensahk!*

"It was," he began, and stopped when he heard his voice quiver.

He took his hand out of the water. Neither hand was bleeding. They felt as if a million ants were walking on them, with hot feet. Careful to touch nothing, he kept the palms down, away from the sun. Torsy needed to be talked to, he thought, because he needed to talk.

"Standing up to run at them would have been stupid," he said. "They would háve killed me too. Someth–something happened. I fell down, and I slept, and dreamed, and then I woke up and I was kneeling beside . . . beside father. And he was bandaged. And you were yelling at me, and I heard you say that I wasn't your brother and I don't think that was in the dream I had was it? But what I want to know is how did I get there, out of the woods and all, and who put the bandage on father? It looked good, that bandaging job. I've watched bandaging, but I don't remember all that much and I'm not neat anyhow. Mother said so. She used to tell me you're not neat, Jarik. You said so too and even Thanamee said so and so I'm not neat, Torsy, and what I want to know is who bandaged father and why won't you TALK TO MEE?"

His voice broke, and he teethed his lower lip again. It had a swollen place from where he'd bitten it when he pushed his hand into the water. He licked the smooth lump, traced it with his tongue. He kept fooling with it while he stared at Torsy and Torsy kept on staring at nothing. She rowed as if she didn't know she was doing it.

If she'd just talk, Jarik thought, *I could worry about her a little and not have time to worry about me.*

29

Being brave and a man is very very hard when you're all by yourself.

He remembered that he'd been whiter than anyone else, or pinker rather, and not as big either. They had called him puny, some of them. *Jarik's puny,* that's what they'd said. He had learned not to fight because when he did he got beat up.

His hands hurt.

Jarik made wrappings for his hands, sort of mittens, or bandages—they were not neat—and he knotted them with his teeth rather than ask Torsy to help. He hated it that his hands wouldn't take it, couldn't take it and do what he wanted them to do.

"I'll go crazy if you keep on not talking to me," he said to the girl he thought was his sister, and he rowed. Push and pull, push and drag and push. . . .

Torsy continued to stare and not to talk to him.

In rowing a boat one faced where one had come from and had one's back to where one was going. Past Torsy, Jarik saw at last that the land had disappeared. He couldn't see Oceanside's bluff any more. He was afraid to look behind him. It was good that the land had disappeared, though because now land would be showing behind him, pretty soon.

How wide was the sea, anyhow?

That afternoon Torsy began to weep and she cried for over an hour. Since the boat seemed to be drifting the way he wanted to go, Jarik left off dragging and shoving the oars. His back was on fire and his hands were wounds that he wished belonged to someone else. He wished he'd thought to bring winter gloves. Now he knew why Othik's hands had been like leather, hard old unoiled leather. He was the man, though, and he had not let Torsy row very much. Her hands were all right. Now he bade her row, hoping it would help her stop weeping. She took the oars and rowed, while tears and snot came out of her eyes and nose. The sea was made of blue-green glass.

Night came. It was cool, and it occurred to Jarik that rowing at night would be a very good idea. He was still thinking about that and what a good decision it was when he fell asleep.

There was no land on the third day when he awoke, and no birds. The only sound was the little *slp slp* of the water against the boat. There were only sea and sky. The world was sea and sky, green and blue and white.

It was awful. Jarik hated it. His was not a seafaring people, and he couldn't understand why any would be. Distance might be a mile or ten (or fifty, or more, he was later to learn). There was nothing to measure against. He knew where *he* was; he was here. Any place that was not here was there.

But where was *there?*

There was no there. Just deeply green sea and pale blue sky strewn carelessly with white. And silent Torsy with huge eyes. She drank a lot of water. She had cried a lot yesterday, and lost a lot of mucus, too.

Jarik rowed.

He tried singing. His voice sounded tiny, and Torsy didn't join in. He stopped singing. He turned around, with trepidation. It was justified; there was nothing there. There was no *there.* He was rowing toward nothing. He continued.

That afternoon Torsy drank the last of the water and Jarik got mad and railed at her and slapped her and almost fell out of the boat. She cried for a long time.

When she spoke, he jerked as if he had been slapped. His heart leaped and began racing. It seemed years since she'd spoken, since he'd heard any voice other than his own.

She said, "That was stupid."

Chapter Three:
There is no There

Wide blue eyes stared into Torsy's large brown ones.

"What? What?"

"I said that was stupid, Chair-ik. They would have killed you too."

"What. Who—what was stupid?"

"Jumping to run at them, silly. You just said it! There were a lot of them, with axes and those long knives and things. They would have killed you."

"I SAID THAT TWO DAYS AGO!"

"I can hear you, Chair-ik. Don't yell." She looked around. "I'm worried about you, Chair-ik."

Jarik was unable to say anything. So he told her the name of the long knives the hawk-men had. "Those were swords. I will have one, Torsy. I shall have a big black one."

Now why did I say that? Who ever heard of a black sword?

"I don't like this much," Torsy said, looking around. "I'm glad we're together. This is spooky. Just . . . water. Not even any birds. It doesn't even look like water. When I woke up, you were putting bandages on father."

Again he had to assimilate and reorient; it was like running to catch up.

"*I* was b— that's silly! Tell me the truth." He forgot to keep rowing. The boat drifted and ghosts whispered along the sides in watery voices.

"You were kneeling over him," Torsy said, looking at him now, "and you were muttering and you were bandaging him, Chair-ik. I came—came out, and

33

talked to you, and you didn't say anything and so I looked around and started crying. You were crying too." Seeing the change in his face, in his eyes, she said, "Maybe it was all the smoke. You know I love you, Chair-ik? I couldn't see very well because of all the smoke, really. I asked you where mother was and you said I was not to look. You sounded all strong and stern and, and *old*, and so I didn't look for mother. Thanamee, I mean. So I asked you what you thought you were doing and you said you knew what you were doing, that you were bandaging father's wound, couldn't I see? And you said that he was . . . was . . . was de-eadd . . . and you could see clearly which wound k-ki—which wound did that, but you thought it wasn't right that he lie there without a bandage with his blood coming out. I said it didn't matter, Chair-ik; *'It doesn't matter, Jarik,'* I said, and 'What are we going to *Do*?' And then you looked up at me real mean and your eyes were all ugly and you said your name wasn't Chair-ik."

You're crazy, he thought, but he didn't say it.

One time Baverinik had gone crazy, that's what they said, he'd gone crazy, and he said crazy things. Torsy was saying crazy things, now. Everything that had happened must have driven her crazy. He remembered how his father had said once, that time the hailstorm came after the drought, that such things were enough to drive a man crazy. Torsy must be crazy. It was a good thing she had a strong brave man to take care of her.

Poor Torsy.

"Jarik *is* my name."

"I know. But *then* you said it wasn't, see? I thought you were . . . were . . . I thought you'd gone crazy."

Jarik laughed aloud. *He!*

"So I thought about that," Torsy said, "and cried, and you went on putting the bandage on him, better than I ever saw anyone do it and after a long time I asked you who were you, then."

Jarik remembered the oars in his hands. He pushed and pulled. "Did I answer?"

"Yes. You called me a fool and a weak little silly crazy, and you said your name was *Oak*. And I was *scared*, Chair-ik!"

"How could I have said that? I was having a dream. I don't remember that."

"You said it, Jarik."

He didn't reply.

"Do you remember putting that bandage on father?"

He pulled the oars very hard and one of them flipped and came up out of the water and he banged back and hurt his back and his elbow. "No!"

Torsy said, "See?"

And then Torsy said, "Did you hurt yourself? Do you want me to row, Chair-ik?"

All boys knew about non sequiturs, but they were accustomed to hearing them from parents, not sisters who were eight months older. Jarik looked at his sister for a long while, but he couldn't think of anything to say. He rowed. Then he remembered to look back over his shoulder. There still wasn't any there.

"There isn't any there," Orrikson Jarik said.

"What?"

"There isn't anything back there but sea."

"I know," Orriksdaughter Torsy said. "I can see that."

"There isn't anything to see."

"I mean I can't see it. Anything but the sea, I mean."

"We have to get someplace. We don't have any more water."

She waved her hand in a world-encompassing gesture. "There isn't anything *but* water!"

"We can't drink this water, Torsy."

"What happened to ours, then?" She shook a leather container. It didn't slosh.

Jarik looked at her a long while, considering. Then the big brave strong man said, "We drank it all."

"We should have brought more."

"I guess so."

"Oak was what they were going to call our new brother, if it was a boy."

"I know."

"Well, you said your name was Oak."

"So you yelled at me because you were scared."

"I was *scared*, Chair-ik!"

He gave her a superior look and couldn't think of anything to say, so he said, "You haven't said anything for two whole days, Torsy. More than two days." He glanced over. The sun was very low and long thick ropes of yellow and pink and a reddish sort of blue were dragging across the sky after the sun. "Almost three days."

"I guess it was because of what happened."

He rowed, nodding. After a time he said, "I guess that's why I was putting the bandage on father, and told you I was Oak. Because of what happened."

"Chair-ik . . . do you think we're crazy?"

"I'd like for you to call me Jarik, like Thanamee. Say it the way she did: Jair-ik. That's my name. Yes."

"Yes?"

"Yes, I think we're both crazy. Or were. I don't think we're crazy any more Torsy."

She thought about that. "Do you feel crazy, Ch–Jarik?" Torsy called him Jarik ever after, as Thanamee had done.

"No. Do you?"

"No."

"Then we're both cured. We're all better now. We were both a little crazy and now we're not."

"I'm glad we're not crazy! I remember Baverinik."

"Me too. I remember Baverinik too."

"He never did get hale."

"Well. We're all hale now, Torsy. We aren't crazy any more."

Inside them, unbandaged and unhealed wounds festered. The time was yet to come when they'd be old enough to know that they could never be hale, not what other people called hale, not after what had happened.

"How . . . how long can we live without water, Jarik?"

"I don't know. We have to get there soon, though."

"Your hands are bleeding."

He looked. The rag-wrappings were reddened. "Just a little," he said.

"I'll row a while."

"Fix us something to eat. Not the salt meat, though."

"Oh, Jarik! That's very smart. I wouldn't have thought of that."

Jarik sat up straighter, and rowed.

By the next morning, though, he felt very strange and wanted a drink very badly and he knew that he was dying.

He rowed hard, and toward noon Torsy let out a shout and pointed, almost getting up so that the boat rocked violently. He looked, not over his shoulder but northish of their course.

There was a there. It was not land, though, and after a time he knew what it was.

"We have to get away," he said, and began a fiery-bodied, heavy-armed attempt at bumbling the boat around.

"*Jarik!* What is it?"

"That's the wing on a big boat. A boat big enough to carry forty men and all the things they steal from the people they murder. That green thing is the big wing that stands up above their boat. Do you see any black spots coming this way, in the sky? Birds?"

"It's not green," she said, "it's blue and yellow striped. It's pretty."

He looked. The stripes had become visible, that

37

fast. The big winged boat was coming after them, and swiftly. He fought the oars.

"Torsy. Those are hawk-men. When they're closer you'll see the big bird's head on the front of the boat. It's a hawk. They're the hawk-men, Torsy! They kill! They'll *kill* us, Torsy!"

"Maybe they don't see us."

The ship was bigger, meaning closer. The vertical wing looked all swollen.

"They see us. They're coming after us!"

Jarik fought oars and boat and sea in desperation. Naturally enough he accomplished less than he had previously, despite the fact that he was now provided some impetus by the breeze that blew the hawk-ship rapidly toward them.

Yes, it was a hawk-prowed ship.

Yes, it was coming after the boat. In a grievously short time for the fearful children, they were overtaken. Even so the larger craft was not so maneuverable as the small, and as Jarik and Torsy did not want to be taken or to board the hawkship, the matter was not easy. The men who gazed down at them with such surprise on their fair-bearded faces could not understand the younglings' obvious fear and desire to flee.

"Ho there, lad!" The man who called, peering over the bulwark of his hawk-headed craft, was hatless and his lightly blowing hair matched the sawdust color of his beard; he seemed to have no brows at all above blue eyes so pale they might as well have been called grey. "Grab an oar and pull yourself against us. Or hold up one of yours."

"No! No! Go away! We don't have anything worth stealing!"

"*Stealing!* Lad, we're not *thieves* . . . you'll die out here!"

"Odd accent," another man was saying, squinting down at Jarik and the darker-haired girl with him.

"Them clouds over there mean a nasty squall by

38

sunset," sawdust-beard was saying on. "You'll be in the sea afore Shralla dismounts, and dead soon after—d'you understand me, lad? *Dead!*"

"We want no help from you, hawk-man! I'd sooner die in the sea than by your sword!" Jarik raved, made the more fearful by the gold-bearded man's odd accent.

"I don't even *have* a sword!" called back the man, whose language was Jarik's and yet appeared to have no r's. He turned his big sawdust beard to his companions. "Delirious. Just a temporary craziness. The sun—and probably no water. We'll have to fetch them on board and likely get kicked into the bargain."

"Leave 'em there then, I say!"

The man with the sawdust-hued beard glared. "You'll not sail with me again, Slore."

"I'll go in after 'em," another man offered. He was youthful, slim and, like all his companions, tall.

Sawdust-hair shook his shaggy head. "Likely the boy'd hit you with an oar, Strode. The lad's just dafty right now. He'll be hale enough anon, once we've got him aboard." He clapped a big freckled hand to his face. "Pox and hailstones! How to rescue a boy what don't want to be rescued!"

"Barish—mayhap we—"

"Hush; let me think."

By genius and maneuvering, the hawkship captain accomplished the mission he had set himself. The process scared Jarik and Torsy the more; their determined rescuer contrived to get his ship about and close again, after which he ordered portside oars up and out; no, over there a bit, aft-ward; that's better, better. . . farther aftward. . . down! Easy now, don't want to hit—ah!

And two enormous oars neatly caged the little fishing boat that had been Othik's of Tomash-ten.

The boy was panickally dithering as to whether to wield knife or the big boar-spear, a sapling to which was securely bound a broad iron blade like a broad

39

leaf. He actually had a knife in his bandaged hand, then dropped it in favor of the spear—while the slim young man went knees-and-hands down on an oar. His hair was enough like Jarik's so that he might have been an older brother.

Torsy screamed when his strangely-shod feet struck clumping into the fishing boat, and she screamed again when the powerful young man caught her swiftly up in his arms. Being tossed up into waiting hands the size of small hams took her breath so that she went soundlessly, swallowing a third scream.

"Here now, m'girl," a big friendly voice said from a big friendly face with enough old-yellow beard for two men, and that huge man hugged her up. "I've a grand-daughter nigh your age, I'd wager, 'cept her hair's more brass than pretty old copper like yours! She'd be wanting a hug and a good cup of ale about now, with may be some honey in it."

What Torsy heard: "Heeh now, m'gehl. I've a grand-daughter (-word?-) your age, I'd wajah, 'cept huh haihd's mwa bdass than pdetty old cuppah like youahs! She'd be wawnting a hug and a goo' cuppa ale abut now, with may be some honey in 't."

Torsy was torn between fear and the desire to squirm and the enormous comfort in his enormous arms against an enormous chest that radiated warmth like a sleeping sheep in winter. "You talk funny," she said, and then she said "Ale?" for she'd been allowed only water and milk, and then, "JARIK!"

Jarik was taking care of himself, barely usable hands or no.

Despite the hands and his weariness and weakness, he managed to swing the haft of the mighty boar-spear hard enough to catch Torsy's rescuer in the side. The slim young man went overboard. As soon as he came up, spluttering, laughter burst from his fellows.

"Strode the Weaponer's found his match!" someone yelled, and the laughter rose to a new crescendo.

And Jarik remembered how the hawk-men had laughed while they slew his people, and he let go the unwieldy spear to catch up a knife. His sore and bandaged hand wouldn't hold it properly, but he tried. Panic and the supposed need for defense boiled in him like a pan on the cook-stove in the dryness of cold winter. The captain still held Torsy, fondly; his companions gazed down at the boy in the boat, and the floundering Strode.

"Ah piddle," a man with cloudlike hair said, and leather leggings, gaitered buskins and all, he jumped into the sea. Water splashed high and Jarik's little boat rocked violently.

With the newcomer on one side of the boat and the slim young one on the other, Jarik was hard put to defend his unstable keep. When the second man put a hand on the boat's side, Jarik stabbed at it. The man only just avoided being impaled through the hand—and Jarik lost his grip on the knife. It went into the sea.

"Ah piddle," that one said again, and slapped his hand back onto the boat. He rocked it hard toward him, and then thrust it back, as hard. Jarik was catapulted flailing into the arms of the young rangy man called Strode.

With him flailing, scratching, biting all the way, the pale-haired, pale-eyed man got him aboard their ship.

The huge man in whose arms Torsy nestled was the first to speak. "We're no thieves and all your goods are yours as soon's we get 'em aboard, lad, and you need water, and we don't kill people nor eat 'em neither, and you're not too big to spank. Now my name's Barrenserk Bearpaw, and that's Kilwarkson Strode who tossed up your girl here and brought you up too, and we've saved you because we love boys and girls. See there—she's a happy girl with a bit of honeyed ale, and I'll wager you'll not dislike the same. And smoked salmon, too. Hail and pox, boy, I never saw a

41

youngling so in need of a hug and a lot of sleep in all my days!"

Jarik's eyes were large and uncomprehending and his face worked. He gazed and gazed at the big grandfatherly man with the yellow hair and the huge hands and the name without r's: Baddensehk Beahpaw.

Then Jarik embarrassed himself: he collapsed and began weeping.

He cried for a long time, great rending sobs jerking out of his twitching frame all surrounded by men tall as trees; and he resisted only briefly when Barrenserk Bearpaw came to enfold him in a pair of arms big as treestumps and twice as strong.

"Your werk gone to the bottom and all your folk gone with her, is it?" Barrenserk murmured, holding the boy and rocking him. "And you and your fellow lambling the only survivors and all alone! Been being the man, haven't you, taking care of you both and rowing with hands about to come off. Barrenserk Bearpaw's lived a long time, m'lad, and I understand, oh I understand. There boy, there there, let it out, let it all out of you and none aboard this werk will ever ever twit ye for't." The big man looked up. "Home lads, home with these poor dears of lamblings. They can tell us who they are later when they're warm and feel a woman's hands on 'em."

"That's the bravest boy I ever saw," rangy young Strode said, gazing at the boy who'd gone so tiny in Barrensark's arms. "He'da fought us all, Barish!" He rubbed his side and above a ruefully smiling mouth a skimpy mustache twitched; it was nigh white. "Caught me a good one with that boar-spear, too!"

Jarik heard, and he remembered the words, but no matter how brave he was and how much he wanted to, he could not stop his gulping sobbing just then. Nor did he know that his huge comforter was gazing at Strode Kilwarken's son. Four years married Strode was, and nary a youngling to show for it.

"Your Mejye'll be glad to see him, I'll wager," Barrenserk said thoughtfully, quietly.

Thus was Jarik rescued, and soon after adopted, by others of the same land of those who had orphaned him, and his mind staggered in anguish. Nor was it the last of the anomalies that were worked into the twisted, knotted threads of his life. And the weavers wove.

Chapter Four:
Strodeson Jarik

Their land was Lokusta and they were the Lokustans.
They had not yet begun to swarm like locusts; not yet
were the hawkers everywhere dreaded; the raid on
distant Oceanside had been the first. Barrensark Bearpaw and his people knew nothing of it.

Lokusta was a northward land, ringed by cold
waters that extruded mountains with hoary heads.
The short agricultural season was more than pleasant
enough; the winters were an annual attack by a
nature gone all inimical and hateful only to emerge
guiltily blushing and demure in spring. Flowers of
summer were abloom when Torsy and Jarik came
there, sailing up a deep-cleft inlet right into the land
like a sea-filled ravine.

There was no king over Lokusta.

How was that possible? Well! We are all free men
here, under the God on the Earth.

There were no barons in Lokusta. But. . . . Ah, no
buts; we are free men here, under the God who lives
on the mountain called Cloudpeak.

Each *wark*—community; territory—was autonomous.
Nor did they always forego raiding one upon the
other, for exogamy was good for the race and a man
was born to arms, surely; else why was he given bravery and strength and the joy of battle?

The land of Barrenserk and Strode was called Ishparshule-wark, and it lay on the far fringe of Lokusta,
across the impassable mountains so that these people
were *almost* not Lokustans. They were different. They
said so, and felt so. They were the same people,
truly—but, separated, these did not engage in hawk-

raids. So they said. Chief over Ishparshule-wark was Ishparshule Rednose, who was called First Man and who was not bowed to. Wark—which they pronounced "wahk"—was the same as the word for ship: werk ("wehk"); it was merely that over the years the pronunciation had changed to accommodate the two different meanings. Thus were some words born. The language was at once that of Oceanside, and different. The tongues were as two children who left the parent and dwelt long apart, and changed.

Here the letter *j* was so soft as to be a form of *i* or *y*, and the *r* was not said as Torsy and Jarik said it, but was at times a sort of *d* and at times an *h*, or nearly. Jarik wasn't just Jaddik here; he was more Iairik or Yaddik, and when he insisted on the *j* sound he became Chaddik. Torsy was "Tahsy," which was almost "Tossy," but not quite. Here Orrik would have been Oddik. Many words were different, too, and expressions, and slang and colloquialisms. Shrally of the sun-chariot was Shralla, and *that r* was almost pronounced.

Such matters did not long confuse a pair of eight-year-olds. They spoke daily more as Lokustans than as . . . well, Jarik had never known the name of the whole land of which the barony of Oaktrees was a part, and none in Ishparshule had been there. To Jarik and his fellow land-grubbing peasants, a broader name had not been important.

Here the name of the whole land was important, though there was no king to unify it. Anomalies.

"Youah a Lokustan, Jaddik boy, and don't you fahget it!"

And so he appeared to be. The skin of these people was fair, as was Jarik's. The eyes of these people were blue, as his were; some were almost grey in their paleness, but still the blue was present. The hair of these people was fair, like his; some few were bright yellow unto the jonquil. Others were white or nearly,

45

white as sheep's wool at least; and some were like brass.

Torsy's hair was not all that different; her eyes were.

What color was Orrik's hair?

Brown; very old copper.

And his eyes?

About the same.

And his wife—that is, his first wife?

Hair lighter, Jarik recalled and replied; eyes about the same as Orrik's, though Jarik remembered gold flecks, or something like.

There then, y'see boy? Torsy's theirs. You are not. You were a foundling, that's obvious; one of ours. Floated to their shore after a shipwreck, no doubt. Doesn't *jair* mean reward? And *ik* must come from *yik*, the shore! Y'see? They found you there and named you accordingly; Reward of the Shore, or That Found on the Shore.

No no, all the men of Tomash-ten had names ending in *ik*; it was the Way.

Ah and ah, what dull people—and Jarik raged and afterward sulked darkly, for he had never been certain that he belonged in Tomash-ten, and here he did not want to belong. Despite the kindness of Barrenserk, the cloying kindness of his wife and the kindness too of young Strode, this land of Lokusta spawned murderers. *I could not be of these people? I will not!*

Nevertheless, the Three decided and Ishparshule Rednose proclaimed it: Jarik was of The People of the founder, Lok; Jarik could be adopted and would instantly be known as Lokustan and woe onto him who said elsewise.

Torsy was not, and could not be, saving only through marriage. Torsy must be servant; she'd not be enslaved, as she had come here with Jarik and had not been taken in honest raiding. And Jarik raged. He would fight! They would run away, he said! Then Barrenserk took them to his home, Jarik and Torsy, and it was builded of wood and hung and carpeted with the furry hides of bears and wolves and the yellow fleece of sheep and even a wild mountain goat, and a soapstone lamp burned with the oil of some sea monster that fountained water. There Jarik and Torsy met their rescuer's fat wife who was benign and beaming and solicitous to a fault, and his grown sons and daughter, too, with two children among them, for Barrenserk and Kilye had wed at not-quite-thirteen and were not yet forty, but were grandparents twice over.

Barrenserk and his Kilye would take Torsy in as servant, for there was much room with their children grown and steading on their own. Jarik's face went dark at that and his fists clenched into knobby little balls, for all the tender pinkness of their new palms.

—but Torsy would be raised, he was hurriedly assured, as daughter or grand-daughter.

"Look ye here, Jarik, hailstones and pox on your clamoring, you're not too big to spank! What's a child? What's a son or daughter? A servant, soon's it's old enough to help its parents. You think you'll idle about as guest, with Strode and Mejye? 'Course not! Besides. . ." Barrenserk paused to grin fondly at Torsy, and Jarik noted that. "Besides, Strode and Mejye are very young and without experience with children—we've had six and raised three, remember— and you my lad are a fox with a knot in his tail! Haw haw, Torsy'll be like having it better than you, you'll see Jarik old Jarik with your knotty fists, you'll see and not shut up and help us get rid of some of this nutcake and milk."

And Torsy said little, as ever she said little, but watched big-eyed and ever was malleable and seemingly complacent.

Jarik became Strodeson Jarik, Lokustan.

Torsy remained Torsy, and lived, unadopted, with Barrenserk and Kilye, which meant Spring Flower. Servant or daughter; son or servant; where was the difference? Both had to go to school two mornings weekly with other children; both had duties and chores; both were subject to correction and punishment and rules. Freedom was not for those ungifted with reason, whether offsprung or adopted or servanted.

Jarik heard remarks about his size—for he was the smallest boy in his classes and two girls his age were taller and larger of bone—and he fought, and was beaten. Jarik heard remarks about his sister, the strangeling, and he fought, and was beaten. Nor did his new father, himself so young and rangy and weapons-fascinated, try to point out to him the uselessness of bravery without strength to back it. Jarik learned. Jarik heard remarks about his size, his height, his parentage, his pronunciation, his stupidity, his foreignness, his un-belonging-ness. And he suffered black eyes and twisted arms and bloody noses and cut lips and once even a sprained left wrist (Isparsek was punished a *lot* for that).

And he learned to take it, to keep it pent within, to rage silently, and he knew that he did not belong and strove to be invisible and to please. Within the smoke-and pain-darkened corridors of his mind he scarred, and festered.

He was one of them and yet he was not.

Nor did he want to be one of them. These were the people who had killed his parents! Never mind from what wark those others had sailed. They were Lokustans, descendants of the father Lok. Lokustans were hawkship men; Hawk-men. Why, even to set to sea was to "go a-hawking" in the big hawk-prowed ships with their tall striped sails. Jarik had no desire to be a hawk. Indeed, he wanted to be a wolf. And he did most of his suffering in silence. He would not bear tales against those who teased and hurt, even though he had to go indoors among adults to escape them.

When he was assured that he and Torsy were not

siblings, and the words suggested immorality, he fought.

His total rage and all-out fighting on that occasion shocked all who saw and later those who heard. It brought him stern punishment—and much impressed these people who were so different from his own, with weapons hanging on the walls of every home. In his attack on the other boy and on his teacher—whom he knocked down, an astonished man an inch above six feet—Jarik was as if mindless in rage, vicious, ruthless, without morals or rules.

He was punished sternly, aye. Yet the folk of Ish-parshule-wark respected what he had done, and the way he had acted: outside himself, a machine-that-fights: *morbrin*. It was the way of the wolf. The wolf was respected, for he minded his own business and tended his family and survived on his own, and no wolf had ever been known to attack a human other than in self-defense.

Jarik's father Strode was not so huge as many others in Ishparshule-wark, and so was fascinated with weapon-*skill*.

Jarik's training began soon after, with weapons. . . along with feeding the pigs and cleaning up after sheep and carrying wood for cook-fires—and for heat, over half the year—and seeing to his lessons. He was in his ninth year when his weapons training began, and shorter by inches then his fellows, and more rangily built. Indeed, the woman that Hardhead brought in from another wark thought that Jarik was the son of Strode and Mejye by blood-birth.

He and Torsy had made agreement between them: they would not tell all that had happened to them, nor of Kiddensahk. As time passed, though, Jarik did ask certain questions; he was no longer the newcomer seeking information for questionable purpose.

No, no one knew of a hawkship named *Isparela*: "Snow-lady." It was a natural enough name for a Lok-ustan hawker. Must be called after the god Herself.

For here, astonishingly, the Fog Lords were unknown! Here was the God on the Earth named the Lady of the Snowmist, and she was a woman.

"And you have *seen* her?"

"Father and mother have."

"A *God* on the *Earth?*"

"Aye. People where you come from never saw her, Jarik?"

"No. And it was not a she. *My* people had more than *one* God on the Earth. The Lords of Fog."

"Hmp. But they never saw them?"

"No. The gods stayed. . . at their place, and did . . . what gods do. You know."

"Not I! None knows what gods do, Jarik!"

"They made us, didn't they?"

"They made Lok, and his wife, and Shralla and Serames and even Bodmor. Since then—" A loose gesture. "The gods don't seem to work as hard as we, do they?"

Jarik shook his head, smiling a little—and glancing about. To talk of the Gods! How strange! How . . . deliciously wicked! The Gods were not to be talked of, in Tomash-ten that was no more. But then everything was lighter here: freer. The Way was different, and it was looser. It was odd, because this weather was hardly so friendly. These people were just *different*. Freer, less rule-bound and more friendly—and yet combative. Imagine weapons training in Tomash-ten! Never! Inconceivable!

"Anyhow, you don't know if these Lords of Fog— brr! Who likes *fog?*"

"It's the same as mist, isn't it?" Jarik pointed out, ever defensive. "Just without the snow? Snow mist sounds mighty cold to me. Who likes snow?"

"Huh! What would you expect, in Lokusta—the Lady of the Asphodels?"

"May be all gods are the same. Or one, or just a few; the same with different names."

"No no. We know different, Jarish. And not just because of what the Three tell us, either." -

"Those old women," Jarik said, but he had lowered his voice and again he glanced around. So the Three were, old women; they were to be spoken of and treated, though, only with respect; they spoke for the god.

"There are the Iron Lords. We know about them. They are Gods on the Earth too. They rule in Lokusta, too—and out to sea as well."

"With the Lady of the Snowmist?"

"No no, in different parts. *We* know about the Iron Lords, Jarish. They are not the same as the Lady of the Snowmist, oh no."

Jarik said nothing. He saw no reason to admit he had not known there were so many gods.

"What I was going to say though, Jarik . . . you don't know if your Lords of Fog are hes or shes or its, if none of your people ever saw them." Hair the color of barley-straw fluttered atop a shaking head.

Jarik considered, and shrugged. "It didn't matter to us. It still doesn't. But . . . to *see* a God on the Earth . . . what does she look like, Bounder?"

"Who knows? I haven't seen her. Besides, she wears a mask."

"A mask? The god?"

"All gods wear masks, Jarik! Everyone knows that!"

"Oh. . . yes. But is hers white like the snow, or . . . what have you been *told* she looks like?"

And Bounder started to tell him . . . and Jarik's eyes widened as he heard. . . and he interrupted.

"And she has wings on her helmet," he blurted; white wings!"

Bounder looked at him. "But . . . how did you know?"

Jarik could only stare, and then tell the other boy that he had to go and be at weapons practice with Strode. He did not. He did have to be alone, and to ponder.

The day in Oceanside, when *it happened*, and when he had started up and fallen down unconscious: he had dreamed. He had seen the Lady of the Snowmist in that dream, though he had never seen or heard of her! How was that possible? *Was* he of Lokusta, perhaps even Ishparshule-wark? Had he remembered, back in his head somewhere, without remembering? Or . . . perhaps he had not, but she had come to him in the dream, because he was hers; because, again, blight on the thought: because he was of Lokusta? Had she made him fall down unconscious—and Torsy too, he remembered, wondering—in order to save him? Had it been she, this God on the Earth who reigned over—part of!—Lokusta, who had sent forth the ship of Barrenserk so that he and Torsy were rescued hours from death either from no water or from drinking the undrinkable?

Jarik did not know.

"Lady of the Snowmist! Am I your servant? It is Jarik who speaks—Jarik who begs an answer. Who am I? What am I to do? Where do I belong? Am I to serve you? Am I ever to have—" he broke off, and glanced around. But he was out behind his home, Strode's small cozy home with well-chinked logs, and just behind the oblong little building that was Strode's one-holer . . . that had to be cleaned out in the spring. No one was around. He was alone.

Alone.

"Am I ever to have my vengeance?" he asked, more quietly. He looked all around, scanning sky and earth; mountains and buildings, wondering where dwelt the Lady of the Snowmist. . . and the Iron Lords. . . and the Fog Lords. . . . "Who am I? Who is Jarik? *Why was I sent that dream?* Did you send it, my Lady Snowmist? Where. . . *where does Jarik belong?*"

Chapter Five:
Jarik Elk-slayer

Torsy abode, and fared well though silent. She continued strange and was not good at her lessons. She was loved by her "grandparents," and she loved them as well, though she strove ever to cleave to Jarik.

She grew little, and yet was taller than her brother. Because they did not have to live together, they were friends rather than as siblings. Strangeling Torsy, who made others nervous. A good, silent, dutiful young-ling, far more alone than Strodeson Jarik who had been Orrikson Jarik (or had he?). But the story concerns her but little, for she had had no dream, and had "seen" no god ere she beheld one, and had no great soaring imagination complete with intelligence as had her brother (or was he?); nor was she to meet and serve the Iron Lords, and the Lady of the Snowmist, or look upon Osyr or meet and become as one with Jilain of the Isle; nor would Torsy be the One who was Two and then the Three who were One.

Jarik, who was to do and be these things, grew in intelligence and in knowledge. He improved too in the use of weapons—a natural, Strode said, and so too did others.

The Strodeson was not happy, though, for among children there was no premium on intelligence nor could he shine with weapons skills. And worst of all, he remained short and thin of arms and legs, among a tall and big-boned people.

He became ten, in Ishparshule-wark of Lokusta, and eleven, in Ishparshule-wark, and that year he was chosen from among all the others. He would be Voice at the festival of Snowmelt! Another, Berjanderk who was three weeks short of his twelfth birthday and thus only just eligible (and only two inches short of six feet), was Third Brother, but Voice was the better part; the best part of all. Jarik rehearsed and rehearsed. Many were envious; envy oft became enmity. Jarik, misfortunate Jarik, was accustomed to that. He rehearsed. He would be the best Voice ever to speak at Snowmelt in Ishparshule-wark. He would be so much better than Berjanderk that Berjanderk would hang his head in shame even until high summer. And though the air remained cold and spring seemed reluctant and far away under skies filled with lead and mountaintops heavy under their burden of winterfall, the cakes were baked and the animals double-fed and clothing made and mended and costumes made and fitted and sewn and adjusted.

And Jarik rehearsed, even while he fought the swinging bear-post in the barn. It was much battered, that practice opponent, and a year had passed since it had swung back and knocked Jarik down.

The day before the festival of Snowmelt he attacked it with the old boar spear that had been Dundrik's, and bare it far in, so that when it swung back he was borne off his feet and flattened. But still he clung to the spear's haft, which was thick as his wrist.

All Ishparshule-wark gathered then, as were gathering that same night all the people of all the warks of Lokusta. The fires were kindled and blazed up tall as a woman. Solemnly Ishparshule Rednose was brought through the vent in the circle of all his people. He wore green, all green, and his ceremonial sword and badge of Firstship was not at his side. He was escorted by the Three. They were tall and thin and misty-ghostly in their rich silver-shot robes of palest grey, broidered all with white, and in their eerie white masks. Ishparshule's breath puffed into the air, but cloaks were not worn on Snowmelt Night.

They conducted him to his seat, at that part of the circle of people opposite the fires.

54

"Behold the Three," Ishparshule called into silence ameliorated only by the crackling of flames and the popping of gassy wood, and he looked about at all the people of Ishparshule-wark that they might all see his eyes (which, in the darkness, they could not).

"Behold the Three," he said again, "who speak for the God on the Earth!"

"Behold the Three!" the reply rose, from the throats of all old enough to speak words.

"Behold Those who speak for the God on the Earth!"

"Behold Those who walk among us for the God on the Earth!"

The Three stepped away from Ishparshule then. They lifted six bony arms in silver-threaded sleeves of whitish grey. Dry old voices crackled like leaves in autumn and one was very hoarse, for all knew that one of the Three had been very ill through the winter.

"Behold the First Man," the Three chorused, "who speaks the Word of those who speak for the God on the Earth!"

"Behold Ishparshule!" the people of Ishparshule-wark chorused, and with a murmurous rustle of clothing they sat, every one, despite the coldness of the ground. Spring was coming; never mind that it was recalcitrant this year; it was the time of Snowmelt. They would bring the spring, this night.

The Third Brother came then; though all knew he was Serashule's son Berjanderk, he was eerie to their eyes and napes prickled at sight of his robes and mask of dead black. A child whimpered and was peremptorily comforted. The Third Brother spoke from between the fires that were not quite so tall as he, and they flickered yellow and orange on his robes, but not white.

"Behold the Third Brother who is Death," ne called in his voice that was about to change, "for it is He who truly reigns!"

I will be louder, Jarik thought. *And better.* Even so the same shiver went up his spine as it did all others, for the word *death* was not spoken among the people of the warks.

"And the Third Brother need not patrol the skies, day or night, for all know he is supreme. Mateless, lonely: pity the poor Third Brother!"

The people of Ishparshule-wark chorused the groaning sound of disapproval and contempt. Jarik had often heard the sound; not tonight! Tonight the applause was for him—or rather for the Voice.

"Mateless and lonely," the Third Brother, the Dark Brother called again; "he who is the Lonely One, the Nightshade, the Raincrow; the Grave-lord." For the name of Death was not spoken; among Lokustans those who left the earth-plain answered or went to join "Him whose invitation cannot be denied."

And for the third time:

"Mateless and lonely, he ever seeks company and recruits it from among humans."

The dread black mask turned this way and that, then, seeking company, a recruit; and everywhere he looked he saw only the ward-sign and the yellow lifestone worn this night outside the tunic. He drew back, but Jarik thought he could have done that better.

"The Third Brother," the Third Brother called out, "may call you to him at any time, with you of any age; ugly or beautiful . . . good or bad . . . high-born or low-. And once one comes to visit and relieve his tedium and the dark, that one bides there, so that he or she never returns among men. And the—the color of D—of the Third Brother is BLACK, and his abode is the cold dark, and his time is WINTER!"

Hmp, Jarik thought amid the groaning, *he forgot his lines and stumbled!*

Then he felt the touch, and he rose. As he did so his hands went damp about the dry branches and his armpits went wet and he felt cold and prickly as though the blood had run from him. His heart pounded and rushed within him. Nevertheless he paced solemnly forward in his robes of green and his mask of yellow below his yellow hair with its green-tinted strands, and he bore the branches.

Death stood betwixt the fires. Death faced the newcomer. Winter and the dark faced spring and the light. Jarik ignored him in accord with his part, and hurled a branch on either fire. (At the same time, on the fires' other sides, men hurled huge dry branches into the flames, which of course crackled and snapped, gave off sparks, and leaped up much higher.) Tongues of yellow and white licked at the sky. The circles of light spread, joined, spread out to encompass the ring of seated people. The Third Brother threw up a hand to shield his face while Jarik swiftly realized that his role was to contain some discomfort he had not considered; the hottest place near two towering fires was between them!

The Third Brother slunk back, back. . . and then Death turned and, half-bent, fled away into the darkness while the people of Ishparshule-wark beat their palms on their thighs in a slapping cacophony of applause.

They went silent. The fire crackled and snapped.

Jarik took deep breaths and hoped he could be seen there between the fires. It was more than very warm.

"The SUN," he called out shrilly, "is a fair-haired woman astride a golden horse!"

And the people beat palms on thighs.

"Her skin is of fresh new cream from the first-bearing heifer and her hair is the butter of that cream!"

Applause again, and from an unseen throat, that of Climinje the Singer, they all knew, came the golden cry: "*She is Shralla!*" She carried the final sound out and on and on, in a long-drawn "aahhhh."

"*Shralla!*" erupted from every throat in the circle, saving only seven that belonged to infants and someone who coughed rheumily.

"And her steed," Jarik cried, "is *Serames*, the Light! He who was turned by his envious brother Bodmor—"

Almost Jarik went on, but early groaners reminded him to pause and wait for the Bodmor-jeering to rise and ebb and cease.

" . . .Bodmor the NIGHT!" Jarik called, and his voice cracked so that he paused and tried to be silent about clearing his throat. Monstrous embarrassment came on him, but never mind that; he was chosen Voice, and must continue.

"Tell us again!" came the chorus of youthful female voices; with their part thus done those girls looked both smug and relieved.

"He is Serames, the Light, turned by his envious brother Bodmor the Night" (some over-exuberant youngling groaned and was shushed and cuffed by an embarrassed mother) "into a horse, so that he might not have Shralla, his one beloved."

"Shralla, Beloved of All," came aureately ringing the voice of Climinje the Singer.

"Daily does Serames carry Shralla of the Sun, in eternal pursuit of her who reigns over the gems besprent on the cloak of night" (almost Jarik forgot to make his skyward gesture, and it was hasty and jerky and his knees turned to melt) "Laralla, the Gemstone Lady, for she is beloved of Bodmor. And all love Shralla, light-bringing, nurturing Shralla and her ever-faithful steed and lover, Serames. And few love Bodmor, who is the second brother. And NONE loves him who is the Third Brother!"

From within his green, green tunic then Jarik brought forth the sprig of the ever-green mistletoe. He handed it to the girl who ran fleet-footedly out to him, white hair and white dress blowing behind her in the wind of her own passage, and she carried it to place into the outstretched hands of Ishparhsule Rednose.

"Welcome, green and gold," Ishparshule called out, and Jarik heard the big high-voiced man's voice crack worse than his own had done. "Welcome, lady of light! Welcome. . . SPRING!"

The shouting and gaiety and dancing erupted and the carcasses were soon roasting, porkling and lamb, while ale flowed and men lurched and fell drunk even though coupling continued through the night. Spring was come to Lokusta—though it was contrary, and waited nearly three weeks more that year, with some muttering that it was because an outsider had taken the role of Voice. And that fall Jarik participated in another rite in which he had the prime rôle. He was twelve, and he was named a man, and busked as a man by his mother and girded as a man by his father, and his gift was a lifestone of yellowest yellow.

Next day he wore a sword all the day, though it was long and heavy on one of his height, and clanked when he essayed to sit or squat. He loved the weight. He swaggered. All others knew one thing of certainty, and he knew they knew so: Strodeson Jarik could use that sword.

And the weavers wove so that in winter of that year, Barrenserk Bearpaw died of the rheum. Though both his sons and his daughter asked, his widow Kilye elected to remain in the house she had so long shared with the Bearpaw. Now she shared it only with Torsy.

Jarik went to his father. "I would bear wood for Barrenserkwife Kilye."

"It is well," Strode said, looking proud. "But first you must ask permission of their first son."

That Jarik did, and was told by Barrenserk's firstborn that his help would not be needed, nor was he asked within the house. Pain and bitterness were thus put upon him anew, nor did he play the stoic role. Jarik saw that Torsy learned of the words said to him and the way of them. Torsy told Kilye Barrenserkswife, who was not pleased with her son and let him know so. Nor did he play the manly stoical role, but spoke to Torkes Ridgerunner, and Torkes Ridgerunner spoke with his daughter right sternly, so that as a dutiful daughter she no longer looked with favor on Strodeson Jarik.

A few months later the Ridgerunner's daughter wed the son of Stride Elk-slayer. Cold and dark filled the heart of Strodeson Jarik, and all knew it.

He disappeared from Ishparshule-wark next day before dawn.

With him went his own good knife given him by his father, and the sword that would be his when it was needed, and his foster-father's heaviest cloak of doubled fleece both outside and in, and too the boar-spear Jarik had brought with him from a far, far wark called Oceanside. He took only jerked meat and no water or ale.

Jarik did not return.

Snow fell and wind howled, and Jarik did not return.

Strode and Mejye mourned their son, gone in his grief to accept the invitation of the Third Brother, who was ever more lonely in winter so that it was then more went to join him. The scarlet-spotted bed-sheet hanging outside the door of the New-weds' hut froze, and cracked in the wind, and Jarik did not return. Days passed, and Jarik was mourned. Nor spoke the strangeling Torsy so much as a word, so that her "grandmother" was both sore grieved and afraid for the girl.

Seven days passed, and the wind dropped and ceased.

On the eighth day the sun shone as if next week's Snowmelt rites had already been held.

On the ninth day, at eventide, a half-alive figure staggered into Ishparshule-wark. It was Strodeson Jarik, even more diminutive in the heavy swaddling of his father's long, long cloak and his snow-mask and his heavy flapped cap of fur. He staggered half the length of Ishparshule-wark, dragging a huge carcass

60

frozen stiff and heavy. Its branching horns gouged the snow. His hands bled within their fleece-lined gloves so that the gloves were never good again. By the time he reached the door of the New-Weds' hut, many people were watching, all in silence, while from his own home Strode was moving toward his son in a long-legged walk. People remembered afterward that Strode was bareheaded and wore only his home-tunic and fur foot-mittens.

Jarik knocked at the gaily decorated door of oak, and it was opened by a very surprised couple. They stared.

"A wedding gift for the son of the Elk-slayer," Jarik said, and gestured to the great elk he had slain, and turned away. He walked three paces before he collapsed, just before Strode reached him.

Racing, calling Jarik's name, Torsy was there just as Strode lifted his son in his arms.

Chapter Six:
Out of the body!

In his fourteenth year, Strodeson Jarik Elk-slayer was unwed and without betrothal. Feeling that no fathers would accept a maiden-gift from him, he offered none. Nor was Torsy wed; it was assumed she would not be. Some youths were interested in her, a fascinating bauble so different in her eyes and hair and bone-structure. But she was hardly a scintillant bauble, and any attention given her was surreptitious. She was the strangeling Torsy, and what mother wanted a grandchild marked for life with eyes not blue?

The husband of the beauteous though passing plump Clarje died, and people muttered that Clarje had smiled at and made certain gestures to Jarik Elk-slayer son of Strode. Nothing came of it. Some said it was because Jarik paid no mind to the childed woman of sixteen who outweighed him nigh double.

"I feel no desire for the widow Clarje," he told his father, when Strode at last introduced the subject.

"But Jarish. . . a man must have a wife."

"Perhaps I will raid into another wark and fetch home a bride, then," Jarik said, though in truth he had not yet experienced puberty and did not feel himself ready to consider taking a bride.

"Oh Jarish," his mother cried out, "no! You might be slain!"

He gazed at her, and at Strode her husband. "Look at my mother Strodeswife Mejyish," he said. "Here is the best womanly form in all the wark. Clarje!" he snapped out scornfully. "I shall bring home no well-fatted hog, as my father did not."

Strode gazed upon him with misty eyes, and Mejye bowed her head and wept at the compliment and affirmation of her youthfulness of form—which she'd have traded for a child from her own womb. Nothing was said again of the widow Clarje (who scandalously wed the son of Stride Elk-slayer, the following spring, but a scant six weeks after the death of his wife in childbirth).

In casual manner and without being specific or straightforward, Strode made certain approaches, hints, suggestions to fathers of three several maidens of age or nearly. Nothing came of that. Strode had taken care and none was so careless or cruel as to say him an open nay, when he had not openly asked. Thus were friendships preserved, among decent people. Strode did not tell Jarik of his explorations into the possibility of the boy's marriage. There was time, Strode told himself.

Spring came a bit late that year, and down in Fox Valley the wark of Seckharden was badly flooded. Four young men from Seckharden-wark came to Ishparshule-wark araiding just after summer's beginning. They were rebuffed by three. Two were Strode and his son called Elk-slayer, and the latter wounded and knocked down a man of Seckharden's people so that the fellow fled moaning and holding a uselessly dangling arm. The third defender of the wark was the son of Stride Elk-slayer, also called Stride.

Battle-blooded together in defense of wark and maidenhood, Stride and Jarik looked at each other. Stride bowed, then. After a moment, Jarik bowed to Stride. Strode saw each bow, so that no feud remained between them.

"I am your brother, warrior," Jarik said.

"I am your brother, warrior," Stride son of Stride said.

Saved from the carrying-off to Sechharden-wark were Sijye youngest daughter of Stride Elk-slayer, and Aspen daughter of Osorth Straightback; the latter was not even of age. Sijye looked upon Jarik then, and did not drop her eyes. Both her brother and Strode saw this, and looked at Jarik, and at each other. And they smiled.

Two days following Jarik and Strode and the two Strides went hunting together, and Jarik returned with them to bitter disappointment: he had missed the visit of the God on the Earth!

She had merely . . . appeared, they said. It was her first visit to Ishparshule-wark in seven years, and Jarik was terribly disappointed, even angry. She had said nor done aught save to Choose Brathis of the mighty arms, who had swaggered and gone to her while all watched. And she and Brathis had vanished.

"Vanished," Jarik repeated.

"Aye. Vanished, Jarik. Disappeared. Poof."

Jarik shook his head and looked sad to have missed seeing the Lady of the Snowmist. Having come so soon after the repulsed raid from the other wark, he thought, she would surely have chosen him, not Brathis . . . though, true, Brathis was the finest physical specimen among the young manhood of Ishparshule-wark, if not quite the most handsome. Stath, who thought he was, was as unhappy and resentful as Jarik.

Already Brathis was back, swaggering as if he now owned the wark. He did not; he did own the attentions of its maidens and even of some shamelsss wives.

As had been the case with him the Lady of the Snowmist had Chosen eleven years previous, Brathis remembered nothing of his sojourn with the god on the earth. He had been gone two days. No one knew what milady Snowmist did with these young men— but all knew what later befell him she had Chosen last time. He was five-and-twenty now, was Flint the God-favored. Able to choose from among the maidens of Ishparshule-wark, he had married late after having sowed wild oats unto scandal. Some said that she-whose-name-was-not-said had killed herself over him, when he wed another. Flint the God-favored was unaccused and unharmed—and had not been other than exceeding hale for eleven years.

It was the gift of the God; he whom she Chose enjoyed health all his days.

Jarik grieved at having missed the God and could take solace only with Torsy and with her nearly everyone called Grandmother Kilyish: Barrenserk's widow Kilye.

Sijye Stridesdaughter did not offer solace; she could see only Brathis the God-favored.

A few nights later while Jarik slept something happened, so that he awoke to find with some fear that he was stuck to the bed. It was something Strode had spoken of, "warned" him of, years ago; it had not happened, and Jarik had forgotten. Nor was that nocturnal emission all that occurred that night, for on finding it he was afraid, and sore shocked, and he became very hot and then cold and then what happened was this:

A bell jangled and a hundred, a thousand, a milliard bees buzzed. The sound was not deafening, but was awful; it bothered him terribly. Wind whistled and a spinning black well opened before him like a round doorway into midnight. For a time he thought that it was rushing at him, and he sought to flee.

He could not flee.

Then he realized that the well—a horizontal well, its dark maw facing him like a cave into the mountainside save there was no mountain—was not moving at all. It was not rushing at him; without sensation of movement, he was falling into it. And he fell and fell. The well's mouth widened but Jarik remembered how the ship of Barrensark and of Kiddensahk had seemed to grow as they neared, and he knew that the well was not growing but was nearing him—rather, that he was nearing it. Falling. He fell and fell. The darkness within the well deepened and spread out. It broadened until it encompassed him and there was nothing else but the dark.

The bells ceased jangling; the seemingly infinite swarm of bees remained.

Rapidly he rushed through the well or cavern. Though there was no way to measure—no *there* to measure against—he knew that he was rushing at an impossible speed. It was as if he were being sucked, rather than falling, as though falling were a mere slow matter, a prelude or mere hint of the rushing he was experiencing. He was aware of no weight, of no wind or of aught of flying and snapping of his hair, but he knew that he was rushing through—nothing.

The words were not there. To describe what he experienced and saw? No, he could not do so in words, mere words, for there were times when one realized that words were not only finite but very few, and that those that existed encompassed but three dimensions.

All was black, utterly black and yet it was not: there was neither sight nor color. He knew that his eyes were open but he saw nothing. He wondered if he breathed. He did not know. Headfirst, he fell down and down, in and in.

A point of light appeared.

It grew, like a slowly opening eye. *I am coming to the end of the whatever-it-is,* he thought. *That is the bottom of the well I see. . . or the top . . . the other end. I will soon be out.*

Another thought came, and with it brought the clamminess of terror: what then? What lay at the bottom of the well or this tunnel through a mountain?

I will fall out into the light, he thought, *and I will wake. For surely I will wake. I will be awake.*

Yet how could he, for he knew that he was not in his body. His body lay behind him, in the house of Strode and Mejye; his own home. His body was surely asleep. He was not. He was very very awake. He thought that if he looked back he would be able to see his body, far and far behind; could see Jarik lying there. He did not like that. He would very much like to return to his body.

Am I dead?

No, no . . .

The blackness became greyness as light bled into it. Once again he was aware of the whirling, the swirling of the very well he was in. Nothing touched him. The grey lightened. It became pearly, barely transparent, murkily whirling. And he was out.

He felt neither hurt nor heat nor cold nor the stir of air his rushing through it must cause, so that he knew that he had indeed separated from his body. At that instant he had the extraneous thought that he certainly hoped he would be able to find his way back to himself, and inside, so that he could be one again and no longer this strange and discomforting *two* that he was.

He was alone, very alone. Now he did not even have his own body for company.

Jarik saw the man, then.

He was a tall and slender man, with arms and legs well rounded, and there was aristocracy in his face. He was of no color that Jarik could describe, or later remember, this man who seemed waiting for him. A slim, plaited beard covered and depended from his chin only, so that his well-cut face was hairless and smooth. He bore in one hand a sword, long and black and shining; in the other he held a staff, crooked at one end; the staff was the length of the sword, but white. The man's eyes seemed to glow red, but of course that was impossible, and his serpent-mounted crown was surely of gold. The man was naked, and his genitals were huge.

Come, my son. You come to manhood at last.

The man's lips did not move; indeed, he was as a statue. The words had been formed, Jarik realized, within his mind. (*They have to be. Without my body, I have no ears to hear!*)

He took hold of the man's white rod, though Jarik

67

was not sure with what he obtained that grip. His hands were surely back with his body, back there, wherever *there* was. Now he was here.

Here was the night sky, and he could not look down to see what he and his guide stood upon; he thought that it was on nothing. The night sky surrounded them: blackness speckled with white dots. Realization came upon him that they were not all white, the gems of the Gemstone Lady of Night. He saw several colors, saw how they twinkled and seemed to wink. They faded, as he and his guide seemed to rush toward one.

It grew until it filled much of his vision, much of the sky; a great flaming circle of fire, yellow-white. Streamers of flame leaped from it into the . . . the sky; the space that surrounded it. Jarik could not look at it. Eyeless, he squinted.

Then something happened, and he could see beyond its glare, which had grown not so great. He was sure that his guide—his Guide—had accomplished that, for he was sure that he was in the company of a god—a very great wizard, at the very least.

Four circles—no, spheres, stones or pearls that were not-quite round—moved (rolled?) around the white circle of flame. No, there were five. No six—

Four interested him for some reason; perhaps because these were the ones his Guide wanted him to note.

One was smallish and red, farthest from the central flame than any. It circled the central flame, and now and again, as it came around again, it was large, not small. On this side of it two others circled, like twins, smallish and blue-white—one was red-tinged only. They circled together, in concentric paths. And finally there was the outermost pearl, which was not blue-white or pearly but definitely blue and white. Like the others, it turned as it circled that great central circle of flame.

Jarik wondered if somehow these spheres rolled on

the sky, as if it were a flat surface for their support. What kept them moving? He did not know. They went around and around, four spheres on concentric paths; like gems or eerily pulsing lights, all against a background of grey and the great flaming circle. It reminded him of Shralla; would she and her steed look so if one could somehow fly and draw closer to them?

Jarik had, he recalled, flown. He was flying now. Wasn't he?

Somehow suspended, somewhere and somewhen, Jarik watched. He watched the two small . . . pearls . . . develop little wobbles, as though they had been in tracks and had worn them down by constant movements and might now slip out of those set paths, those orbits around the circle of flame. Now he saw that their paths intersected at two points, and he gritted his teeth, but they passed each other, seemingly narrowly.

He watched as if his eyes were locked by chains to those two spheres.

He saw them stagger out of their fixed paths, which had grown more and more erratic. They raced toward each other. Flashes of light sprang from them and he felt, without being sure or knowing why, that he was seeing fire.

The pearls were rupturing. The red sphere and the larger blue and white one circled on, unperturbed by the predicament of their fellows. The central flame blazed, untouched and unmoved. The pearls were being drawn irresistibly toward each other, bulging now as if longing to join.

Closer they approached, and a streak of light leaped from one of them to flash across the blackness toward the huge blue-and-white ball that turned slowly around the yellow-white fire. The light flew straight as a thrown spear.

Thus did I depart. With me I brought life, though I was alone on the ship.

Other streaks of light sprang up from that pearl—

and fell back. Jarik waited for another comment in his mind; the Guide made none. The pearls raced closer to each other. Closer they approached, and closer. Then they were merging—

No. They did not merge. They collided, and neither rebounded.

Terrible flashes of flame leapt from them in what Jarik knew—without knowing how he knew—was a cataclysmic impact of two mighty forces. The two tortured spheres came together, and they were shattered. Shards flew in all directions, trailing flame, though he had heard no crash, no thunder, no crunch or even thump of impact. He did hear a sound, a horrid soul-shrinking sound that he realized was the death-scream of a billion people. That awful sound penetrated his brain and soul like the blade of a newly sharpened knife of the best iron.

Thus our world died, in collision with its sister world.

The words were in Jarik's mind. He no longer saw his Guide, though he was there; Jarik was clutching his staff. Knowledge came into his mind, without words. He knew, with that knowledge and understanding that was to be but fleeting, temporary: he knew that two entire worlds were dying, had died, with all the people on the one; worlds that had lain between his own and the dull red one that could frequently be seen so clearly in the sky of night. Bodmor's Eye.

Pieces of the two destroyed spheres flew spinning and tumbling out . . . and were arrested, and, tumbling, began to circle just as they had before, when they were unified into a twoness rather than hundreds of thousands.

Jarik tensed, watching the moving dot of light approach the large globe that was blue and white, and then it was there . . . and nothing happened, absolutely nothing that he saw. It was there. Something had left one of the departed spheres; pearls, worlds; it

70

had crossed the intervening space and arrived at the white-and-blue one. And Jarik remembered that his Guide had said, *Thus did I depart.*

You are a god on the earth.

I am a god on the earth, (something) *son Jarik.*

Jarik tried to ask, *What have I seen?*

It is your birthright and your conception, Jarik. You saw two that were as one, and when they became one they shattered and were nothing. You are a twoness that must be a oneness, and that can come about only by your taking on a third part, which will unify you into one.

I–I do not understand!

Nor will you, nor can you. It will be agony to you that you do not understand, and are two both at once, (something) *son Jarik, and for that I am sorry. Yet the agony will continue when you are whole—three as one, although it will be a different sort of agony and you will know happiness. Some happiness. A part of you is a tree, and a part of you lies on an island, and you—you lie in the home of Strode, Jarish. You and I will meet again.*

And the Guide was gone, and Jarik lay in the home of Strode, his home, in his bed, and it was no Guide's staff he clutched, but his own.

Jarik was quiet and strange for days after and he told no one of what he had experienced or dreamed. Nor did he know whether it had been experience or dream, nor was he happy that a good deal of it immediately departed his memory. He tried to go into himself, and he wept more than once, though with care that no one saw or knew.

Had he dreamed? Or did that which was his very source and kernel of life leave his less important little earthbound body, and travel into another dimension of reality? Had his Guide been real? Was Jarik there in bed, asleep and adream, or had he left his body to travel through shadowy realms of mist and no-time? As before, when *it happened* in Oceanside that day of horror, he was unsure whether he had experienced a dream, or a vision, prescient or post—or . . . some god-sent miracle that might be called alternate reality.

He told no one. He could not do so in words that were not only finite but so pitifully few as well, so inadequate and embracing only three dimensions. Besides, he did not remember it all. He felt sure only that twice now he had seen or "seen" two several Gods on the Earth. And twice now he had heard—or "heard" himself referred to as two, rather than the one he knew he was.

More doubt was thus thrust upon him, and more impatience to be on and know what it was that he would do, and a terrible new driving wish and longing to be no longer different, to be like others, knowing who he was and having a part in things. He wanted desperately to be important, like Brathis.

Thus so did Jarik come late to puberty that was but another trauma and that but added new tangles and knots to the threads of the unfinished fabric of his life. And the weavers wove.

A few days later his voice broke, and after that it would unaccountably betray him and leap up high so that he had no control over it and was near to despair. He wondered if this was his twoness, himself and his voice, and hoped that he found soon the isle whereon waited the third part that would make him whole.

Even within the bosom of his family, he became secretive and ridiculously modest. (Secretly, Strode rejoiced, for he knew that Jarik had come at last to puberty and would now rush into manhood, though so late.)

The weavers wove, and the changes continued.

Within a month tender little pin-hairs gleamed on his face, his voice had dropped into a shockingly resonant baritone, his shoulders were rounding, filling, and he had grown over an inch. His face also commenced to sprout pimples along with hair. Nor did Strode thereafter see the boy's piddler, for years.

Within three months there was a fine, nearly white down on Jarik's legs and upper lip, the hair of his head had somehow glossed, he had more pimples still, hair burst forth in his loins and inside his large, rounded new shoulders, his calves looked positively swollen, and thin arms had become full of rounds. He had but to lift a hand to cause muscles to leap up in his chest and upper arms. And he had grown two more inches.

With manhood and the promise of height and a beautiful body on him, Strodeson Jarik Elk-slayer the Loner did not nevertheless gain the female attention he should have had; Brathis the God-favored got it all. Only Torsy and homely, triple-chinned Sweet-flower—and Mejye his mother—gazed with pleasure on him, and dared tell him of his beauty, and sigh over his new musculature. And he grew more.

He hewed in half the long-battered swing-log, bear-post, in the barn; broke a chair without knowing how he had done it; and two pieces of crockery though he hadn't thought he was being careless. And he walked like a stumping horse on feet now at home in Strode's buskins. And he grew taller still. He alone put up the new swing-log for his practice, and Strode quietly told Mejye that he was not certain he himself could have done that.

Jarik also ate like a herd of pigs.

Brathis tried Sijye, and cast her aside, so that she was most unhappy for weeks. Then, even as young Stath discovered her, she remembered and rediscovered Strodeson Jarik Elk-slayer. Openly then did the smoky eyes of the daughter of the Elk-slayer meet those of the wark's other slayer, alone, of an elk.

He had grown another inch by harvest-time.

Chapter Seven:
Jarik Man-slayer

Jarik was not sure what love was, in the summer preceding his eighteenth birthday. Thus he told himself that he loved Sijye, to whom he gave much attention, who was his girl. He did not, however, know whether he loved her. His mother Mejye worried over that, though Strode did not.

Jarik had had to grow accustomed to his new body, which was tall and classically muscled. The big hands at the ends of thick wrists had to learn anew to use tools; ax and hoe and spear and sword, adze and knife and bow-saw and vake. Strode gave him a ring of bronze with silver band and a bright yellow citrelain—and within a few months his digits were too thick to accommodate it anywhere but on the smallest finger of his left hand.

When he concentrated and gave thought to what he was doing, he was less good with ax or vake or spear, and once he cut his foot with a hoe. That brought him much funning from others. He tried, but he did not take funning well, or correction either; it became hard for Strode to talk with him critically, and Strode sought to avoid it. (Jarik was strange, an ever impatient lad who was quick to anger, but he was a good son nevertheless.)

Jarik learned a way *not* to concentrate, and the results were weird.

Once he learned not to direct his ax and sort of step mentally aside from his wielding of it, from aiming, chips flew and trees fell and ax and wedge drove through logs until they were parted. At the same time he had learned that, to split a standing log, one did not swing the ax at it, or the mallet at the wedge. One attempted to swing *through* it. And the splitting went the faster.

"It should be the same in sword-wielding," Strode told him.

"Sword-wielding?"

"In fighting," Strode said.

"There is no fighting," Jarik said sullenly. "Only this playing at it. I think I should build a hawk-ship and go forth ahawking."

"You are not good with those tools and that sort of patience-work," Strode pointed out, not without some trepidation at Jarik's reaction.

"I could learn, and gain help."

"And then go raiding farmers as your people were raided?"

Jarik's face tensed and he struck at the tree he had decided to sword-chop—the birch was not quite the thickness of his body—with great viciousness. He had so many ideas and hopes—and all, as Strode had just pointed out, seemed to be unreasoned and unreasonable! It was no fun to be seventeen, and tall and muscular with hair like the sun falling down one's back, and to know that one was a fool and *still* did not belong or matter. It was worse than no fun. It was monstrously frustrating.

Jarik knew that he was grievously impatient, though he did not know why, or for what; what he was impatient to do or be.

Not a hawker! No, he could not be one of them, becoming as one with those who had slain his parents. No, he could not be a hawker. Besides, Strode was right. He was not good at fine work, at detail jobs requiring patience.

Kiddensahk! Kiddensahk! I was coming . . . what has happened? Where are you, murderer? No one's even heard of you, murderer! It's been ten years, ten years, and look at me! Oceanside is unavenged and I am big enough to do it! I, a Lokustan! *Like you, Kid-*
75

densahk! I don't even know who I am, much less who and where you are, murderer of my parents.

He had to fight, to twist and set a foot against the tree, to get the sword out. And then he had to take the time to straighten the iron blade.

"No man knows when he may be called upon to be a warrior, Jarish," Strode said. "You know this better than any; you and Stride the Younger and I became warriors one day."

"Once! It was . . . glorious! It was being an eagle, and flying!"

Strode sighed. "I have trained you in the use of weapons, and you want to use them all the time. Such leads only to death, Jarish."

"Then I should have been trained to hoe and vake, or to adze and plane and bow-saw, as a wright!"

"I am sorry I have done this to you," Strode said, looking unhappy. "I have ever worked with weapons, loving them. But no such weening desire has ever been on me to use them and use them! It is enough to know that I am good, and able to protect family and wark if need be. It was enough to be one of three who drove off four, that day the Seckharden-warkers came araiding."

Jarik feinted, half spun with wheaten hair flying, and chopped into the tree—directly into the slim wedge, and without a moment's aiming, for he had looked away to spin. "Hah!" And he had to wrest the sword free. Once again it survived, though Strode was much apprehensive over the future of that oft-straightened, nicked blade.

"A tree is not the best practice object, for a sword."

Jarik looked at him. "You have not practiced with me for over a month." His eyes and voice were accusing.

"It is a busy time, son."

Jarik looked at him. He was rangy as Strode was now, and as tall, but roundly developed in all his muscles. Strode's chest was bone covered with normal

76

thin sheaves of muscle and skin; Jarik's was divided
into two separate halves, like plates or small shields.
Strode lifted his arms and his biceps tensed in tight
thick cords; Jarik but twisted a wrist outward and his
biceps bulged as though an eagle's egg was lodged
beneath the skin. And Jarik was better with arms.
Swifter, more daring—and more skillful. They both
knew it. Strode no longer cared to work out with him,
with weapons. Jarik was not only very good, he
changed when he wielded sword and slipped shield
on arm. Strode feared him, though he had told only
Mejye. Jarik fought outside himself, like the wolf; he
was *morbrin*: the-machine-that-fights.

Jarik had so much anger in him, and so much impatience. He seemed to want to slash and crush and
slay, when he bore arms. Trees absorbed much of that
anger and energy, though a door-hinge had once been
broken by the force of his departing home; other ob-
jects had died in his hands for he was still not in full
control of his strength.

Perhaps he did belong with such as those who had
raided his own wark ten years agone, Strode mused
unhappily. Strode hoped the big lad did not find
them, though. Jarik wanted to kill them—all of them.
And he'd doubtless die in the attempt, savagely
hacked until he dropped and was easy prey. And this
business of postponing and postponing even the pre-
liminary hint of betrothal—! It was not normal.

"A busy time," Jarik said after his foster-father, and
hewed into the birch, which shuddered. And the
weavers wove.

Stath, who was Jarik's age plus a few months, had
turned eighteen in April. He was burly, freckled easily and seemed florid even in winter, and there was
bronze in the long hair he trapped in a smooth
leather fillet bossed with two blue-flashing perisines.
In May Stath and another did something very
strange; they slipped off, armed and armored, to raid

77

Seckharden-wark. They were rebuffed. Stath bore two piddling wounds neither of which left a suitable scar and his companion would never again walk without a limp. They endured the public castigation of Ishparshule and the Three, but both youths knew that Ishparshule's heart was not in the condemnatory words. Was his good strapping wife not of another wark? Had not Ishparshule, at seventeen, stolen her, whelming her two brothers so that he was hailed as battle-victor? Did she not love him and would have been sword-won slave-of-willingness had Ishparshule not wanted her as wife?

Stath was Ishparshuleson Stath. And he decided that he wanted Sijye.

He brought her things. He "came upon" her here and there, and bore water for her. At the same time, naturally enough, he became no friend to Strodeson Jarik Elk-slayer and Loner.

When Sijye asked Jarik if it were true he'd been foundling even of his previous parents, he knew it came from Stath. When Sijye asked if Torsy were really mad, Jarik knew it had come from Stath. To others, too, Stath referred to Jarik as "twice-foundling" and wondered aloud about his true birth and why perhaps he had been abandoned, not lost at sea, and made sneering mention of his "witling sister," and intimated that she might well be available to anyone at all, since she'd had so little attention of them.

"Stath," Jarik said on a day no different from the day previous, for it had been nigh two months since frost had sparkled of a morning, "say no more about my sister Torsy, and stay away from Stridesdaughter Sijye."

"Jarik," Stath said, and his eyes narrowed. "I take no orders from a twice-foundling with a witling 'sister' who does not even look like him. Strange habits, some outlander parents have! Jarik: You stay away from Sijyish, for soon I will take a gift to her father."

Jarik was trembling. There on the birch-dotted hillside under the July sun, he glared at Stath and his fingers vanished into fists. "He will reject it."

Stath smiled. "Will he, Twice-found Jarik? Will he?"

Jarik started toward him; Stath bent his knees. They did not circle, or draw lines with their feet, or trade daring blows. They went at fighting as a business. Jarik closed on the other, and with him. They strove and strained, tore up sod with their feet, and fell. They rolled and strove. People saw. Some called out to each other. Soon the two youths were separated by three men, among them Strode. Both were scratched and bruised, and the bruise high on Jarik's cheek showed how close Stath had come to his eye.

Panting, the two big youths glowered at each other.

"I cut trees down with a sword, Stath," Jarik told him. "Do not come near when I cut trees!" And all knew it was a threat, though made in heat.

"Stay away from Sijye, Jarik outlander!"

"Father," Jarik said, glaring not at Strode but at Stath, "I would bear a maiden-gift to Stride Elk-slayer." And Stath struggled with those who held him.

"Do not do it, Jarik!" Stath cried. "Don't think of it! I will kill you, Jarik."

Thus another threat had been heard, though it too was made in anger's heat. It was very exciting, this striving of two big powerful youths for one maiden; what a thrilling gift it made for Sijye!

Then Stath was cuffed, for his father Ishparshule had come. Solemnly then, before eighteen who heard and more who saw, Ishparshule, First Man of the wark, forbade them to fight on pain of punishment. Many who heard scowled, and the two young men went their separate ways, scowling.

Jarik had issued challenge, though. Too, he had much energy of anger and hate to work off. A few hours later, nearly at twilight, he was hewing at a thick pine with his sword, when footsteps sounded acrackle beneath fallen cones. Jarik turned his head to see Stath, all swathed in a long fox-trimmed cloak of dark blue.

"Go away, Stath," Jarik said, wrenching his sword from the tree. "You are not safe near me, when I have a sword in my hand." But his shield leaned against another tree, with his woods-ax.

Staring silently, Stath drew the pin from his cloak clasp. The little rumple of fabric slipped through the ring and his mantle dropped from him. He had worn the cloak so as to come here, seeking Jarik, without others' knowing that he wore sword.

"Put down your sword, Jarik."

"I will not. I am cutting this tree with it."

"Put down your sword or raise it against me, twice-foundling, doubtless bastard son and part-brother to a witling sow."

Even "sow" was an insult. To have called Torsy a shoat would not have been, for pigs were hardly hated by lovers of chops and ham and thick bacon, full of fat against the winter's cold. By saying sow rather than shoat, however, Strath had intimated that Torsy was no maiden.

Jarik turned to face him full. His sword was in his hand and his face gone dark. Their eyes stared wide each into the other. Stath swallowed, and drew his iron blade by its leather-wrapped hilt of wood capped with a pommel set with the red stone called carbanean, or bloodstone. The sword was shiny and well-forged, the sword of the First Man's son.

Jarik's sword, its pommel the plain iron of the tang that passed through it, was notched and had often been bent. Its grip was of wood, fastened in sections, above a plain cross guard of horn—the horn, like his dagger's hilt, of his own elk.

"I am here to chop this tree, Stath." Jarik's voice trembled. So did his arm, and his face worked.

"Will you take it to your witling sister in trade for her favors?"

That was far too much. No man could hear such and walk again with his head up unless he received apology or blood. Jarik charged.

Neither youth bore a shield. Stath struck at Jarik's blade, and iron rang, and Stath strove to tear open Jarik's chest on the backswing. He failed, for Jarik pounced back light as a spotted pup. His suddenly glittering blue eyes did not even watch the sword flash across, its point missing him by the breadth of two fingers. He was not concentrating; he was fighting. His brain stood aside watching. Jarik had gone *morbrin.*

At once he stepped back into range and his own back-slash took Stath in the neck. The blade hewed into the ring-bones of Stath's neck, and smashed one, so that Stath Ishparshule's son fell down dead in his blood.

That swiftly was the life of Orrikson and Strodeson Jarik changed again, forever; in a moment and at a stroke. Or rather it was drastically changed next day when the Three and the Council spoke, and Ishparshule iterated the sentence.

The sentence was exile, and Jarik heard it spoken. He was pronounced rogue: a vagrant scoundrel without wark. They paid no mind or ignored the fact of Stath's goading, and his going with concealed weapon to where Jarik worked off his anger against a tree. The decision was simply that Strodeson Jarik was guilty of doing death on a man of the wark; the sentence was that he must leave the wark. A runner was bade go to Seckharden-wark, and warn them that a rogue would be loosed, and they had best post watch and stand prepared.

The condemned wondered what the sentence might have been had Stath been someone's son other than the First Man's.

Jarik was Jarik, impatient and hostile and long seeking acceptance that had not come fully, ever. He stood up and spoke so that his voice rang even into the forest.

"I came here not by choice. I was fetched from the sea. You are not my people. *You could not be my people!* People like you murdered my parents! All these years I have had to hear slurs and insults on me and my sister, and now after years of patience I have at last struck back at the vilest of the insulters. And you say Get Hence, you are here at our sufferance Jarik the outlander, and we wanted you—who slew the elk, who saved Sijye and Aspen—only when you were a stray gauntling dog to be teased and kicked!"

Ishparshule rose from the Stump of Judgment. "You are in the presence of the Three and Council, and sentence has been passed. Cease this disrespectful talk!"

"I will not! You are *not* my people. I reject you! I reject the authority of Council and Three and Ishparshule father of him who sought me out to kill me! I spit on your sentence." And he spat on the ground between him and the huge stump whereon Ishparshule sat at ceremonial times. "I leave Ishparshule-wark now because *I choose to!*"

There was muttering, never mind that it was an empty gesture from the lad's anger and for his own self-respect. Best this hot-headed rogue, so very good with weapons, be killed. . .

Strode stood tall then and looked people in the eyes where they lived. He told them that if they would slay Jarik they must first put death on him.

"Unseemly," Ishparshule said, though his voice held a quaver. "Sentence has been passed; it is exile. Strodeson Jarik has not offered violence, and has not yet left the wark. He may not be killed or set upon in any way. Strodeson Jarik is to receive a hand-ax with a good blade, and those clothes and things that are his save for the sword which will be broken, and food sufficient to fill my helmet. He is to go from among us, and let none see him nigh the wark after, lest he

83

be slain as rogue. By dusk let him be gone. It is spoken."

"You miscalled my name," Jarik said venomously. "It is Jarik Elk-slayer, old man, for I am son of no man here and am a doer of deeds."

Then did Strode look wounded and turn away. And Jarik went from that place, and he saw Sijye daughter of Stride. She turned her back so that he saw only her citrelain braids. He called her name, and when she swung back to face him her pretty face was imperious and scornful.

"Killer! Rogue! You brought no maiden-gift to my father, for three long years when you could have done! Now Stath would have done—and you have slain him! What has Stridesdaughter Sijye now, but shame and the scorn of all?"

Jarik was shocked, and was hardly capable of considering the woes of another; none could approach his own. He spat on the ground between them, for none had the pride of Jarik.

There was much weeping and embracing and pulling of hair among him and his parents, and hugging almost violent. So, fiercely, did Torsy embrace and strain against him—but she wept not, or spoke.

Toward sundown, Jarik left Ishparshule-wark. He fared westward—and from that west came the howl of a wolf, and then another.

"He goes to join his own kind," someone said. "Hear? They call to him!"

And Jarik walked west, up the long slope amid the birches and rowans and the few stunty aspen that grew there, and the sun went down on Ishparshule-wark and on the departed rogue.

Chapter Eight:
Let no human misdoubt the odds!

Unstealthy noises awoke the sleeping Jarik, and in the dark he met the quiet-walker with his ax in hand, three-quarter-moon blade glinting dully in the moonlight.

"Torsy!"

It was she, enveloped in a dark cloak; a young woman eight months older than he or so they presumed, and willowy as a girl of twelve, with long straight hair and huge brown eyes that were almost perfectly round.

"Oh Jarish!"

She hugged him long, squeezing hard as if trying to press herself into his body. Then, stepping back and speaking low and urgently in the dark: "At dawn several will come, seeking to slay you. Stride the younger and Bounder have gone out to hunt. They are on Honey Hill, just across the ravine. They will sleep *very* soundly this night; so Stride let me know. They expect to be robbed."

"R—I will rob no one!"

"No no, Jarish." Tears streaked her longish face with its pointed little chin. "Some will come to slay you at dawn, Jarik! Strode is watched, that he may not help you. See you not that I wear Kilye's cloak? I slipped away, Jarish; I had to sneak, by stealth. No one thought that Strider, Sijye's brother would aid you, or Bounder either, so they were not watched. They merely packed up some things to go on a hunting trip, and they did not come the way you did. They bore with them things for *us*, Jarik. We are to go and take them, tonight, now, and escape in another direction.

"Oh, Jarish," she said, with a new sob as she thought of what she was saying, what had befallen him.

"For us! We—Torsy: You are not exiled. You must go back."

"Oh Jarik! Do you ever think beyond your nose or own name? What will happen to me if I remain? Think, and tell me."

He pondered, and his hands clamped her arms, covering nearly all the thin upper arms. Of course. They would make the playgirl of her. Who would protect Strangeling Torsy the rogue's sister? If Strode did, or tried, he'd be set upon. No. Jarik would have no harm come upon Strode, or Torsy, or old Kilye; not because of him!

"I love you, Jarish."

"Yes. Come then, Torsish. We will not let Strode and Bounder take this risk for nothing."

And they collected those things he'd brought, and made their way across the hill's brow and to the ravine that separated it from Honey Hill, and with much effort and slipping and huffing, they got themselves down and up the other side. They found the camp, wherein two men lay rolled in wools and gear was neatly stacked, packed, well away from them. . .

By dawn Jarik and Torsy were so weary that they were staggering. Now they had the added weight of helm and buckler, sword and dagger, flint—and—steel, and wolfskins. Kilye's huge cloak of dark blue woolen was Torsy's to keep, Torsy said; aye, Kilye knew and held much sympathy. His friends had left food with the other things he "stole," but Jarik would take only the loaf. He was fully capable of slaying his own meat, he muttered to Torsy, and he wanted nothing more of Ishparshule-wark than was necessary. Kilye had sent along a draw-bag that housed six other little ones. They contained herbs, various nostrums Grandmother Kilyish knew were effective, for this and that complaint.

They fared south in the night, and by dawn they were weary unto staggering. They had walked all the night. The sky had only begun to grey when they found the low cave.

They went just within, and stretched for sleep. They had eaten of the loaf as they made their way here, miles from the wark, and needed nothing now. Jarik slept because he was too body-weary not to, though his brain was slow to take leave of its broad divagations.

When they awoke, at midday, it was to the voices of plover, teal, and wagtail fluffing their feathers in the sun and supervising their newborn. And just beyond the cave's mouth a very red fox stood, gazing curiously at the two humans within.

"Jarish! A fox."

"So it is. Be still and be quiet, Torsish. He is curious, and shocked that we are in the nice cave he thought was his. He means us no harm, but is young and curious."

Jarik rose very slowly, keeping the fox's gaze locked with his own. His hand came up just as slowly, with him. The ax-throw was only partly successful in those cramped quarters; the animal's flank and hind legs were crushed. While it yelped its pain and tried to snap at him, Jarik retrieved the ax and smashed its skull.

"Gather wood," he said, putting aside the ax and drawing his dagger, just at the low mouth of the cave.

"Jarik! No one eats *fox!*"

"We do, this day. He was sent to us by the god. Go not far, Torsy. Stay within my sight. We will not leave the cave again until sunset. Those you spoke of may be searching for us—probably are, angry that we've eluded them."

Back in the cave, behind the small fire whose smoke drifted out the cave's mouth, they cooked and ate the meat of the fox Jarik had skinned. He was careful to keep grass out of the fire, and all the sticks were dry that there might be no heavy belches of thick smoke. The meat was stringy and tough; it was meat. They remained there, not to be seen by day. It was very cool in the cave. Jarik tried to think rationally.

"I love you, Jarish."

"Yes," he said, thinking. "I love you, Torsy."

"Jarish . . . you know . . . that I am not your sister."

"I know. Not by birth, Torsy; I know. But it does not matter, for I *am* your brother."

"I have never loved anyone save only you, Jarish."

Thinking, he said nothing. How wonderful if he could find a wark whose young men had died of pox or accidents or been slain, and with only old people and young women, in great need of a strapping young man good with weapons, a protector! How important he'd be; how fine life would be for him then!

"I do not love you as *brother*, Jarish. I want you to *love* me."

He sat, slumped for the cave was low, and she was stretched out, touching him, shoulder to leg, so that she was beside him and faced him. He nodded, hardly having heard her: "I love you, Torsish."

"It is not what I mean! I mean . . . I want you to *love* me, Jarish. I want to be yours."

Idly he patted her upper arm. "You can't be mine, Torsy. You're my sister."

"I'm not!"

Why would she not let him ponder their predicament, try to plan for the future? What was she babbling about, anyhow? He looked at her, blinking.

"Torsy, I am your brother, whether I truly am or not. Very well, Strode—I mean Orrik pulled me from the sea or found me on the beach. They raised me as your *brother*, though. I understand that you aren't enough older than I for us really to be brother and

88

sister. I am your brother, whether I truly am or not. Do you hear me?"

"But we can still be sister and brother, sort of, and I can be yours too."

"No, we cannot. We will stay together, though." He squeezed her arm. "We will stay together. Always. We will not be separated again, Torsish."

"But I want to. . . I want you to. . . you *aren't* my brother, Jarish! We share no blood. I don't love you as a brother, don't you see! I love you as a man. I want you to love me that way, as a man loves a woman. To have me, as a woman."

This time Jarik stared, and there was horror in his eyes. Torsy had passed over a bridge he could not cross. "Torsy! You don't know what you're saying! No! It cannot be."

Torsy wept. Jarik was afraid to try to comfort her. He wanted to, and to hold her, but he did not; lest she should think she was being held as a woman is held by a man, her man. No! How could she speak so? She was his *sister*. She always had been; he could not change that, at the twitch of a gland. She was all he had. With each other, they *belonged*. Otherwise, they were unimportant; they were part of no one else, of nothing else; they *belonged* nowhere. For them, there was no *there*. That she could suggest, even think of making love with him—it shocked and horrified him so that his brain reeled and rocked with the impact of such a concept. No!

He felt pain. Belonging, was what he wanted. A semblance of importance, was what he wanted. Life with honor was what he wanted, and to *belong*, and to be needed and *do* things. He floundered about within his mind, within his soul, desperately seeking out and clinging to the bits and shreds of certainty and strength he found within him. He held them up in his mind and clung tightly to them, as a man lost in a snowstorm will be found clinging to a tree and his spear; things that were steady and stationary and could be depended upon.

Torsy was betraying him, adding to his misery and uncertainty. He was no bad person; he was sure of it. *I am a good man. I shall not make love with my own sister. A good man does not do that.*

Besides, he had never had the slightest shred of thought along that line; she was not attractive to him, as a woman.

Just after sunset they emerged, taking the scarlet pelt. Jarik wore the shield on his back and carried the old boar spear on his shoulder. The sword was sheathed at his side. He had strapped the dagger around Torsy's slim hips and slimmer waist, feeling the bones through her clothing. He carried the ax in his hand, naked wood and curving iron.

Again they walked all night. They were forced to avoid what appeared to be a small wark's outskirts, and then a woodcutter's hut, which looked as if it had just grown among the trees, as natural as the trees themselves. With astonishing daring, Torsy fared close enough to snatch a fine new loaf hanging from an eave. They were lucky there was no dog, and Jarik told her so. She kept her silence.

When they crossed a stream, she slipped but did not fall. She had slipped on a fresh-water mussel, which she picked up and stowed in her belt of leather and cowhair. In silence, remembering that Torsy had always loved shells, he vowed to make her a decoration of it.

They fared on, and the moon went away.

They came at last to the coast. It was not of one of the high-sided inlets that probed Lokusta like the slashes of a giant's sword, but of the sea itself. The occasional keen of gulls and terns, even in the night, had drawn them irresistibly back to the sea.

Jarik and Torsy stood and gazed out over the water, dark and dark, and they were wrapped in their thoughts as an oldster seeks comfort in an old cloak or blanket. They had lived by the sea for eight years, and they had not seen it for ten. Both swallowed lumps that formed in their throats, and tears slid down Torsy's cheeks. Somewhere out there was Oceanside, and Oceanside was dead.

Had others settled there, in ten years? Had *Isparela* and Kiddensahk come again?

They descended to the strand, and walked along, delighting in the sparkle of the sand and the quiet sound of the night-sea. Torsy picked up shells until her hands were full beneath the greying sky, and she began discarding some when she spotted prettier ones. Jarik was watchful, a man of weapons with responsibilities. They walked on sand toward a stony cliff that reared up from the water itself, slicing and ending the beach.

"Look." Jarik was pointing.

It was a high-water cove he had found, in the rising granulite cliff they approached. The dark mouth hung open ten feet above the water line, and they must cross a bit of shallow water to reach it.

"There we will spend the night," he decided, and they had to wade.

The rock face rose up out of the water, and Jarik saw that the Tide-mark was well below the cave. The latter's mouth was perhaps four feet in height and a bit wider across.

"It should be dry," he said. "If that's the case, it will be a good place to sleep. We can build a fire just inside."

He had seen plenty of driftwood, well up the sand and some back against the cliff behind the strand, doubtless hurled and floated there during storms and left to dry, for the tide did not come in so far.

The rock face was tilted slightly back from him, and was not so smooth that he could not see holds for his fingers and resting places for his feet. Besides, the mouth of the cave was only about ten feet above the water; eleven feet from his buskined soles. He waded back to the strand, left off pack and everything but the sword that was strapped at his side in its sheath of wood covered with leather and two bands of bronze.

"Do we have to do this?" Torsy asked, looking apprehensively up the cliff's face. "We have the wolfskins and our cloaks, after all. We could sleep on the sand, back against the main cliff. It wouldn't be that cold."

"Let me look after our night-time protection," Jarik said importantly, and set one foot carefully. Stretching, he caught a handhold, and so he went up.

The cave was tenanted.

Jarik and the two vipers stared at each other. They hissed with their heads up and their bodies coiling and Jarik nearly lost the precarious purchase of his feet on the stone. He stood with his chin just above the cave's floor, a hand on either side of his face, and looked at the two nervous reptiles. They were a little farther away then he could reach. He did not try.

The vipers did not strike; thus he need not let go with his hands and fall back into shallow water to save himself from their fangs . . . water not so shallow that he'd not be hurt, in falling backward.

"Stay down, and away," he said very quietly. "I may fall, or have to jump backwards."

"Jarish! What is it?" Torsy's excitement made her forget to whisper.

"Keep your voice down," he muttered. "Two snakes, that's what. They're spending the evening at home, and I think they don't want company." That sounded cool and level-headed, he thought, and was proud. He considered.

Clinging with the left hand and trying to cling with shod feet to grievously short outthrusts of rock, he bowed his body outward so that he could get at his sword. His right hand passed across his belly, which was almost utterly flat. Trading stares with the snakes on their level and watching their nervously darting tongues, he eased his sword slowly out of its sheath. He got it past his body, between himself and the cliff face, and stood straight again with belly against the stone. That was a comfort. He took time out for several deep breaths.

"Come down, Jarish. Snakes! Oh let them have it—we can sleep on the sand."

"No," he said, stubbornly brave, her protecting male. "I want the cave. And the birds deserve it. With the serpents dead and us gone, the birds may shelter here again. Today, we do!"

"Jarish—they'll strike! What will I do if you're bitten?"

"Ah—they aren't poisonous, Torsish."

The vipers stared. One of them kept rippling into new shapes in that shuddery boneless way of reptiles. Their heads looked swollen. Forked little tongues ran in and out with the speed of hummingbirds' wings and Jarik saw the curving teeth. He had lied, for Torsy's sake. Few snakes habited this land. Of those, only vipers were poisonous. And he'd had to go and stumble on two of them!

It's my destiny. I'm damned. Nothing is ever to be easy for Jarik the Loner, the outsider!

Slowly, cranking his elbow outward, he brought the sword up.

He tried to relax his legs to ease the strain, but could not. His toes were trying instinctively to curl and cling, and that bunched his calves under the buskin-straps and loose woolen leggings—which had gone hot. A seabird screamed three times, close together. Well back up the strand, another replied.

"Get back, snakes," he said, and showed them the sword. A dark blue-grey, it flashed in the rays the sun was sending up over the horizon.

One serpent retreated a bit; the other looked from

the bright metal to Jarik's bright eyes and back again to the sword. A seabird squealed and water lapped.

Jarik had realized that he did not want to drive the serpents, or even one of them, back into the cave. He'd only have to search for it in the dark, at great risk, before he and Torsy would dare enter to sleep. Yet there was not room for a good swing of the sword. He could not chop the vipers, for in swinging he'd strike the stony top of the cave's mouth.

He was committed. He wished he'd never seen the cave, now. But he was committed. No one would know if he gave up the dangerous essay—except Torsy and he. That was enough. He was committed, and he had to do it.

It was not easy, Jarik thought, being Jarik.

He pushed the sword into the cave, along its floor, very slowly. He moved the long iron blade—slowly—over to the wall on his right, with the sword flat on the cavern floor. The snakes watched it, and him. Seabirds screeched and mewed. Torsy said, "Jarish. . ."

He began blinking his eyes to hold the vipers' attention. They stared with bright blinkless eyes like strange vertically barred bits of glass. Tongues were going and coming, going and coming, seeming to seek to taste the air or the scent or sound of him. Each snake was partially coiled; each head was lifted on its sinuous, muscular neck. He was better able to see them, and knew that behind him the sun was coming up. He tensed, and drew a very deep breath.

If there is a god who looks out for this land-by-the-sea, he thought, *let him smile on me now. Or her!*

And with all strength and swiftness he whipped his sword leftward, a sharp flat narrow plane two finger-breadths above the floor of the cave. And the sword's edge caught both snakes.

Rolling and tumbling, lashing and writhing, they were swept against the leftward wall. Both were cut; one was halved. Both halves snapped and writhed and tried to coil while the other viper, sore wounded,

94

struck insanely at the sword and the pieces of its companion. Though he held it pressed against the leftward wall with his sword's edge, Jarik could not force the blade all the way through the raging creature. Could he move faster than it? Terns and gulls scolded and seemed to cry *No, no!*

He tensed, sucked in a breath, prepared himself—and twitched the sword rightward to whip it back so rapidly that it was a blur that struck sparks from the wall even having moved only such a short distance. The snake's head and the three inches behind were parted from its body, which did much coiling and lashing, like a snapping whip. Elation was like white light in Jarik's head and in his knotted stomach.

"Jarish?" From below and sounding far, Torsy's voice was fearful.

"I've killed them. Be still." He heard his voice quiver and chastised himself mentally for having answered.

Releasing the sword, keeping his eyes on four eerily lashing snakes only two of which had heads, Jarik pulled himself up. Both feet pushed and sought projectiles to thrust against. On his belly, he was on the ledge, which meant that he was in the cave: its mouth was flush with the face of the granulite cliff. Four pieces of viper snapped while he, keeping close to the rightward wall, rose on tremulous calves into a squat.

With the sword, he hurled the dismembered, moving carcasses of the cave's former tenants out into the sea. One slipped off the blade and fell almost straight down. Torsy squeaked and Jarik heard the splashes as she danced away.

"Eat, sea-birds," he said, grinning. He was suddenly weak and quivery and humid.

When he peered back into the cave, he saw only stone for a distance of at least twice the length of his body; the rising sun was shining almost directly into the gaping hole in the rock. Nothing moved back there, where grey became blackness. Snakes were wont to be found in twos; surely there were no more. He released the sword and turned to fetch up Torsy and their belongings.

He groaned. He'd have to go down. First they'd have to collect driftwood for a little fire in the cave's mouth, and he would not remain here while Torsy went alone down the strand. With a sigh, he looked down. Jarik grinned at her, told her that they had a cozy home for the night, and he was coming down.

Chapter Nine:
Oak the Healer

The cave provided difficulties that made Jarik think
Torsy may have been right; perhaps they'd have been
better off out under the sky on their cloaks and
shaggy hides. The breeze that came in off the sea was
chill, and from time to time it drove the smoke from
their little fire back at them. Twice birds entered.
They flapped wildly about, screeching, until they
found their way out again.

Below the cave, tide slapped noisily against the
rock.

Too, they were in close proximity, with Torsy per-
sisting in remaining so near they touched. She
snuggled. She hugged him. She stroked him. She told
him she loved him. When none of that brought result
other than brotherly touches, she announced that she
wanted to air her clothing. Despite Jarik's protesta-
tions, she stripped.

Torsy was lean, angular, and of course very pale
where the sun had never touched her skin. A hand
could have been thrust between her thighs while her
knees touched. Her hip-bones were less padded than
Jarik's and her calves seemed no_bigger than his
wrists. Jarik was glad that she he called sister was not
interesting to him, as a woman.

Nevertheless, he was a healthy and virile youth
nearly eighteen, and virgin though he'd never admit
it. Torsy was a female and he had never seen one
nude before. He was stirred. He affected not to be; he
affected to pay her no mind. She came to him and
knelt to put her hands on him.

"I am cold, Jarish."

"Of course you're cold, Torsish. You shouldn't have taken off your clothes. Here, wrap yourself in your cloak and get into the furs."

"It's hardly the time of year to be bundling in furs!"

"It's you said you were cold. *I* will sleep in my clothes."

"They don't smell very good, Jarish."

He did not like the silly little musical quality she affected in her voice. "Stay away from me then," he said with vehemence. Jerking his arm from her hand, he made as if to push her away. There was only bare flesh for his hand to contact, and he drew it back.

"Hold me against the chill. Your hand's so warm! It is delicious to be naked, Jarish . . . but a little chilly. . . . Cuddle me, Jarish. You're so big and warm."

"No! I'll not, Torsy. Not! Now leave off crowding me."

She pouted for a while, then sobbed.

Then, "Love me, Jarik."

"Torsy, I love you as my sister. I do and always will."

"That's not what I mean and you know it! It isn't enough!"

Jarik felt desperate in his discomfort. He tried challenging, helplessly on the defensive and so trying an offense: "You spurn my brotherly love, sister?"

"No. It is just . . . I want more, Jarik, Jarish . . . I want you to—"

"No!"

He remained adamant. She made him more uncomfortable even than he'd been made by name-callers in Ishparshule-wark, and he wished she hadn't come with him into exile. But no, he reflected, he didn't wish that. At least, he added mentally, he thought that he did not. She was just a little unloved bird, fearful and all these years more alone than he, while he'd always been her hero, and now they were exiles and she was without a nest and frightened and unsure. Needing comfort, he told himself, just the same as he. Solace. But—*not with me! Not the way she means, the way she wants. . . thinks she wants. No!*

Still, his treacherous plaguey body was aroused. He wished he could go out of the cave for a time, or that he was sure she was asleep, all cloaked and fur-swathed in a lump so nearby.

Jarik's mind and body agreed to give him peace at last, and he went to sleep.

When he awoke, Torsy had accomplished her purpose, at least physically. There was blood on both of them. Jarik stared and cried out in the illogical reaction of horror to violated taboo—and then he seemed to be falling into darkness, falling, rushing into the yawning mouth of a well, except that the well lay somehow horizontal. A cave. It waited for him, warm and dark and snug. He fell into it. Again he rushed through darkness, and again he was soon sure that he had left his body behind.

This time there was no Guide on the far side of what he thought of as the Cave of Separation From Body. Mists eddied, and then bright sunlight bathed him. He knew that he was flying though he had no wings, felt no vertigo or sensation of movement. No wind touched his body.

Of course not, for my body is left far behind!

He hoped that he could find his way back, and into his body.

Realization came that he could see the terrain below, as if he really were flying. There was the sea, and there the sparkly-sanded strand and the mica-flecked grey of the cliffs. There was the talus they'd descended, and he saw a footprint or three, his and Torsy's, and the place where he'd slipped to slide down several feet. He was flying above it. He flew on along the beach, above it, around the big headland of grey rock. To his right lay only the dark, dark sea that stretched out and out to join the sky. To his left was the land. A forest rose a short distance back from the sea; a broad woods that was mostly of beech. The coast curved, and he saw that the strand ended again and again, cut by rocky cliffs with their feet in the sea.

I'd not be able to come along here if I weren't flying, Jarik mused, without marveling. The thought was one of pleasure and some gratitude, in almost matter-of-fact acceptance. And he flew on.

He saw the village before he was over it. A collection of huts, mostly stone, with a number of boats and over there a few goats and even fewer pigs. Even so, the settlement was larger than Oceanside had been; here might be half a thousand people. A fishing village, he realized. That's why the land in crops was so small no more than a few gardens and two fields of grain, neither large. That's why there were so few animals. These people put to the sea in boats, and from it took their sustenance.

It is not far from where Torsy and I are, he thought, *though we'd have to have a boat or come through the forest.*

Nor had he heard of a fishing village. True, it was days from Ishparshule-wark; perhaps no one there knew of it. That fact, with his not having heard of such a coastal wark, indicated that he and Torsy would be unknown here, unheard of. A haven! A place where an exile might be taken in!

I'd like to fly back over the forest, he thought, *to be sure I've got the direction right and see how far it is.*

He did not; he lost his ability to fly and fell crying out, and with a shock came to his body and his senses in the cave he shared with his sister. And her blood was on them both.

Pressed back against the opposite wall of stone well back in the cave, she was sobbing. He heard himself shouting, and told himself to stop. He did. Orientation returned as if he'd walked far through fog and had to redefine his location and direction now that it had cleared.

He sat sullenly staring. How *could* she! And *why*?

"J . . . Jarish?" she said, fearfully, between sobs.

"I am here."

"Are . . . are you . . . all right?"

"Of course I'm all right. You've hurt me, Torsy, but not my body."

"That isn't . . . that isn't what I meant. Oh Jarish you—"

"Stay away!"

Relieved, she had started to come to him, half crawling. She drew back. She sniffed and her body twitched with dry sobs. After a while, she spoke again. Her voice was small and high.

"You were so *strange*! You—you woke up and . . . and found me, and you shouted. Then your eyes went all . . . all bulgey, and you shook all over like you were freezing, but you weren't cold. Then. . ." She paused, sniffling and shuddering. "Then you. . . you just *stared*, Jarish. You wouldn't talk. Your eyes were like glass and when I waved my hand in front of them you didn't see it. And sud—suddenly you said I was bleeding and had to be *healed*, and you tried to . . . to heal me, because I'd b—bled." And she wept again.

I didn't do all that, he thought; *I wasn't even here!*

He didn't say it. Outside, the sun was past zenith, and he collected himself and his weapons.

"I'll go and find us some breakfast," he said shortly.

"Jarik—"

"You stay here. You shouldn't have done it, Torsy. It's wrong! I'll go and find us some breakfast. You stay here."

And he went.

He found them no breakfast. He missed three birds and two fish with the boar spear because it was thick and heavy, not made for throwing, and too bulky for

101

spearing fish. He did hit one tern, though not with the point. It flew off, shrieking in alarm and then in chastisement.

Not happy, he discovered that he had ranged far, around the headland. That made him less happy still, and he returned with anger on his face. He stomped along, dragging the useless spear.

He saw them from a hundred paces. Two men, with Torsy.

They were using her, on the sand just at sea's edge. She wasn't screaming, though Jarik was sure that she sobbed. One of the men held her, a big one with a single braid like woven wheat. Sheathed sword and buckler lay near him and his back was to Jarik. The other one had Torsy; Jarik saw only their legs, beyond yellow-braid.

Jarik ran, bringing up the boar spear. It was made for the two-handed stabbing and pinning of a boar, that it might not get at the wielder with its tusks. It should prove good for a man, too.

A hundred paces were not so many, at the run. Jarik was no more than twenty running steps from them when the one on Torsy yelled, and the kneeling man looked around.

He lunged for his shield and sword, kicking up sand. Picking them up on the run, he kept moving, straightening, getting the round targe's first strap up his arm and the second one in his hand. He shook his sword free of its scabbard.

Jarik had left his own shield in the cave. He continued his charge, holding the spear with both hands, standing out from his right hip.

The man had got himself ready when his attacker was seven or eight paces away. The other one was fetching his own swordbelt, and shield and spear. The one with the braid took up his stance with his left side to Jarik, shield up and ready to receive the charge, sword at waist level and held out a bit to the side, ready to chop.

Down on him bore a maddened, powerful youth, six feet tall and with close to two hundred pounds on him, with a long running start. He held a wrist-thick spear with both hands, and its point was of iron, tip-sharp, wide as his hand behind, and a foot long.

Jarik did not slow.

An instant too late the man saw that his assailant was a madman who'd not terminate or even slow his charge with a weapon against which there was no standing. Now the braided man had no time to try to move aside. He should have kicked himself into a dive; he did not.

He moved just enough so that he threw away both proper stance and balance. The spear-head struck his shield just to his own left of the center boss with no less noise than that of a woodsman's hard-swung ax biting into a big dry log. The blow to his shield came with the terrible force of strength and momentum. Neither shield nor wielder could withstand it. The spear was borne violently rightward, so that the man's sword-arm was fouled. Surely he did not even know that his left arm had been broken.

He fell, and the spear's haft tried to whip up and away from its wielder; the head was wedged fast in the shield. Jarik hung on. He had to change his direction to avoid falling. He was a near-flying object at the end of a pivot anchored in the shield, which was strapped to the fallen man's broken arm.

Jarik grunted when the spear reached the limit of its rush and tried to stop or return. With it against his hip now, Jarik's momentum carried him on. The man with the braid cried out at the grinding of his broken arm beneath his buckler. His fingers were wide open, but the shield's position relative to Jarik was such that the straps would not slip off the braid-man's arm.

Jarik could not force the spear free. True, he could hold the man pinned, but that was not his purpose, and besides there was a second enemy. He was

103

through with spear-work; the thing was caught fast.
Though the shield's wound gaped, it was not riven.

Jarik released the boar spear and drew sword. He
ducked under his own spear haft to get to the fallen
man.

The sprawled man was partially covered by his
shield. A leg was showing. Jarik chopped it. The man
screamed. Kicking with one leg while the other rilled
blood, he struck with his sword at his attacker's leg.
Jarik chopped the forearm and the other blade just
touched his sword's guard with a smallish ring of iron
on bone. The guard was not struck hard enough to
break; the forearm was.

The man's eyes rolled loosely and he fainted in
pain.

At the same time, Jarik's eyes reported other movement. He looked at the other rapist just as that man,
at a distance of fifteen or so feet, hurled his spear.

Jarik didn't try to duck or strike at the rushing mis-
sile with his sword; he fell flat. One hand squished in
blood from the ruined arm of his first foe. Hard-sped,
the spear rushed over him to strike the sand with a
grating sound and a clatter, far behind him.

Jarik scrambled up. The man had his ax's thong-
loop over his wrist and was coming.

Jarik was without shield while the man advancing
on him held his up and ready. Jarik could have fled,
or called out for mercy or parley. The other man's advantage was great. Neither occurred to him. Nor did
trying to battle without a shield a man who had one:
the moving wall would ever range between the antag-
onists, while Jarik had no defense but his sword.
Using a broad blade three feet long for defense left
little opportunity to strike with it, particularly when
one had been trained with weapon-and-shield, and
particularly when the other man would keep his in
the way while he struck from behind its protecting
wall. Nor had Jarik the reach to try to chop away, un-

scathed, the brass-bossed, round shield composed of three planks bolted crosswise to another.

He did have a little time; seconds. He used them to chop through a useless arm, jerk up a spear-sundered shield, and shake hand and spear free. Now the contrary buckler easily relinquished its grip on the boar spear's long point. The spear fell to the ground. There was no time to pick it up and use it. The second man had broken into a trot when he saw what Jarik was about. There was only time to slip arm and hand through the bloody grips—tight—and present shield and left side to the attacker.

"You bloody vicious *boy*! You've ruined Roke forever!"

Jarik merely glowered in silence, and waited.

What the older man saw in those blue-ice eyes in the open-lipped, teeth-grinding face made him stare—and cease trotting to the attack. What he saw told him to respect his intended victim, now warrior-opponent.

The man moved to his own right. Jarik slowly turned with him, eyes ever on his, shield up. He carried his sword low, at the hip, point angled downward. Man and youth kept their gazes locked, studying, waiting for the moment to essay a swift attack.

Jarik's antagonist wore huge long mustaches that drooped into his beard. Both were so blond as to be nearly white. His flaxen hair was but little darker, bound by a twisted circlet of bronze. He wore another around his thick neck, and a sleeved tunic of faded blue woolen over old leather leggings. These were loose and dark with years of soil and grease. Long ago his shield had been painted red. A few flakes of red still glinted here and there; otherwise the buckler had gone pink over the years. His ax-edge shone from a recent sharpening.

He jiggled his shield and feinted with his ax; Jarik's own shield rose an inch and his sword-arm quivered.

Otherwise he was still, while his eyes glared over the targe. The pink-shielded man moved on, having crouch-paced forty-five degrees of a circle around his foe. Two-man combat was a slow business, between two who knew what they were doing. Circling, changing positions, and feinting occupied most of the time. Awful wounds or death came swiftly, and took no more than two seconds to inflict. There was no constant hack and swing and chop and thrust; blows fell one or three at a time, followed by more pacing, feinting, shifting of feet.

Behind the man now was the sand running back to the cliff; Jarik had turned half around. He took a small sideward step to clear his feet of the sand he'd ground down with his heel, and the man instantly attacked, hoping for the advantage of an off-balance foeman. He struck, low, and while Jarik's shield went down to catch the ax, Jarik's sword swept up.

Both weapons thudded loudly and rang off shields. Both opponents arrested backhand strokes when each saw that the other was prepared. The flurry was over. Again they moved, peering at each other over their shields, their right arms constantly amove, ready to swing fast and hard.

Now it was Jarik who moved in little sideward paces, taken from the crouch. Pink-shield stood almost in place, turning slowly. Jarik feinted. The ax leaped up, coming in overhand, and Jarik jerked his shield up while he moved in a pace and chopped high.

He had lifted his shield enough to save his head and, because he had also stepped toward his opponent, his buckler's iron rim caught the ax-haft just back of its head. With frightful impact the gleaming convex head dropped its lower half over the shield. Jarik was sure he felt it touch his hair. But only his hair—while the impact jarred his arm so that his clenched teeth hurt and his shoulder felt wrenched. Nevertheless his arm had been rising, and yielded under the blow only a few inches. Jarik's biceps bunched and he thrust the shield up again.

His sword, meanwhile, had struck a chunk of wood from the other's buckler. The blade skittered off. Jarik put some pain into his own side then, straining a muscle to lunge backward with a simultaneous pivot to his sword-side. All this in seconds.

During those seconds Pink-shield had not yet reoriented himself to jerk his arm high and free his ax. Caught over the top rim of Jarik's shield, it pulled the man forward with Jarik's back-step. The shield was round and the ax would not remain in place; it slid down along the outer rim with a horrid screeching grating sound.

Meanwhile Jarik completed his rightward pivot and struck again.

A long broad blade of gleaming grey-blue iron swept around the once-red buckler and took its owner in the side, at the ribs. The edge bit well in. The fellow did not cry out; he made an ugly throaty noise as he sucked in a breath sharply, in shock and pain. He was already off balance and the blow staggered him.

Jarik slammed his shield forward, despite the thing's weight. He had borne his own aplenty, to accustom his arm to its presence and drag. Nor hereafter would he be going out for breakfast or anything else without it!

The bucklers clashed; the wounded man staggered but did not fall.

He jerked back his ax and swung it for a swift looping sideward stroke. Jarik thrust his shield as far leftward as he could while he struck again; that stroke was shield-caught, too. The iron rim of his buckler was very late in reaching its goal, and missed the ax; it struck the torc-wearer's forearm. A heavy grunt was wrenched from the fellow's guts.

Fingers came open and wrist-thong slipped. The rushing ax passed behind Jarik, narrowly missing him. He did not see it. He was busy chopping a leg of his disconcerted antagonist. The man grunted again. He dropped, but caught himself on his other knee braced by grounding his shield's rim. The shield did not prevent Jarik from cleaving his skull to the pale, pale eyebrows. They went swiftly red.

The man shivered and rocked. Jarik freed his blade. The dead man's face, already sheeted with blood, banged into his own shield. He fell on it.

Jarik man-slayer went to the other man, who was groaning in his pain. Jarik chopped three quarters of the way through his neck.

His swordblade bore two nicks and was slightly bent, but he turned—and saw that Torsy still lay on the sand. She was not quite naked, though her tunic was rucked high on her chest. She lay on her side, and her huge eyes stared. Jarik saw with horror that blood smeared her loins and was coming from her left nostril as well as that corner of her mouth.

He stared in horror.

His sword slipped forgotten from his fingers. He shook off his shield as

he started for her. She was hurt and bleeding. He must help her. "Jarish," she said weakly, and she was sobbing, poor Torsy. He went to her, squatted, and pressed her back. "Be still," he said, almost harsh in his single-mindedness. His hands ran over her, checked her blooded loins. She was not injured; the blood was hours old and the new had already stopped; it was but the last tissue of her maidenhead. He touched her nose with fingers light as down. It was not broken. Her lip was cut, bleeding. Blood from nose and lip mingled. "Be still, very still," he said, and carefully, gently, tugged her lip out and turned it. "Gaaah," Torsy said in her throat, staring up at him while he discovered that the tooth to the left of the two front biters was chipped. They hit her in the face, he thought, rather coolly, and the broken tooth cut her lip. It was cut, and bruised so that it would swell and stay swollen for some time. Nevertheless there was

108

no permanent damage, nothing to disfigure her face, and he knew that the mouth healed itself better than any other part of the body. With her head back, her nose's bleeding was ending. The tooth should be filed, to get the sharp edges off. He had no file. Later, then. With her head between both hands, he closed his eyes. He pressed in only a little, seeing. She snuffed, swallowing blood. Her head was all right; he saw no other injury. Eyes closed, he passed his hands down her body, as though lightly stroking. She quivered, her eyes fixed a wide gaze on him. He saw no wound. She was hale. He would not use the herbs; both her mouth and her loins were well-equipped to take care of themselves. Ah—the one Grandmother Kilyish had called hart's tail, he saw, might be useful on her lip, for he saw that it reduced swelling.

"Jarish—"

"*Call me not Jarik! I am Oak, the Healer!*"

She trembled, blinking, and kept the huge eyes of old leather fixed on him while his hands traced down her willowy body, all the way to the feet.

"You—you saved me! You killed them both!"

He was horrified. "No! He killed them, the bloody vicious barbarian—Jarik! His heart pounded and his blood ran high and hot the while, for he loved it! Jarik killed them, his second and third human kills! And he enjoyed it! I had nothing to do with it. I am no killer. I have nothing to do with killing. I heal; I am the healer, Oak."

Strangely, the confused patient sought to comfort the healer, then: Torsy came lithely up to a sitting position and clasped him in her arms. He quivered in rage. She felt him limpen, and she held him as she would a child, rocking him while he trembled. She murmured softly to him. And all the while, Torsy shivered in fear and incomprehension.

Poor Jarik, oh Poor Jarish!

Chapter Ten:
Blackiron

Terns and gulls wheeled and mewed and screeked, and the sea made gentle whishing sounds. Kneeling, enfolded in Torsy's arms, Jarik seemed to wake. He pulled away to look at her. *Her mouth and nose were ugly with coagulated blood, but they were not bleeding.*

"Torsy? Are you all right?"

"J–Jarish?" She talked oddly sidewise, against the pain to her lip.

"Oh Torsy yes, yes. Don't you know me?"

She burst into tears and fell against him. He held her while she sobbed hard. He was hardly aware of her nakedness, now. At last she broke into her own sobbing to straighten, and look at him with searching eyes

"Of course I know you, Jarish," she said with a sigh and a quake of dry-sob. "I'm all right. They didn't hurt me much—he just hit me once. You *saved* me, Jarish! You slew them both!" A light seemed to dance in her eyes, and then her face darkened with a frown. "You remember?"

It was his turn to frown. "Of course I remember. How could I forget battling two men?"

"And winning!"

He glanced over toward where a brace of corpses sprawled on the sand they had reddened. "And winning," he said murmurously, thinking about that. And winning! *It was to the death, real combat, and I bested and slew them both! I am a warrior!*

"Jarish. . .what . . . what else do you remember?"

He blinked uncomprehendingly at her. "Remem-

110

ber? Seeing you. Coming to you, with blood on you. Being here, holding you—being held by you."

With her lips slewed to one side she told him what he had done, then; told him of Oak, who called himself healer, and Jarik neither remembered nor understood nor quite believed, and she reminded him of that day in Oceanside, the day *it happened*, when he also had remembered nothing but had, as a healer, bandaged his father as though trained to it. In some fear for its own sanity, Jarik's mind began to consider believing her.

Still he understood and comprehended nothing. Oak? The *healer*? And he . . . "he" had railed against *Jarik? Me?*

"You are a twoness that must be a oneness," the Guide had said, on that journey into another . . . another *something*, to witness the collision of. . . of something; worlds? "It will be agony to you that you do not understand," the nameless Guide had said, "and are two at once."

In agony Jarik thought, *And I will not be whole until I am three? O Guide, how can I bear it!*

Jarik needs help! I need help!

The Guide had made no reply then; he made none now. In this agony, Jarik Man-slayer had no guide. The sun that was Shralla on her horse who was also her beloved rode imperceptibly on its daily course, and gave no reply. The Lady of the Snowmist, a God on the Earth, made no reply. And the weavers wove, and the Guide had been right: Jarik, who was two, knew agony, and fear for himself.

At last, decisively despite confusion and indecision, he rose. He must be at the doing of something. He must always and ever do somethings; to be idle and to think was agony unto a hand in the fire. He looked about.

"They dragged you out of the cave?"

"Th— they found me down here. I was—I was looking for you," she said speaking sidewise. "I—I saw some lovely shells—"

"I told you to stay in the cave, Torsy!"

She looked down, and her swollen lip made her look silly. "I will never disobey you again, Jarik who saved me."

He was forced to drag himself back up into the cave again. There he bundled their few things in a cloak and settled it into the wolfskins. He passed that down to her. She waded over to place the pack on the sand, and when he descended and went to her, she was staring at the dead men.

"They have some things I need," he said.

"It was awful." A great shudder leaped through her. She was tiny, Torsy who was not his sister.

"Stop looking at them, Torsish. They do have some things we need. Then we will go from here."

"Need? Oh Jarish . . . from the *dead?*"

"I slew them in fair combat. What is the law of combat?"

She nodded, spoke low, twisting her wounded mouth: "To him who wins goes that which was the loser's."

"So. Re-bundle these things, Torsy. We'll sip a bit of our water and soon be on our way."

And soon they were, under the sun and with the seabirds soaring and wheeling, screeking and mewing. Jarik moved with deliberate steps, for he was heavy laden. Torsy, too, bore more than she had previously.

Two shields were slung on his back, his own and the once-red one, and their weight was over thirty pounds. Though he could not use two shields, he could not bear to leave such a good one. It was of value and besides he had won it in combat. He wore his belt with sheathed sword and two other belts, baldric-style and crossed over his chest; from one depended a sheathed sword that was spoils. He was ridiculously armed with two axes, two swords and two daggers—he had given Torsy one. The head of the captured ax was covered with the dry, cracking hide of the fox he'd slain and was snubbed close to his belt by its wrist-thong. The big three-quarter-moon head was a patch of bright orange-red fur beside his knee.

The pouch of one man had contained a hare's foot on a thong—protection against the colds of winter— and flint-and-steel, a bit of bright green glass intended as a jewel setting, and two pearls. Their worth was a sword, surely, and therefore considerable food; axes were so often weapons because the making of swords was a high art and they did not come swiftly or cheaply.

The other man's pouch Jarik hung, unopened, on Torsy's belt of woven leather and cowhair. He carried the boar spear and made Torsy bear the other one, that had belonged to the wheaten-mustached man with the once-red shield.

Jarik now wore that man's neck-torc, which was of twisted bronze, plain. Its weighty presence soon ceased to bother him.

"Jarish!" Torsy had exclaimed excitedly when he showed her the pearls. "So much has happened—I forgot to tell you! I opened that mussel this morning!"

"What mussel?"

"The one I picked up in the stream we crossed last night—night before—whenever it was, Jarik! And guess what was in it!?"

"A gold bracelet."

"Oh, Jarish! A pearl—see?"

He saw. It seemed a good one, milkily opaque, smooth and seemingly perfectly shaped. He knew that pearls could be found sometimes in fresh-water mussels, though he had never seen one until now. Was this a good omen?

How could it be? She had found it right before she had been attacked by two men bent on rape!

Climbing up from the beach was no simple matter with them laden so, even on the shaley slope. He made it. Torsy used the spear she bore as a staff, and she made it too, panting and proud. Already her legs were tired, she avowed. Jarik pointed to the woods and told her that they would walk anyhow.

"Why the forest, Jarish?"

"Because it is here and we can't walk on the sea."

She smiled, and winced when that brought pain to her inwardly cut lip. "But—I mean, why not walk along the strand, then?"

"I went around the headland this morning. The beach ends less than a mile from it, with a big cliff rearing right up out of the water. There's no place else to go."

Frowning or perhaps squinting against the sun of morning, she said, "But why through the wood, Jarish? I mean—to where?"

"Beyond the forest lies a fishing wark. A wark of fishermen, I mean, on the coast."

Torsy looked at him. "How do you know?"

"I know. It is there. There is a score of boats, and one is an extremely bright red, with yellow oars new-painted..You'll see."

And Torsy, who understood no more from that than she had before he'd made reply—and indeed understood little less than Jarik himself—was silent. They entered the woods.

Around them pressed boles of trees dark as night, dark as the mind of Jarik who was Two. Above their heads branches met and crossed and their foliage commingled intimately in nature's weaving. The rays of the sun did not pierce that thick canopy of deepest green. Only light did, and only somewhat.

Trees crowded close, and bushes and hardy shade-greas impeded the way of their feet. Now and again their burdens caught on or thumped against this or that tree or foliate bush. Often they trod on moss, which nestled close to the trunks of the beeches. They fared into the woods, and through the woods. Birds warbled and cheeped and shrilled their way and the air they breathed tasted green, smelled green, redolent

114

of bark and moss, leaves of trees and bushes and the berries some of them bore. The way was not easy. The going was slow, in the coolth and mid-morn twilight of the forest. With his sword Jarik hewed away barriers raised by nature. With his hands he held aside branches until Torsy came abreast him, that branches thrust aside and released might not strike her as if in attack. Branches and long tendrils of some ambitious bushes caught at their burdens and clothing, their calves and thighs, and whished free as if reluctant to let go.

Of animals they saw none.

The rough edge of Torsy's chipped tooth bothered her lip, which bore a small cut and a goodsized swelling. Jarik sympathized absently, whilst trying to think. Jarik. Oak. Jarik who was Two. Jarik Manslayer; today he'd fought his second and third true opponents, in the death-combat, and both were gone to Him whose invitation could not be denied (*Both*, he thought firmly and with his lips compressed and his eyes slightly narrowed while deliberately he thought the taboo word, *are dead.*)

His pondering did not help. Neither did Torsy's talk, ever rising from behind him. Once he released a whippy low branchlet apurpose, so that she'd have something else to think about. That switch made by nature for the backsides of recalcitrant or errant children struck her just above the knee, and Torsy had something else to think about, and to talk about. She did, and Jarik apologized—and felt guilty, for that too was one of his curses. Besides, the nasty little ploy had not silenced her at all.

They fared through the woods, and hours passed. Each of them fell once, under heavy burdens, their packs and the combat-spoils Jarik was determined to keep and convey to—wherever they were going. Those mishaps were painful to the faller and ludicrous to the watcher. Each was so laden that the falls

115

were noisy and each had to have help in getting up. And the weavers wove thus:

They came upon a path. Jarik halted until Torsy was by his side. He shifted his pack and grounded shield. That arm twitched.

"Is it a path?"

"It is," he said, squinting along it to the point at which it vanished in the crowding cool of the wood.

"An animal trail to fresh water?"

"Perhaps. I see no deer tracks; those sharp little hooves print deep. It goes the way we're going. Perhaps it's a human path. Perhaps it leads to the fishers' wark."

"Jarish—how *do* you know there is a wark beyond the wood?"

"I do. It is there. You'll see."

"But how do you *know*?"

He told her, though simply. "Whilst you say I was . . . Oak, I felt that I was me, and had . . . left my body. I flew, and I saw the wark from the air."

"Flew!"

"So it seemed. Don't question me. You know I don't know."

"Oh Jarish; perhaps when Oak comes into your body you have to leave."

How easily she said those words, talked about the confounding and mind-shaking! "Perhaps," he said, "when I leave, Oak comes."

After a moment Torsy said, "That's what I said."

"No," Jarik told her, "it isn't the same. Come—Let's follow the path. It will be far easier."

"Suppose it's an animal trail, to water. A bear might . . ."

He showed her a smile, carefully arranged. "We are certainly well armed, Torsish! The trail goes our way. Should we avoid it, plunge on past into the woods and then turn and parallel the path, for it goes our way? That were silly. If it is a beast-trail, and there is a beast coming, it will hear us anyhow."

"I suppose. It will be less easy walking—wait!"

For he had set off along the path. It was fairly well trodden, though not to the bare earth, and perhaps a foot and a half wide. It was man-made, he soon knew, chiding himself for being slow at spotting the signs: he saw the scabbed ends of truncated branches and bush-stems that had been hacked off, not merely broken by the passage of an animal's body.

They fared along the trail. It was easy to follow and now their way was so much simpler for their burdens caught on nothing and were far easier to bear. Naturally the path wound a bit, weaving among the trees. Those remained mostly beech, with the dark grey-green bark, whole and uniform even on trees that were manifestly very old. There were few beech-nuts; either the wood housed animals that today stayed clear of the two human invaders but normally snaffled up the fallen fruit of the many beeches, or the people of the fishing-wark gathered them for their own diets and their animals'. Now and again one did crackle or try to roll underfoot ere it broke, crushing, but these were small and rotten or rotting.

"Jarik—how do you know this path leads to your wark? We can't even see the sun!"

"I just . . . know," he said, and was glad she was behind him and could not see his face, and its frown. How did he know? He . . . *knew*.

Oh! "See the moss?" he said, as though in boredom. "On what side of the tree does moss always grow?"

"A lot of this is ground moss, Jarish, and grows all around the trees!"

He pointed triumphantly. "Ah but see? —on the tree itself. North!"

Indeed though, he knew that was confirmation of the direction he took, not the reason he *knew* they were headed for the village he had seen while departed from his own body. He just knew, as surely as he knew that the village really was there.

Though they heard occasional sounds, they heard

117

no animals. Nor were human nostrils sufficiently well developed to pick up the animal scents that abounded; Jarik and Torsy smelled only green.

Of other humans during that trek they saw but one, and that after hour upon hour of working their way and then walking, with more ease, along this trail. And then they came upon the man, for so, surely, had the weavers woven.

He was older than he was young, this man with the wedge-shaped face, long chin, and haystack hair going grey, though he was neither old nor young. He lay still, just beside the trail so that the hand of one outflung arm lay in their path. The fingers of that hand were curled though moveless, and their tips and nails were encrusted with dark red-brown stains. Blood. His eyes were closed under thin, pale brows, and his chest moved in breathing just as ragged as those brows.

"Jarik! Is he . . . dead?"

"Breathing, see? Dead men's eyes don't close, Torsy, unless they die in their sleep, or unconsciousness." Jarik squatted beside the man. "He's hurt. He— *uh!* His leg—it's all over blood. Ah."

"Jarik?" She was hesitant to come close, and lingered on the path a pace or two away.

"I . . . think he must have been setting a trap for some big animal and it tripped and the spear went through his leg. *Through.* It's torn a terrible hole . . . uh! I don't know what to *do,* Torsish!"

"Let me see. Ooh. We—we need to stop the *bleeding,* Jarish. Uh . . . I don't know either. Oh Jarish! Why are we so helpless? He may die, and we might be able to save him!"

She was squatting beside the unconscious man, beside Jarik, bending forward with one hand braced on the ground by the man's leg. The hand slipped. With a little cry, Torsy partly fell, sidewise. Jarik's hand leaped out to enwrap her nearer arm. He steadied her, straightened her, both of them still

118

squatting. Her other hand came up then and he saw that it was all over blood, and dripping. He thought she had slipped and cut her hand open on the trap's spear, and he knew horror, and

"*Let me see that hand,*" Oak said. "*Quickly.*"

"Jarish, it's not even—"

.."*Don't call me that!*" *Oak said, with vehemence unto viciousness.* "*He kills, I heal. Ah! Silly little girl . . . this isn't hurt at all. You just slipped in his blood. Here, get out of the way and let me see this man. Umm. See that plant—there, with the funny leaves. Yes, that one— Of course! Pull it up. Don't break it off; pull it up, and find more. Bring me them. Go along, girl, Go! Now . . . um hmm,*" *Oak said, lifting the man's eyelid, letting it slip back over the blue eyes.* "*The shock . . . he's unconscious. Blood-flow is slowed but it won't stop. with that clean-through wound. We must stop it.*"

With one of Jarik's knives, Oak cut the thick cord free of the spear, then of the truncated sapling that had provided the trap's anchor. A few seconds later the finger-thick cord was wrapped around the man's injured leg and twisted about a short stick, until it was terribly tight.

Torsy was rather longer at her task, and Oak went impatiently to her. "*Give me those,*" he said, and without another word snatched the leafy plants she'd collected. He slapped the roots violently against Jarik's sword-sheath as he strode back to his patient. Dirt flew. Muttering angrily, Oak discarded several plants that Torsy had failed to pull up but had kept, broken off, anyhow. "*I said just the roots,*" he called over his shoulder in a voice more surly than not. He proceeded to waste water from dead Roke's pack: he washed the dirt-dribbling roots, and his hands. Next he made a thorough mess of roots and hands by rolling the tuberish things between his palms.

"*Should be more like a paste,*" Oak said, but applied the ruined roots to the fallen man's wound anyhow. The cord-and-stick arrangement had slowed the flow of blood to a scarlet ooze. It soon thickened; the semi-crushed roots were doing their work. Torsy came with more. She stopped, staring.

"You . . . you fixed him!"

"Hardly. Remember that plant. It thickens things, liquids. Such as blood."

"What—what's it called?"

"I don't know. Spare me silly questions. This cord around his leg stops the blood. Won't let it flow to the wound at all. The root is a thickener. We will have to loosen the cord every now and then. Remember that."

"Why?"

He stared at her; no, he glowered, this businesslike, Jarik-hating healer called Oak who shared Jarik's body. *"It's important. I have said it. Blood has to flow through the body. Otherwise the skin dies; rots. He should stay here a while. A long while, in truth, but he'd best be got to his own wark and folk. For that at least two men will be needed, with a litter. The path is too narrow for him to be pulled on a one-man litter; he'd be jarred too much."*

He was very wise, Torsy thought, this unfriendly healer who shared the body of her foster-brother and hated him the while. She said, "What—what do . . ."

"Either you and I construct a litter, and carry him to his wark—however far—or one of us remains with him and one of us goes to his wark, shows them . . . this—and brings back two men with a litter to carry him. A door. A fisherman's net. Anything; whatever they have." He handed her the amulet he removed from his patient's neck; a stag's head carved from wood, very handsomely, with skill.

Frowning, staring, Torsy put her head on one side. "O-Oak?"

Oak the Healer glowered at her.

The man was called Toodibahk, which was of course Turibark and meant Groundspear, in this lan-

guage that was the same and yet slightly different
from that of the inland warks Jarik knew, as theirs
was the same and yet differed from that of the
Oceanside of his birth. The village, just where and as
Jarik had seen it from the air, was Harnstarl:
Blackiron.

It was Oak the Healer who entered Blackiron with
Turibark, who was indeed a trapper among the fishermen. Even before Turibark recovered his senses it
was obvious that Oak had repaired him; that Oak was
a healer beyond compare; that he had saved
Turibark. However youthful, he was a most valuable
person. Oak was welcomed in Blackiron, and Oak's
woman Torsye, for none of Harnstarl seemed able to
say the name without that feminine ending.

After giving a long series of instructions concerning
Turibark's care—and snarling at a woman who
brought him a colicky infant, hardly worthy of his
skills—Oak fell down and lay asleep for a long, long
while and when he awoke he was not Oak anymore
and knew nothing at all about injuries, or illnesses, or
healing.

Chapter Eleven:
Jarik Outlander

Jarik became, naturally enough, Turibark's aid and apprentice.

Torsy of the filed-down tooth returned to sewing, and learned to clean fish, and to salt them and make and mend nets, and she gathered beechnuts with others of *Harnstarl*: Blackiron.

The village of Blackiron seemed to have grown around the huge chunk of rock tall as a ten-year-old and fatter than the fattest person of any village. It shone as if its many spiky excrescences and surrounding hollows were facets of a great blue-black-and-grey jewel; as if it had been heated beyond the highest possible temperature. The people of Blackiron said that it was of iron, not stone. Obviously it was fabulously heavy and had never been moved from where it rested. Blackiron Stone, the newcomers were assured, was a sphere; the rest was buried in the earth. A bit more than a hemisphere stood above, in the air.

Blackiron Stone was not touched. It was an altar. Four times annually the fisherman Blut, him called the Priest of Iron but never the Lord of Iron, presided over the wark's ceremonies. These involved gathering about Blackiron Stone, of course. For the rest of the year Blut fished with his sons, in his newly-painted red boat with its yellow oars.

Blackiron Stone was an altar then, and a shrine. Yet no structure had been raised about it or atop it, nor rested there any sort of idol or icon.

The stone—or massive single chunk of incredibly heated iron—was jagged, frequently pitted. Some of the pits were deep. The one atop it was deep, Jarik—who would not allow himself to be called Oak—was told. Imbedded well in the pit or natural niche was the point of the sword. It stood atop the stone as though someone had slashed it down into the mass, and left it there.

The Sword.

It was not a god, the Black Sword of Blackiron Stone of the wark of Blackiron. It was an object of veneration, not worship. Standing above the Blackiron Stone, the Sword was black and shining through blade and hilt and guard to pommel. The Sword was gift, and symbol, and perennial reminder of the gods of Blackiron.

Gods, aye. These were the Iron Lords.

Horrified villagers prevented Jarik from touching the Sword, which he was easily able to reach and which he coveted instantly he saw it. The Sword was the gift and mark of the protectors of Blackiron, the warkmen said; the Lords of Iron.

Nonsense, a too-arrogant young Jarik Outlander said. And who were these Iron Lords who presided unseen over Blackiron-wark and its Blackiron Stone surmounted by the Black Sword?

Gods. The Iron Lords were among the Gods on the Earth.

Long ago the Lords of Iron—who were three—had come here to the settlement that would become Harnstarl. As a sign of their favor, they left the Sword. Its presence protected the wark, which had existed ever in peace since that time of the First Visitation.

The Iron Lords had much Power.

"You can yet see the mark with which they blasted the mountainside, in demonstration of their power to those hundred-and-eleven first people of Blackiron."

And Jarik went and looked at the mountainside, and saw there a great long rent down its side, in the very rock, like a wound made yesterday in the face of an old man and not yet closing. And he knew that he looked upon the completely impossible . . . or a sign of preternatural power. For a time, the outlander youth was impressed into silence.

Then he turned to his instructor, who was she called Seafoam, at that time most interested in Jarik who had been Oak Turibark-saver.

"And the Iron Lords did that."

"Aye, Jarik."

"And they protect Blackiron, with that mountain-riving power."

"Aye. Can you not see? It is a happy wark, ever peaceful, and we all eat well and never know hunger. We prosper and abide and our children are healthy. We owe this to the Iron Lords."

So had Oceanside, he thought, on another shore far from here, and without these unseen gods. Yet, he could not help thinking that mayhap had Tomaz-ten, Oceanside, been under the protection of the Lords of Iron, it had not been murdered and burned and destroyed by the Hawkers.

"And they ask nothing in return, the Iron Lords?"

"What should gods ask?" She gestured at the mountainside with the clear inference that beings who could do *that* need ask naught or aught of anyone.

"Why should anyone do aught for nothing at all?"

She regarded him for a time without speaking. Seafoam was not swift enough of brain to recall that he as Oak had done for Turibark with no apparent thought of recompense. Nor would she take issue with him for his brain was very good—and besides, at that time Seafoam was most interested in Jarik, whom she did not call Outlander.

"What does Blackiron do for the Iron Lords, Seafoam?"

She did not answer that day, and eventually Seafoam wed a youth of about Jarik's age then, for Jarik said nothing to her father, nor bore him gift.

Jarik had his answer another time. He had it from Turibark, who mended though he kept a limp. That which the Iron Lords required of Blackiron was similar to that required of Ishparshule-wark by the Lady of the Snowmist, and yet very different. They must have a youth, the Iron Lords had said, a male: the strongest and most hale in the community. And, just as the Lady of the Snowmist did from her northward protectorate of Ishparshule-wark, the Iron Lords took that youth. Unlike Brathis of Ishparshule-wark and those before him, this youth of Blackiron was never seen again.

Some, though, Turibark told Jarik, said that when next the Iron Lords came—nineteeen years later—some said that the voice of one of them sounded like the voice of the taken youth, had he aged nineteen years more.

Jarik thought on that.

At last he asked, "And when the Iron Lords came that time, nineteen years later . . . did they take again the finest youth of Blackiron—and keep him?"

The answer was aye, they had. This Turibark had seen with the two eyes that were his, and Ganter Greatchest had not been seen again. A youth every nineteen years was hardly a dear price to pay for the eternal favor and protection of such as the Iron Lords, gods on the earth!

Jarik, who was ever rebellious and coveted the Sword besides, did not agree. "You are *Fools!*" he cried, the Outlander come to Blackiron as heroic healer to remain as trapper's aide and apprentice.

No no, they were not; he did not *know*, for he was not of Harnstarl. The Iron Lords possessed *power*; one youth every couple of decades was little sacrifice to gain the protection of such power.

"And no one has ever taken up the Black Sword?"

Turibark looked shocked, but replied equably, with his accustomed patience that was sometimes, to the never-patient Jarik, maddening. "No one has had to," Turibark, Groundspear, said. "There has been no need for the Sword, for any sword, in Harnstarl."

And a day later Jarik ever Outlander stood in the proximate center of Blackiron, and looked upon the Sword that stood above Blackiron Stone.

"I would take it up," he said, for he was cocky still, and Seeking, with impatience heavy on him as a leaden mantle, and as ever he was an outsider, and so unsure.

Those around him were shocked. He who was fisherman every day of the year save four, when he was Priest, was worse than shocked. His eyes rolled and he seemed to stagger as if at a physical blow.

"Do not even think such," Jarik was told. "It is forbidden!"

On that day Jarik said "You are all fools!" and he went from among them. They talked of him, much in mutters with frequent dark glances after him and even at his foster-sister, and it was not so long after that Seafoam's mother announced her betrothal to another, and she wore the pearls that were betrothal-sign in Harnstarl.

Another time he thought to reaffirm that there were three Lords of Iron. True. They were the Lord of Destruction, and the Lord of Annihilation, and the Lord of Dread. Even Jarik Outlander fell silent at the sound of such fearsome names.

And another time Jarik asked what was the appearance of the mighty Iron Lords, who had scarred a mountain and took away an occasional son of Blackiron and returned him not, and whose names were so fearsome.

Big men they were, all in armor of blueblack iron like the skin of a serpent in sunlight. Because masks were attached to their helms, curved and carven plates unlike the serpentish mail, none had ever seen the visage of any of the Lords of Iron. Nor even the hands, for they wore mailed gloves. Faceless men then, all in iron. So dressed the fisherman-priest Blut, four times annually during Rites.

"And when next they return, these faceless men,"

Jarik said, "do you think one will sound like him they took on their last visit?"

The people of Blackiron, he was advised, did not think on that, nor was it spoken of.

Everyone in Harnstarl wore pearls; Torsy had strung that one she had of the freshwater mussel. It was different, and envied, and she was very glad. Jarik wished that he possessed that which was envied, and he tried too hard, in the manner of any unhappy, unbelonging, Seeking youth. He even sought to will himself to leave his body, that Oak might return and bring honor and praise and envy on both himself and Jarik. He was unable to accomplish it. Jarik's going out-of-body and Oak's advent had been something that just happened, and he could not induce the phenomenon. It occurred to him that Oak came when Torsy was hurt or Jarik thought so, but she came to no harm, in Harnstarl, nor would Jarik deliberately hurt her who was at once his sister and not his sister. And so he abode in Harnstarl; Blackiron. He thought about Kiddensahk from time to time. *Live*, Kiddensahk, *until I come for you!*

Was Jarik happy?

Few could have told. He pretended. He sought alternately to please and to gain attention by shocking, by being the rebel and scoffer. That proved no more successful for him than for any other youth who tried too hard. He but suffered being friend and aide to the grateful Turibark. Jarik was superb with the sword; here there was no need of such. He was fascinated by the Black Sword of the Iron Lords, and coveted it; it was untouchable. Not even Jarik would go so far as to break such a taboo; he was unaccepted still, and here on sufferance. That he was now and again reminded of that did not aid his mental state of maturing, not at all. He worked out with his sword and his captured weapons, axes and the spear and shields. This activity, unknown and so alien in Harlstarl, drew watchers. Naturally there were some who were so fascinated that they wanted to learn. With a single exception, these were other youths, male. He taught them, secretly cursing the Iron Lords for affording this wark such protection that it had no need of men of weapons.

He accompanied Turibark, and was thought a trapper, though he knew that he was not and would not be. Yet he did not know what he would do, what he would be. Nor did he know what he awaited. Something. A change. He did not forget Kiddensahk, and his dream of vengeance for dead Oceanside. Discovering to his great surprise that part of the costume Blut wore in rites was real, iron rings linked and attached to a coat of boiled leather, Jarik learned the name of its maker. He went to that man, Steed Bighand the Blackwelder or Ironworker. Jarik found him huge, and not young. Steed remained ox-strong, and showed the youth.

"I should not care to fight you," Jarik said, for he wanted something and understood somewhat of persuasion through flattery, "Steed Bighand!"

"I do not fight," Steed told him. "In Blackiron we do not need to fight, Outlander."

"Such a one as you need never fight anyplace," Jarik said. "Strong men with swords in hand would flee you, Steed Bighand!"

They came to a bargain. Jarik would provide Steed with meat, twice every ten days, and promised too the services of his un-sister, who would mend Steed's clothes, for he had no wife and he and his daughter were not friends. And so Steed the worker in iron began the slow and lengthy business of making a coat of mail for Jarik the Outlander. He would need a mail coat, Jarik told himself, when he went for Kiddensahk.

Jarik saw Torsy, and he avoided Torsy. Jarik feared her, though none other did. He did not want to lie with his sister, even though she was not his sister. She resigned herself to a lack of companionship with him, much less that which she desired beyond friendship, and she continued to esteem and worship him almost as a god. He saw to it that, for the most part, she esteemed and worshiped from a distance.

He wished that the Iron Lords would come, and choose him, and he wished that they would not. He wished for a chance to be Jarik, *Jarik*, JARIK, not Orrikson Jarik or Strodeson Jarik or Jarik the Exile or Jarik Loner or Jarik the Outsider, but Jarik; a person, a man important, known and respected.

Was Jarik happy, then?

Of course not; he was miserable. He covered, relatively well. Some few knew; most did not. He trapped, and he worked out, and he checked on Steed's (secret) progress, and he reveled in teaching the use of arms—for which he was criticized. Arms were not needed in Blackiron, they said, and so they were not wanted. Only trouble, they said, could come of this outsider's, this Outlander's teaching their youths the weaponish use of swords and axes and knives. He was even discussed in Council, as he had been before, in Ishparshule-wark. They had taken in among them not Jarik, but Oak—the healer. Where was he now? Jarik could not heal. Torsye knew more than he, and had at least taught them to recognize and use the weed they called Thickroot, and she remembered the manufacture of some of those things in the remedy pack she had of Grandmother Kilyish; some of them were unknown in Blackiron, and she led women to find and fetch in the ingredients, from the wood. Jarik knew nothing of such matters. The big sun-haired hulk had disappointed many who had sought his help with their injuries, until at last the people of Blackiron ceased to ask medical aid of Jarik the Outlander, who was taller than any of Blackiron and more muscular than all but three.

We do not know how long Jarik and Torsy abode in Harnstarl before the Hawkers again entered his life, and then the Iron Lords. Some say it was but a

129

year, while the weavers wove. This is unlikely; surely more time passed. Other stories claim years, and there is one that purports to tell us of Torsy's being wed to a man of Blackiron, a widower. Little credence is given that story or the one that Jarik, too, wed, and that his bride died within a few months in her pregnancy, after and during an assortment of omens and signs doubtless accreted long after his time. That he wed there in Harnstarl is surely not so. What is so is that we are not sure, and so Jarik's age was lost track of in Blackiron, and never again can we be sure of his age at various stages of his life. Perhaps the matter of Rander and the Lord Cerulean occurred only in his twenty-first year, and perhaps he was five-and-twenty or, according to some estimates, even older—though that is an estimate in which there is placed little credence. Tales that the voyage to and from Osyr's Isle was a matter of years can surely not be correct.

Torsy and Jarik abode in Blackiron, and surely it was for more than a year. No occasion arose or could be induced for another appearance of Oak, nor did Jarik experience his leaving of the body as he supposed it, or, so far as is known, any other mystical experience. In time he came to assume that all such was behind him, with his early youth and puberty. He was not sorry.

It has been said that there exists a partner for everyone on the earth—and some say that few find that partner, but settle for another. Despite his ever being not only youth but *boy*, and an individual apart and lonely and Seeking, Jarik was tall and strong and favored with good looks of the face. Many more than few women looked on him with favor, although his sexual life seems not to have existed. In the case of Alye of Blackiron, the attraction was mutual. None but admits sureness in this; Jarik had high fondness for Alye.

The weavers were weaving.

The day came when Alye, with Torsy and Nevre,

went from Blackiron into the woods to gather nuts, for they must be there before the squirrels and wild pigs. And that day, with his mind on a liaison with Alye, Jarik also went into the forest, to inspect the traps, his and Turibark's . . . or to "inspect the traps."

Alye was not there to meet him at the assigned place. He did not long wait, for patience was a virtue he did not possess.

He went looking, and found the trail of the three young women. He followed. Still he did not find Alye. Instead he came upon Nevre and Torsy, who was his sister and yet not. They were all over blood, the both of them, and lay in blood, and they had been chopped with iron blades and did not move. A trail led away from them, through the forest.

Oak did not appear on this occasion, for there was no need of him. Torsy lay on her back with her eyes open, and Jarik saw the fly that walked on her cheek, and trod on her eyeball, and Jarik saw that she did not blink. Nor on this occasion, the second most shattering of his life, did Jarik collapse, or even waver in indecision. He knew what to do, as though a horrid fearsome calm had come upon him.

A youth not quite sane returned through the wood to Blackiron. His was a grim and purposeful face; he was a bleak and horrifying figure from which people drew and backed away, when he returned to the wark. He strode through that little village of fishermen, and to its center, and there he stopped. His eyes were like glass, frozen in ice.

No; it was only a pause.

None had ever taken up the Black Sword from the Blackiron Stone in Blackiron. There had been no need, and after a century the standing sword of gleaming, unrusted black iron was an object of superstition encrusted with injunctions; it was taboo. None of Blackiron ever took it up or even considered it; none even so much as touched it.

Jarik the Outlander touched it, without stretching. He did more; he drew it easily from its niche and rushed it through the air; sharp, and shining, and rustless.

Those who were there—women and the young and very old, as the men were out with their nets—were struck with worse than dismay. Shocked, scandalized, they sought to stay him. The sword itself, and Jarik's dreadful face, dissuaded them. They fell back, only following him to the very edge of the wood with their constant imprecations mingled with pleas. With the long black sword of the Iron Lords, Jarik stalked away, and many many eyes gazed after him as he disappeared into the beechwood.

When he came upon Torsy's killer, over a day later, the trio of men from hawk-head ships was as half a man against the maniacal animal who came ravening upon them with his awful black sword.

Chapter Twelve:
The Black Sword

Surrounded by corpses in the little glade, Jarik turned to look upon Alye.

She shrank back against the broad-boled tree, tremulous hands to her mouth, and she but shrank the more when Jarik held out a hand to her.

In his other hand there was strangeness: Hawker blood ran down the sleek blade of black metal in the manner of colored water running off glazed pottery, or off an oiled surface rather than a blade exposed for a hundred years, unoiled and untouched, to all the elements. As the blade had refused to rust, it now bore not so much as a nick. This despite the fact that a shield of one of the three Hawkers was cloven from ironbound rim to boss.

Shrinking still as though from the foulest demon rather than the youth she was so fond of, Alye slipped slowly down the tree's bole. She sank to the ground. There she sat loosely, back against the tree. Blood stained her thighs, which were bruised. Spittle drooled from the mouth she seemed unable to close. She had been crushed, defeated, mistreated and degraded, brutalized by the armored men driven only by lust to the callous use of her. They had paid with their lives ... and what had Alye paid?

Blading his sword in the blood-splashed turf, Jarik went to her. Horror was a dark clawing force in his brain as he started to bend to her, and it rose up like ground-mist, and whelmed his mind.

Bruised, bloodied, much ill-used, Alye appeared to be in shock. Oak, tracing his fingers over her while she cringed all ashudder, learned more; he saw within

134

her. She was internally torn and ruined of body and mind; she was hopelessly insane. Oak the Healer could do nothing. He rose, with tears rilling down his face, and retreated from the brain and body he presently commanded. This time, he let Jarik know with certainty what he knew. Then Oak was gone, and the body fell to the ground.

Now there were five such bodies in the glade; a destroyed young woman, and the corpses of her destroyers, and an unconscious young man.

Jarik awoke, and *knew*. He gazed on Alye, and the tears Oak had left to dry on his face were joined by fresh ones. He blinked hard while he turned and drew the Black Sword from the ground. Then he turned back to Alye and did what he must; he ended a helpless animal's permanent misery.

After that Jarik went wild.

He hacked the three male corpses to pieces. Armor and torcs, a helm and the big brass buckle of a belt, skin and muscle and bone; all these the Black Sword clove, and it remained free of bend or nick while the blade remained sharp as ever. The madman who wielded it was aware of this and yet unaware, though he knew that the Sword was far from ordinary, beyond even the very best blade his people could create, and he knew that the Iron Lords who'd shaped and forged it must indeed be gods.

Even a madman respected the blade, though, and Jarik used ax and sword of the slain Hawkers to dig the grave. In it he laid the Alye he might have loved, or have come to love.

Then, sweaty and spattered with gore not his, he stood in that hideous glade and looked about. The glazed stare of madness left his eyes, like ice before the warming sun of spring. And Jarik wept. And, as he was Jarik and a man of weapons, he took spoils. He took up the excellent buckler he had so admired when it rode the arm of one of Alye's violators, who was now nigh-headless.

135

With it on his arm, Jarik returned through the forest to Blackiron.

It did not occur to him until he was well nigh there that Hawkers sailed asea on ships, and three comprised no crew; where there were three there must be more. He was right. There were more, and they were raiding Harnstarl.

Perhaps forty were attacking, armored in helms and shirts of metal-studded leather or iron chain, armed with spear and sword and ax wielded by experts from behind round bucklers. The wind age, the sword age, the wolf age had come upon Blackiron.

Blackiron was a larger community than had been Oceanside—and its people even less capable of defending themselves. They could but die. A few of those Jarik had been teaching had snatched weapons and were faring forth in defense of the others of that peaceful fishers' wark. Steed, too, held off attackers, by dint of his size and strength: with a great bar of iron in either hand, he let none near him by the simple means of constantly whirling himself and both awful clubs. Jarik saw a spear-haft splintered while the force of the blow knocked its wielder nearly off his feet; saw another Hawker duck low and drive in, to be brained by Steed's leftward club of iron. A Hawker down!

And several villagers down in their blood. A spear drove into the back of a boy of nine, and people shrieked; in attack and glee; in fear, horror, and pain.

From the woods then came ravening a ferocious beast on two legs, and yellow hair flew behind him as he charged. The Hawkers did not know he was upon them until three of their number had fallen to him. He wielded a strange and refulgent sword of sheer black, and bore a shield some of those hawk-shippers recognized as belonging to one of their scouts.

The people of Blackiron had no word for a man become as the animal that, occasionally and only in highest summer, grew suddenly fearless so that, drooling foam, it attacked anything, even itself. The people of Blackiron had never seen kill-rage, in a human. The Hawkers, among whom the phenomenon was hardly common though known and recognized, had two phrases for it; in the battle-rage and the machine-that-fights.

Now they were mindlessly attacked by one caught in the battle-rage: a young yellow-haired man become *morbrin*: the machine-that-fights.

It came from the wood upon them like a lean killer wolf on snapping lesser foxes; like a rut-roused stallion on geldings in the wrong place at the wrong time; like a blood-mad man of weapons on normal weapons-trained warkmen who had assumed a few hours of easy slaying and rapine, followed by the taking of booty.

A small army attacked Blackiron; like an army of one, Jarik attacked the army.

The Black Sword hewed an arm nearly off, just below the shoulder, and withdrew in a great splashing wake of scarlet to chop half through a buckler, ringing on the iron boss. That man's stroke was spoiled by the tremendous shock to his shield-arm and he suffered, helplessly, the indignity of having a foot slammed into him; thus Jarik gained leverage to free his sword of the shield. It tore free with a shriek of wood to leap across and *shear through* another sword, with a brief clang that left a Hawker staring goggle-eyed at the few inches of broken iron standing forth from his fist. Then he was struck by a shield swung madly by a *morbriner*, and while he fell another was made to stare, too—at nothing, for the awful blade in the hand of the awful maniac sheared more than halfway through his neck. He was dead before his heart knew it and before he fell Jarik was at another. The Sword seemed to tremble, to achieve life in his hand.

A hand flew on a long trail of dark blood, and the hand still clutched the ax it had blooded in a fisherman's chest. Hawkers fell and legend was born while,

137

incredibly, others turned from easier prey to rush to the aid of their yowling comrades—horribly menaced by a single man who seemed to have them surrounded. He was tall though hardly a giant; ice was in his eyes, and cerulean glass; and his white teeth gnashed in his raging mouth that loosed saliva to glisten on his chin. Blood splashed his face, and his powerful arms and his striving, fast-moving legs, and flew from his ghastly preternatural blade even into the mass of his wheaten hair, which was long unto his shoulders and caught back by a strip of unornamented leather. He wore the plain torc of his second victim, and the dagger of his third, and carried the shield of his fifth; and now he doubled that toll, and more than doubled it. For none of the blood on him was his own.

A sideward-rushing ax almost missed him but not quite, and now the blood that sheeted down from high on his shield-arm was his. He did not notice, or even turn on that attacker; he was busy hacking nearly through the leathered thigh of another.

Encouraged, even fired by this fantastic and seemingly gods-sent intervention, some of the long-peaceful men of Blackiron joined their wark's savior. And now the Hawkers, seekers of easy victims and spoils, were in a real combat. One of Jarik's students even split open a man's face, lengthening his mouth to his right ear.

And then *they* were there.

Each was armored all in scintillant black that was like running black water in the sun. Boots of it shod them and rose above their calves; from their tops rose leggings of it to vanish beneath the skirts of their long-sleeved coats or shirts of it; gauntlets of it covered their hands to mid-forearm and were reinforced by small plates of blue-black iron. The armor looked like woven metal, and like cloth. An unornamented helm of black iron covered each head, and a pendent drape of the strange-serpent glistening armor covered necks and ears and both cheeks, like a three-quarter facial arras. Masks attached to the helms obscured their features and curved to vanish within the helm-arras on either side. Of blue-black iron, the masks had eyeslits, and strange straight "noses," and grim mouth-slits fashioned into them; the last was merely a thin horizontal line in each, into which a finger could not have slid.

No eyes showed within the eyeslits of those fore-boding iron masks.

Nothing showed anywhere of that grim and horripi-lating trio's flesh or features; only their forms. And each carried a sword like unto that Jarik wielded and did death with: black and shining and glassy, reflec-tive as water or jet gemstones or the wings of ravens in the rain.

"I am the Lord of Dread," one said, for they were identical, all three. He extended his sword then, and the Hawker at whom it was pointed burst into flame, though he was eight paces away. He emitted but two terrible high-voiced shrieks and died where he stood, consumed in clothing and in flesh and hair and bone.

"I am the Lord of Destruction," another said, and his voice too was metallic and hollow, ringing dully within his iron mask and helm. And he pointed his sword, and another Hawker became a pillar of flame so hot that his fellows did not edge, but sprang away.

"I am the Lord of Annihilation," the third said, and extended his sword, and twitched it to one side, so that not one but two men of the hawk-prowed ships died in roaring white-and-yellow flame.

The field of battle, which was the wark of Blackiron just above the beach, went silent while spines crawled and eyes bulged and gooseflesh erup-ted. Then a Hawker whirled and fled. His spear was heavy; he dropped it. Another followed, and then they were all fleeing down to the strand—those who could. Still caught in the blood-mad rage, Jarik pur-sued them.

The Hawkers raced down toward the sea's edge where their ship waited. Its prow was the giant head of a predatory bird whose eyes were yellow circles, carved so as to bulge, and each the size of a big man's fist. Behind those men followed Jarik, with the Black Sword, and he struck down a man from behind before Jarik stumbled and fell in his headlong *morbrin* charge.

The Hawkers ran on. Not one of those terrified men would spare the few seconds necessary to tarry and slay him who had done such bloody work on them.

Beside Jarik when he lifted his head lay Turibark's nephew Berik, and he was wounded and bleeding. He was one Jarik much liked. On his knees, Jarik stared at him. He groaned, reeled, dropped the Sword, clutched his head. . . *and bent over the injured young man. He began examining the wound, though seemingly superficially; Oak the Healer had no need of probes.*

Explanation was made to the Iron Lords by highly nervous Blackironers, who had oft discussed the phenomenon since Jarik's coming here. This was Oak the genius, they said; Oak the healer, who was also Jarik—if that ravening rabid wolfish killer had indeed been Jarik and not some third dweller in the darkened chambers of his brain. Nor, the Iron Lords were told while they stared, would Jarik remember having been Oak.

The Lords of Iron, dread fire-kindling swords in gauntleted fists, tramped down to where Oak labored.

"Torsy!" Oak called. "Bring the remedy kit!"

"You are Oak the Healer?"

Oak did not look up at that voice that sounded as if it came from the deeps of an iron-walled well. "Aye."

"And are you he too who took up the black sword and slew these attackers?"

Now Oak looked up. It was with a jerk, and horror overlaid his face. His reply came in a shout, even to those who were Gods on the Earth: "NO!" *And wear-*

140

ing Oak's surly yet intent, singleminded expression, he proceeded with his business, which was healing.

The Iron Lords exchanged a look. That is they seemed to; the iron mask-helmets turned each toward the other.

"You need not mind that, Healer," oné said. "We will take these wounded and heal them, for our power is great."

The mouths of the people of Blackiron formed O's, then, and that sound emerged from many. They stepped or shrank back while, one by one, the wounded of Blackiron rose into the air. While the Iron Lords stood silent as though in concentration, those bodies floated eerily away toward the mountain atop which the Iron Lords were said to dwell.

While this was transpiring, the Lord of Annihilation vanished. (Or perhaps it was Dread, or Destruction. Who could say? the point was, he *vanished;* one moment three stood there, like scintillant blue-black statues, and next instant they were but two.)

With some care, almost daintily, his brother-gods roasted the sprawled Hawkers. Dead and wounded alike sprang into flames when the swords were pointed at their sprawled forms. One was left, and he was dead.

"Do not move him or touch him," an Iron Lord said, and none would.

Save for that one dead Hawker, naught but ash remained of the others, and little stench or smoke. And the wounded were all at the mountaintop, and now were but specks in air. Then those specks were gone, and then the Lords of Dread and of Destruction also vanished.

Staring after them, Oak started to rise, staggered, seemed to liquesce at the knees, and collapsed.

For nearly twice ten minutes the people of Blackiron had stood like statues with glass eyes. Now they began to move.

Chapter Thirteen:
The Iron Lords

By dinnertime, the Iron Lords returned with Harnstarl's wounded . . . healed. Tears flowed as in a rainstorm.

"They will require rest, for though they have healed, their bodies and minds have suffered terrible shocks," one of the iron-clad gods said.

The people of the fishers' wark wept, fell to their knees. They babbled their thanks—and, strangely among their number were two of the several whose relatives were beyond restoration even by the power of the gods on the earth; for they had been slain and death was forever.

The Iron Lords looked at Jarik, who had washed or been washed, and wore clothing not splashed all with gore and the blood of others. His arm had been bandaged.

"Healer," an Iron Lord said.

"I am not Oak the Healer. My name is Jarik, who was Strodeson Jarik."

"Ah," that Lord of Iron said as if in an aside, "once there are none to tend, he reverts to his main personality, then." The helms of his brother gods nodded; only they, however, understood what had been said. "Well then, Jarik, Strodeson Jarik, it is you who has dared take up the black sword of the Iron Lords?"

Jarik met their gazes. Or so he supposed; there were only the mask-slits, without visible eyes. "I dared." In truth, he now wore the Sword by his side, and none of Blackiron was sure what to do about it. "The Iron Lords were tardy in coming to the aid of the people who look to them for protection. Had it not been for me and this Sword, all would have been slain ere you arrived."

"In order for us to know that danger threatens the wark, the sword must be nigh to the village," he was told, hollowly, metallically. "We came the moment we knew there was danger and anguish here."

Those words brought silence. Jarik stared. As if without his knowledge his left hand moved to the black pommel and hilt that he now knew were not mere iron, despite his knowing not what else they might be. "The Sword . . . tells you?"

Three helmet-masks nodded in silence.

The silence remained, and hung thickening, cloying the air like prickly heat.

A woman's shriek swept away that laden quiet. "YOU! AAAAHHH! YOU! Had you, Jarik, not taken the Sword—my husband Tola would be ALIVE!"

An instant of the new silence of shock. . . another . . . and then another of the wark cried out: Aye, and her son, chopped dead by a Hawker, and the lad but thirteen . . . but for Jarik, he'd be alive still. And weeping loudly she fell to her knees.

Dismay smote Jarik, and worse. He was staggered, and paled visibly so that his eyebrows seemed to disappear. Yet he wheeled on them, the peaceful fisherfolk of Harnstarl.

"You! But for me! Let me tell you what I found in the woods!" And he did, so that the new wails rose at news of the deaths of three young women thought to have been fortunate in their absence. And tears shone on Jarik's cheeks. "Now you understand why I took the Black Sword! I went mad! I took it up for Blackiron's vengeance and I *took* that revenge, all on your behalf—our behalves!"

His words brought on a thoughtful new silence. During it, eyes far from friendly continued to stare at Jarik. He felt the gazes; he seemed to feel the very eyes, and the weight of the thoughts behind them. He was not a hero. He was an Outlander still, and not

143

only not accepted but hated. He felt their rage—and he felt guilt, and its weight. It was true. Had he not taken the Black Sword, the Iron Lords would have come the moment the Hawker attack began. Under those circumstances there would be but three dead, of Blackiron: Torsy, and Nevre, and Alye. Or perhaps only two, he thought, his agony deepening so that he felt even more weight; perhaps there'd have been but two dead. Had he rushed at once after those three men, bearing his own weapons; had he not returned here for the Black Sword; then he might have overtaken those raping murderers before Alye's mind gave up to the dismay and revulsion at what they did to her . . .

Jarik sagged under the weight of dread knowledge, real or supposed, and of guilt. He sagged physically. The tall chesty blond Outlander with the big arms and thick wrists seemed to grow smaller before the gaze of many, many eyes, including those invisible ones of the Iron Lords. He felt that he saw detestation in all of them.

Had he doomed Alye himself, as well as slain her? Had he slain these five dead of Blackiron just as surely, and forever changed the wark and the minds of those who had been wronged? For mental wounds would remain, no matter how miraculously their bodies had been healed by the magicks of the Iron Lords.

Jarik pled, in a voice that broke.

"Lords. . . Lords of Iron. . . I beg you to take this sword from me. . . and my name. . . use your great powers and let me be Oak! Oak, forever, to remain here and serve these people as healer, always."

"Jarik."

Was one of the Iron Lords spoke, a god on the earth. Jarik did not know which it was. They appeared equally tall, that awesome trio, and of the same build—large—or so their armor indicated, at any rate. They were equally faceless and the masks were

144

identical. One of the Gods on the Earth spoke to Jarik, nor did Jarik know which.

"Strodeson Jarik," that god said again. "Why did you return here for the sword we left here so long ago, Strodeson Jarik?"

"I . . . don't know," Jarik said "It just . . . came into my mind. It seemed what I had to do. I did not *know* what I was doing!"

The mask-helmets turned. Presumably, the Iron Lords exchanged a look. A different one asked, "Strodeson Jarik: is it true that you pursued them alone, and slew all three rapists, alone?"

"Lord, it is so."

"You attacked three men, warriors, alone, and you did death on them, alone."

"It is so, Lord."

"Aye. It is so."

The helmet-masks turned each to the other, back to Jarik. Someone started to say something and one of the black-armored trio moved a gauntleted hand, no higher than his waist. The voice stilled. That Iron Lord spoke, to Jarik.

"And how many, Jarik, did you slay here, among the attackers of Blackiron?"

Thought was given to that, and muttering counsel taken. So many had seen, and yet none could be sure. A raving, ravening maniac had attacked the attackers, and with such swift fury that none could be sure how many he had hacked and of those how many had fallen dead. Jarik had downed three even before he was discovered, and after that there was agreement that he had laid low no less than six others, though surely he had not slain them all. No matter; all were gone now to the Dark Brother. He would have the comfort of much new company this night, in his thrice-dark domain. If the Dark Brother appreciated the company of murdering Hawkers.

An Iron Lord spoke.

"You have done much for Blackiron, Jarik. First,

you saved the life of its trapper, our servant Turibark. How can this be forgot?" (How, Jarik wondered, did they know this? And others wondered too, though all knew they would never know the answer. These were gods; Gods on the very Earth.) "You avenged the violation and deaths of three Blackiron maidens. How can this be forgot?" An awe-inflicting iron mask turned to the warkmen, seemed to gaze into the mind and soul of each. "You saved the wark today, and many lives, by attacking the attackers. And you were an army of one! Yet you bear but one wound—which we leave you, for you have earned the battle-scar, Strodeson Jarik who is Oak."

Into that impressed silence a woman shouted, "No!" and faces turned to her in astonishment, aghast. "No! The mother of a dead son cries out NO-O! Blackiron owes him nothing! All here were well and peaceful until *Jarik* came! *He* brought this on us! He saved us only from what he himself brought about!"

"Woman—Ashye—we know and understand your bereavement and sorrow at the death of your son Yash." Thus spoke an Iron Lord, and all wondered that he knew Ashye's name, and the name of her dead son. "Thus we curb anger, for you have said No to the Iron Lords, disputed the words of the Iron Lords! Had we not come today, do you think Jarik could have slain them all. . . to protect you? The brain fares better when the ears are wide and the mouth shut fast." And the black mask of iron—no, of god-metal, Jarik thought—turned this way and that, so that all knew they were being looked upon, and they were as smaller. "Let all be silent for a time, and wait. *All.* The Iron Lords confer."

So they did, while Jarik and Harnstarl waited. The Iron Lords drew close to one another, identical faceless man-shapes all in black. Only the murmur of their voices could be distinguished; none discerned a single word.

After a time he who had spoken detached himself

from his brother gods, and went to the Hawker whose body had not been cremated. His neck had been sheared over half through, so that his head lay at at a shuddersome angle, in a lake of his blood. The Iron Lord squatted by him, and Jarik saw that the scintillant armor was indeed like snakeskin; it bent and folded as easily and gracefully as wool or russet. The Iron Lord straightened, and bore something of the dead man's to his fellows. Again the gods conferred. Jarik kept his eyes on the one who had lauded him, and chastised Ashye, and who had brought the amber-sewn pouch of dark leather to the other two. It was he who turned first, but Jarik saw that it was another who spoke. For a moment, he wondered if anyone else noticed. It did not matter; all listened to what the Iron Lord said, and new guilt rose—not in Jarik.

"Now we know this, from the body of this slain raider. These men had a means of confounding the power of our sword to call us." He displayed the pouch, very briefly, before enwrapping it again in that big iron-plated gauntlet of supple god-armor. "We would not have been summoned even had the sword been here, atop Blackiron Stone. Hence you see, our people, that this one you have adopted, this Jarik who is best with weapons among you, *saved* Blackiron, not betrayed it."

As the weight was lifted, Jarik seemed to sag even more. Other faces were sore stricken. An apology or two was muttered. Rebelliously, he who had first joined Jarik and widened a Hawker mouth, now drew sword and saluted Jarik with it in an unmistakable gesture. Steed the Blackwelder came, so huge and burly, and placed an arm on the shoulder of Jarik, and then Turibark came, too, to stand there.

Jarik stood facing the Iron Lords while on him surely rested the eyes of all in Harnstarl. He was still, standing straight with the extraordinary Sword sheathed at his side.

One of the Iron Lords unsheathed his own sword, black, refulgent as if liquescent, identical to that one at Jarik's side. He strode, unclanking, to Blackiron Stone. The people of the wark drew away before him. Atop the Stone, into that ancient niche, he slid his own sword's tip, which was swallowed to the length of a forefinger's first two joints. And the Iron Lord turned back to face—to "face"—the gathered people of the wark of Harnstarl: Blackiron.

"This sword is my very own, from my side, from my own hand. It will never fail you. Trust in it. Trust in us; trust in the Power of the Iron Lords."

And then that mask and its eyeless slits were turned toward Jarik. "Jarik! The Iron Lords have conferred. No. We deny your request. You will not remain here as healer. There are other things for you. You will come with the Iron Lords, Jarik, outlander to Blackiron."

Jarik gazed upon him, and upon his brother gods, and Jarik knew fear. Yet that fear did not make him quail; it imboldened him.

"Those who go with yourselves are not seen again, Lords of Iron," he said, careful to use the formal pronoun of respect that he had not employed for years, for even when Jarik respected it was hard for him to admit it. "I have no desire to accompany the Lords of Iron."

A murmur ran through the people of Blackiron like the buzz of home seeking-bees. The Iron Lords surely stared. The turning of their helmet-masks each toward the other surely betokened an exchange of meaningful looks—direful looks? One raised high his metal-gloved hand and many shrank back. He received the silence the gesture demanded.

"Jarik will be back among you in Blackiron ere the sun rises on the morrow." Thus he spoke, and that hollow-reverberating, metal-tinged voice rang loud that all might hear.

More muttering rose. Not instantly, but after a moment of shock. And then the people of the little fishers' wark were murmuring among themselves about how Jarik had dared challenge the gods themselves, and how they had loudly made a promise . . . to alleviate Jarik's nervousness; to placate *Jarik!*

A hand gloved in god-mail stretched forth, and the fingers were open. "Come, Strodeson Jarik. The Iron Lords have need of you."

"Need!"

"Need! The Iron Lords *need* Jarik!"

"He said they have *need* of him!"

While those who called him Outlander exclaimed so, staring in awe first at the Iron Lords and then at Jarik and back to the gods, Jarik could but gaze upon these gods upon the earth.

One of them approached him with a series of even, majestic paces. The Iron Lord came to him, and Jarik saw that the god on the earth was but a fraction taller than he. That was comforting, somehow, that the god was hardly taller than the tallest in Blackiron. Perhaps to the people of the wark the effect was not comfort; perhaps the effect was the reverse of comfort. Jarik did not know. Indeed, Jarik did not care.

Torsy . . .

Torsy is gone, gone. Gone with Barrenserk and Stath and Alye and Orrik and Thanamee; gone with Oceanside and . . . and all that I have been before, which is nothing!

Standing before him, the Iron Lord removed his big black gauntlet. It was flared widely at midforearm and was plated with rectangular pieces of iron like the round or hexagonal bosses sewn on some leather coats to increase their value as armor. The action revealed not flesh, but another glove within the gauntlet. This one fitted closely what appeared to be a normal hand, large and male. The inner glove was of some most strange and exotic *cloth,* silver and yet dark, tightly woven; shimmery, as the black armor was. Metallic, Jarik thought with wonder on him; metallic cloth!

That silvery hand was extended, palm up. "You are safe, Jarik. Come. Your hand, Strodeson Jarik."

Jarik gazed at the invitation and demand of that extended argent hand. *A guide*, he thought, and was reminded of that other Guide, who had led him to what were seemingly other realms—and to Blackiron.

No, he mused, this was different. This was a guide, but not the Guide.

Guide.

The guide. . . Torsy . . . Alye. . . gods, the world has fallen apart; everything is different. . . am I sane? How can I be? O gods . . . ah, gods indeed! And here they are! And here am I, Jarik, poor ever-outlander Jarik, and surely if I take this strange silver-colored hand nothing will ever be the same again. But. . . when, when has anything ever been the same for Jarik, save unpleasant and unhappy?

To me—me!—now is extended the hand of a God on the Earth . . .

Not without misgivings, Jarik reached out to the hand of the Iron Lord.

The silver glove *was* metallic, and it was cold.

Chapter Fourteen:
Iron Lords' Keep

Jarik staggered. The transition was dizzying, as was its means. One moment he had been in Blackiron, surrounded by its people. Then he had taken the oddly-gloved hand of the Iron Lord. At once there followed a tingling and a sudden darkness and pinwheels behind his eyes. As swiftly he knew a great rushing and a sensation of nausea, as if his internal organs were floating whilst he . . . flew. *Really* flew, in the body, not out of it as with that other guide, the Guide. And then the jarring, with solid matter beneath his feet.

He staggered.

Quivering, holding one hand tight-pressed to his stomach, he retrieved the other from the clasp of the Iron Lord. Jarik looked about himself, and his eyes were wide in awe. Nor was he aware that his mouth had sagged open.

"Where . . ."

"We are within the mountain. This is our keep, Strodeson Jarik."

"Within . . ."

Aye, they were. They had . . . conveyed . . . him to the great pile of dark rock that towered so high over Blackiron and the surrounding land—and inside it. He was within the mountain riven as a sign by the Iron Lords; within the keep of the gods on the earth. Jarik looked about him, and was astonished at the demesne of the Iron Lords.

The sprawling hall was neither round nor square nor wholly rectangular at all, for the walls curved and recurved. There was but one corner. And they were of living stone, those walls that could have contained most of Blackiron. He remembered the scar on the mountainside, and the way the four Hawkers had burst into flame, and later the corpses, and Jarik thought Aye, the Iron Lords do indeed have Power!

The Iron Lords had *carved* this mighty chamber—as well as what other rooms lay beyond the two arched doorways he saw. Nor had they done so with minds fixed solely on utility. The hall of the Iron Lords was most esthetically pleasing, in shape and in furnishing.

So too was the profusion of rich hangings, and fine furniture, and carpets the likes of which Orrik's son and then Strode's son had never beheld; he who had never beheld a baron, much less a king, much less a god—and now the keep of three several gods was laid open to him! Surely no king lived so well, Jarik reflected. He was both impressed and awed, he who lived and dreamt of vengeance, who had ever been outsider, Outlander, and so relied only on himself and had defied all, all—and had lost all, even Torsy—and had never allowed himself to show awe, or that he was impressed.

Now Jarik was impressed, and awed.

Chairs and couches were wrought of dark wood, some of it nigh red, and inlaid with wood of a lighter hue. Cushions were strewn over them, and on the carpets, which were woven in patterns and colors that were, like those of the hangings, unbelievable. Sun-yellow he saw, and the blue of the sky in June and in December and August as well, for these were three several shades. There was a red so light it was like unto clover and one so dark it reminded him unpleasantly of dried blood. Other shades there were, ranging between. There were emerald and jasper and mosstone and amygnant, and the color of grass in springtime, and tawny and ocherous and quin and aged gold, and frosty grey-white and purest new snow. Aye, and silver and bronze. Two colors he did not even know, could not give name to. There were

152

both red and blue at once, a mingling. The one held more azure and the other contained more of the hue of old cherry wine by lamplight.

Jarik marveled, and felt small. Once he had seen three cushions in a house, and had thought that domain of Ishparshule lordly and luxuriously effete. The farthest wall of the keep of the Iron Lords—hung with a sun-splash tapestry all shot through with twinkling silver thread—must have been distant to the length of his body twenty times over.

Here within the mountain the air was sweet and neither chill nor hot, dry nor wet.

He stood on a balcony or gallery, he and the three gods who were covered over all in blue-black metal that was surely not iron, but something far smoother and sturdier even than iron. The sort of gallery ran around two walls to the sprawling chamber. Two doors left it. No, three. The floor with its bedazzling carpets lay well below, twice the length of his body. (Over twelve feet, as the people of Ishparshule-wark measured; over thirteen, by Blackiron measure.) Nearly that distant above was the ceiling; a ceil of stone, living rock, not smooth but left in its natural state—or somehow carved so!

The hall was peopled. Below were . . . women and girls.

Jarik gazed down upon them, and his blood and his body stirred. All, all were lovely, all bright and scintillant with the marvelous gauds that bedecked and bedizened their shapely forms. Those forms were his to see and inspect whilst growing the warmer, for the women and the girls wore very, very little indeed, though they were covered with jewelry set with many flashing stones and bright colorful glass, as well as pearls and amber. All, he noted—and he noted them well—possessed hair and eyes much like his own. They were paler, though, for Strodeson Jarik the Outlander was sun-ruddied into a stag-like tawniness. Their ages appeared to range from eleven or so, just pre-

153

adolescent, to . . . who could say? Many women, most, were temptresses at thirteen if not younger—and hags at thirty, with swollen bellies and vein-streaked legs and dangling dugs from childbearing and from work, their skins roughened and lined and made dark from cookfire and sun, needle and thrèad, hoe and ax, mortar and pestle, wheel and loom. None of these looked to the staring Jarik to be above a score of years in age, and none, incredibly, appeared to have borne.

He wondered if they had to work, these women of the gods. And—did they bear? Were those mothers and children below, their children—and none of them male?

"Our servants," one of the Iron Lords said, for he was a god. "They serve us in all things. We have no families, for we are gods on the earth. There are only we three here, and our servants. What man has need of more—or what god?"

Jarik had not supposed he could cease looking on the massed femininity below, but at those words issuing through a horizontal slit in a metal mask he wheeled from the gallery's rail of fine smooth walnut.

"I!" He slapped his chest. "I could want for more, and do. I have need of a place to be and to belong! I who have been called Orrikson and Strodeson and yet am the son of neither. *I* need more, Lords of Iron! It's people, people I can be calling my own I have need of . . . and vengeance, the vengeance I've dreamed of."

Iron helm-masks nodded. "He will do," an Iron Lord murmured, low.

"And. . . I have need to know why your three selves have said the lie on me, and on the people of Harnstarl." Despite his brashness, he would continue to use the respectful impersonal pronoun, for he knew he had found at last those who were—*that* were—worthy of his respect.

They stood staring at him—he supposed, for they were eyeless or seemed to be in the masks attached to their shining helms of black metal. One of them asked his meaning.

Aye, one of them, still, for though Jarik sought to distinguish voices, he had not. They were identical in their all-encompassing armor, their gauntlets off now to reveal the close-fitting silvery gloves on hands that looked of normal enough shape, and Jarik knew not which was Destruction, and which Dread, and which Annihilation who had slain two at once. He no longer knew even which of them it was had taken his hands and fetched him here in manner unnatural; supernatural.

"Yourself has said that my taking the Sword was not the cause of the deaths in Blackiron; that the Hawkers had a charm against the Sword's power to call yourselves thence. But this is false, Lords, for it was only a Lokustan bag of flint-and-steel yourself was holding up. And too when I drew near the wark and saw what was happening, it seemed that the Sword saw too, for it was as if alive in my hand. When I reached the village—in seconds your three selves came. The Sword, then, brought yourselves— and had I not had it with me, the Lords of Iron would have been in the village far sooner."

"You are too wise," an Iron Lord said, in that voice that was at once hollow and metallic and muffled. "Yes. We told you that lie for your own good, Jarik-Oak, that you might not feel guilt, and gnaw at yourself the more. And that the villagers would think you their rescuer."

"Then. . ." Jarik paused long, not wishing to say it, to hear his words and the answer he knew must follow. "Then those of Blackiron *were* slain because I took the Sword."

"Had the sword been there, Strodeson Jarik, it would have summoned us at the first sign of true danger."

After a moment Jarik, who did not want to know

155

and yet had to know, said again, "Then those of Blackiron are dead because I took the Sword."

"Yes."

Jarik took that and the pain it brought in silence. His lips firmed; he aged a bit.

"Why?" Jarik demanded, his voice rising. With anguished eyes he stared at those gleaming masks. "Why did I take it? None has *touched* the Sword in generations. What put such a thought into my head?"

"You *knew*," The leftmost mask said. "You are different, Jarik-Oak. You know that. Come, tell us of yourself."

Jarik glanced over the railing, and down.

"We will go below, and sit," an Iron Lord said. Was his voice touched with age? "Perhaps this Man Who is Two Men would like wine, or ale."

They went along the gallery then, and came to strangely suspended steps that were of metal, not wood. Nor were they solid, but slim horizontal strips of the god-metal attached and *suspended* betwixt two metal poles that ran from floor to gallery, and them not of the girth of Jarik's wrist. Yet this was a stair, not a ladder. He did not like these steps, and the empty space behind each as he descended; he clung to the rail and kept his eyes on the women. They looked up at the descent of their masters and the youth they had brought back with them. Many eyes looked upon Jarik then. All were set in comely female faces, as all were blue or at least, blue-grey. All save the one, with the interesting look of gauntness on her cheekbones and yet of over-ripeness in her breast and hips; her eyes, Jarik saw with wonderment and great appreciation, were of that newfound color that was blue with a tinge of red in it. In her eyes the red was only a hint, a droplet of red in a cauldron of blue, but it was there, as the color of the fox gleamed in her hair, so that it was orange rather than yellow.

Strodeson Jarik had never seen purple, or red hair,

as he had never seen the demesne or even the clothes or person of a real lord, much less gods.

The carpet, of yellow and cerulean and the green of appletree leaves in latest spring, was soft beneath his buskined feet. He saw women gazing upon his strong bare calves, with their muscular roundness that was not knotty. The women did not rise at the approach of their lords and their—guest, though the pre-adolescents did, and stilled themselves. All watched. Their eyes shifted constantly from their lords to Jarik.

"Take that seat, Jarik-Oak."

The slim young woman with the honey-hued hair fairly sprang from the chair to which that Iron Lord pointed. It had an attached backrest, and furthermore to it scarlet fabric was sewn, a carbanean hue, while a red blue pillow cushioned its seat.

Jarik hesitated. Two of the Iron Lords sat at either end of an armed, backed chair that was long enough to accommodate four—for Jarik had never laid eyes on a couch, either. The third god seated himself then, gingerly. And their guest sat. He was amazed at the softness of the chair. He was much aware, too, of the warmth left in the cushion by its occupant, and her seated now on the carpet near the Iron Lord in the chair.

"I was about to ask you to tell us of yourself, Jarik Who is also Oak. Doe: fetch wine, the—" and he said a word Jarik did not know.

A young woman scurried. The Iron Lord waved a hand and another thrust herself lithely up to accompany the first, her named Doe.

Jarik, swallowing, dry of mouth though not in anticipation of wine, watched their departure with the helplessly magnetized gaze of a virile youth; one wore only a girdle of colored pearls or perfectly sphered bits of glass, from which in front only there depended a single strip of jeweled cloth, while the other's hindcheeks churned within a skimp of yellow cloth that left bare the beginning of her rearward cleavage. Dressed only for the indoors, they were— and for the eyes of men. Rather, gods.

Jarik was accustomed to seeing women in tunics and long skirts and, in winter, more. He had not thought of attire as holding the possibility of being erotic, and did not know the word exotic. Now he knew its effect on him. He swallowed again. In the keep of the Gods on the Earth!

"You do not know your parents, do you?"

Jarik looked at the speaker, him in the chair-for-one. "No, Lord, as I must not be Orrik's son of Oceanside. Lord. . . would yourself be telling me whether yourself be Destruction, or Dread, or Annihilation? For all your masks be the same."

"None may look upon the face of a god and live," one said, and Jarik remembered.

"Disconcerting," said he who was on the leftward end of the chair-for-four. "It is not necessary that we discomfit this bereaved and disconcerted lad more, is it?"

"I am the Lord of Annihilation," the god in the yellow chair said.

"I am the Lord of Destruction," the god on the left end of the couch said.

The other, though Jarik looked expectantly upon his mask, did not speak.

"One learns not to utter the profoundly obvious," Annihilation said, from the yellow chair, and Jarik remembered.

"And not to ask the profoundly obvious," Destruction said, from the couch, and Jarik remembered.

"And I asked a question of you, Strodeson Jarik-and-Oak," Annihilation reminded their guest.

Jarik began to speak. Brought wine, he sipped and marveled at its wondrous fine flavor, and told them the story of his life, insofar as he knew it. The Iron Lords listened in silence, nor did they drink. Jarik wondered, even while he spoke: did gods drink? Did

158

gods eat? Did the gods on the earth remove their masks, ever? Did they remove their "iron" carapaces; did they bathe, or have need; did they so much as sweat? Gods. Did they retire in armor—indeed, did they have need of retiring at all? *Do gods require sleep?*

And so he told them what he knew and thought he knew of himself.

The while he knew nothing of them, save that they were unequivocally strange, and not earthly, and showed no skin or hair whatever, and had Power. Ah—and that their armor *rustled*, rather than clinked though it was metal, resembling the loose yet fitting skin of a dog; and even though they seemed identical, hollow and metallically echoic behind their masks, the voices of the three were different.

"You are of the people of the Hawkships, Jarik-Oak," Annihilation told him, when Jarik had done. "You are of the land—a large sprawling island actually—called Lokusta. You must know this."

"No!" Jarik burst out without thinking that it was a god he refuted; the words brought response from him as though his knee had been tapped. "No! They are murderers! They slew my parents and my sister!"

"Both Ishparshule-wark and Blackiron are parts of the large isle called Lokusta," Destruction said, "and neither counts itself a part of that land. You need not, either. Endeavor to use your brain and not your juices, lad."

The Lord of Annihilation said, "Your *foster* parents. Your *foster* sister. You must have been a foundling, Jarik-Oak. Abandoned for some reason. . . some imperfection, perhaps. Or because your parents had already more get than they could manage to feed."

"Perhaps because he was a male child," he on the right end of the couch said, and Jarik remembered that he was Dread, who had not stated the profoundly obvious; once his brothers had identified themselves, he remained silent. And was not silence an ally of dread?

Jarik wondered, looked his questions. To no avail; none of them explained the remark. He pondered. He knew that some peoples exposed and abandoned female offspring. It was not unknown in Ishparashule-wark, where it was a matter for little condemnation or even reprobation. But—to abandon a *male* child? That, surely, was not the way among any of the warrior peoples of Lokusta!

The Lord of Annihilation said, "We understand, however, that this does not assuage your grief nor make you desire revenge the less, Jarik-Oak. What do you know of the slayers of your . . . parents?"

"We called our home Oceanside, within the barony of the Lord Parderik, of Oaktree. The Lokustans call that land—an isle, they say—Akkharia." (The word meant simply Land of the *Akkhs*, with an aspirant, or *Akkhas*. It was meaning less to Jarik. He had never heard anyone in Oceanside use the word *Akkh* or *Akkha* in any context.) "What do I recollect? That the commander of those Hawkers was named Kidden-sahk. The name on his ship was writ in characters different from those of Oceanside, but now I know it was *Isparela: Snowlady*."

"Ah," Destruction said.

"Yes," Annihilation said. "It is what we would speak of with you, Jarik. Tell me: the people who raised you—the Lokustans, I mean, not the previous foster-parents, of Ak-Oceanside. Spoke Strode or others in the wark of Ishparshule of . . . *Elye Isparanana?*"

"Aye," Jarik said. For in the tongue of the people of the warks and the hawk-prowed ships, *Elye* was "Highly respected woman; Lady" and *isp* was "snow" and *arnan* meant "mist"; "fog" was *arnan* or h*arnar*. And Jarik said, "The Lady of the Snowmist came once to Ishparshule-wark while I dwelt there."

"Ah," Dread said, and Jarik was sure now that his
160

was the voice of a grumbly old hound. "Tell us of that."

Jarik thought he detected both age and some excitement in that voice of metal from down in a well. He told what he had been told of the Lady of the Snowmist, the god of Ishparshule-wark and other warks nearby, and he told them why she came now and again to Ishparshule-wark, and what she did. He told them of how she had Chosen Brathis, so that he became popular with the maidens of the wark and would enjoy good health, always. At least, so had others she had chosen.

Three shining blue-black helms and masks nodded. Though he could not be sure, Jarik thought that they were disappointed to learn that he had not *seen* Elye Isparanana. It was the Lord of Destruction who spoke, leaning a little forward.

"We cannot tell you what she does with those youths, Jarik; we dare not tell you, mortal lad. For what she does with and to them is horrible, revolting. A monstrous thing. The Lady of the Snowmist is pure evil, Jarik; reddest, ineffable evil! She is dedicated to ridding this world of men as we know them, all humans, to be replaced by . . . something else."

Staring, Jarik swallowed. He had heard of men who were not, who were beast-men, though he had never seen such. Experiments on the part of the gods, some said. Perhaps it was true, then! Ishparshule-wark's god . . . evil!

"She must have sent those Hawkers today," Destruction was continuing, "in direct challenge to us. She sought by her minions to slay our chosen people: Blackiron."

"Evil," Dread muttered, in his deep voice of dread.

Hoping that they did not see his little shudder, Jarik showed the Iron Lords his grim face of anger. How did he look, he wondered, when he was *morbrin*?

"You are powerful, Lords; why then have yourselves not imprisoned or slain her?"

"Ah," Dread said, and leaned back.

"Gods may not slay gods," the Lord of Annihilation said; "it is a law of the Universe. Too, long and long ago the Lady of the Snowmist wove a powerful spell, and it keeps us here, confined. As she herself is confined to her territory, her demesne, a mountain above a portion of Lokusta. We cannot leave here to extend our protection to others as we wish, for she prevents us. The power of the gods wanes in proportion to the distance from their own territory. And now she sends her minions to attack those we protect!" A gloved hand fisted; a mask-helmeted head shook as though in helpless anguish. A god!

Jarik saw, and he thought, marveling: *a god!* Anguished and frustrated—a god! And Jarik remembered and was a little wiser. But only a little.

"She is a sorcerer?"

"She is a god."

"As yourselves be."

"Even as we are, Jarik. And it is hardly unknown that often the gods must ask the aid of mortal men."

It was unknown to Jarik but he nodded wisely, and gave listen. The Iron Lords had said, in Blackiron, that they had need of him. Now they told him why, to what purpose.

It was simple enough; they wanted him to slay the Lady of the Snowmist.

"Slay! A god?"

"Once you are nigh her demesne, the mountain of Lokusta called Cloudpeak," Destruction said, "the sword itself will lead you to her."

"This—"

"Yes. That sword. Our sword."

Jarik touched the hilt of the marvelous Black Sword he had taken. "And—does it hurl fire, Lord, like yours?"

"It does not. Nor will the one I left below, in

Blackiron. That is a Power of ourselves, Jarik, not of the swords."

"Lord? How can she be slain? A god? I am only a b—a man." He would not say "boy." He was very young, but soon he was to belong, and be important. *I cannot be a boy then, can I!?*

"You must tell her your story. She will want to examine you—you bear some mark to distinguish you from others?"

Aye, myself, for I have ever been apart from others, Jarik thought, but he said, "No, Lord. None I have knowledge of, no."

"A trifling mark may exist that *she* knows and will recognize," Annihilation said. "She will know the identity of your parents, Jarik. We are convinced that it was at her bidding that you were left to die, as an infant."

"I? The bidding of the Lady of the Snowmist—I?"

"Yes." Annihilation's helm-mask nodded. "For reasons known to herself; Jarik; doubtless it would somehow further her plans. Perhaps she foresaw that it would be you who would come in time to end her reign of evil."

"Not for vengeance," Destruction said, whose voice was less low than those of his brother gods. "For all of humankind, for men as you know men."

And Jarik felt great importance on him, while the weavers wove. Nor do the weavers apprise either gods or humans of their plans.

"Karahshisar knows much," Annihilation said, with a sigh, "of both past and present. And of the time to come, as well."

Frowning, Jarik asked, "Karah-shisar?"

"It is her name," the Lord of Annihilation told him.

"What does it mean?"

"It is a name. It has no meaning. Does the name Eskeshehir have aught of meaning for you?"

"Esksh—no, Lord."

"It is my name," the Lord of Destruction said,

163

"which we only may use, one to the other. And the Lord of Annihilation is Nershehir, and the Lord of Dread is Seyulshehir. They are our names. They have no meanings. For these are the names of the gods on the earth."

Strange, Jarik mused. All names had meaning. His own—in the language of the people of Oceanside, which differed somewhat but not wholly from that of the people of Lokusta—meant "Strand-reward" or "Beach-gift." Indeed, he had long assumed that it indicated merely that he had been born on the beach below Oceanside, or conceived there. Now, with sure knowledge from these gods on the earth that he was not of the Oceansiders, and a sense of importance permitting him to think logically, he admitted the real meaning of his own name. He had been abandoned, by *Lokustans*; the Oceansiders had indeed found him on the strand!

Jarik noted too that the four strange words, the names of the gods on the earth, bore much similarity each to the other. He asked, "She is of your kin?"

"She is of our kith," Annihilation said, rather swift in his modifiication. It might mean nearly anything; Torsy, Jarik was sure now, was not of his kin—had not been—but had been of closest kith. *Torsy, oh Torsy . . .*

Jarik was not gone, and somewhere, he fervently hoped, Kiddensahk was alive and, all unknowingly, awaiting the coming of Jarik the avenger.

"She is of our people," Dread suddenly said, and Jarik swung his head that way, for he whose name was Seyulshehir said little. "*Was.* Now, as you have seen, she is our enemy. The enemy of your fellow men, of all humans. Like you, Jarik, we are exiles; homeless, kinless on this—in this place. Because of her."

"She is of your own kith and imprisons yourselves; she is god of my people and bade them leave me to die."

"Aye," Dread said, and so did the Lord of Annihilation.

Jarik expelled a sigh and started to rise. That impulse he curbed; he remained seated, for he was in the presence of gods and hardly so sure of himself as he hoped they thought.

"Then she is not sister or kith of yourselves, Lords, and she is no god of mine. She is our enemy."

He heard himself say it: *our*. The Iron Lords sat, faceless but watching from behind their masks of shining blue-black. *Surely*, Jarík mused, *they smile now within those helmasks of harsh iron. For they want me to do death on her, and I have renounced her, and said "our," allying myself with the Lords of Iron. I! Jarik! I am important! I belong at last! Ally and agent of the Iron Lords!*

Thinking, he glanced around—and must tear his gaze from the women and girls who were the servants of the Lords of Iron. He brought his gaze to rest on the Lord of Dread, on Seyulshehir, for he said but little and Jarik would hear him speak.

"Yourselves will be aiding me in the finding of Kiddensahk!"

"Aye," the Lord of Dread said, and that was all that he said.

"Kirrensark," his brother Nersesehir who was Annihilation said, "is a servant of the Lady of the Snowmist. Doubtless you have her to blame for both your abandonment as an infant and for the slaying of the people you called your own, who called you son. Kirrensark's wark is in her demesne, which is on the other side of Dragonmount."

Jarik realized then that there had been no "Kiddensahk," all these years. He had heard the Lokustan raiders call the name of their leader, in their way of speaking that did not pronounce the letter *r*. Kirrensark! *I will come soon, Kirrensark, murderer!*

"Dragonmount is impassable!" Jarik blurted. *And*

on the other side of that long towering range is . . . Kirrensark, *who is not Kiddensahk at all.*

The Iron Lords made no reply, for they spoke not the obvious. Jarik was embarrassed and knew shame, thinking them again asmile within their masks, and this time *at* him. No mountain was impassable, when one was allied with the Iron Lords—or for the matter of that when the sea was but a little way distant.

"Lords, yourselves placed another sword on the altar in Blackiron. This sword is mine, now?"

They did not so much as glance at one another. The Lord of Dread said "Aye" and Strodeson Jarik was the possessor of the Black Sword, a marvelous weapon of god-magic.

He nodded. "I will keep the Sword. With it I will avenge my parents—my foster parents, whom I loved as father and mother. After all these years, I shall slay Kidden—Kirrensark of the hawk-prowed ships. Then, Lords, will I, Jarik, be slaying the Lady of the Snowmist. Karahshisar." Deliberately, in the presence of these gods his allies, he pronounced her true name, that only the gods might use one to the other. "My enemy. . . our enemy."

Jarik spoke ebulliently, he who was not then aware of all the properties of the weapon that had come into his possession. He felt very good indeed. Strodeson Jarik had a fine weapon, the finest of weapons, and knowledge, and purpose—and he was allied with the gods on the earth, who had Power. Over the years, the so many years of not-belonging and misery, he had nigh forgot his vow to exist for vengeance; that he did indeed exist for vengeance. *Kirrensark, monster—I come!*

Three gleaming dark helmets nodded.

Jarik remembered, and spoke not so ebulliently now, though he allowed no plaintive note to tinge his voice. "And how can it be accomplished, Lord Gods? —The Death of a god?"

The iron heads looked at each other. Annihilation spoke.

"The Black Sword will slay her, Jarik, even a god . . . and those she raises to menace and do death on you, though you must have as much care as ever . . . *warrior.*"

"Ah," Jarik said, hearing that word meaning "Man-of-weapons" while thought lay thick on his much-laden brain. "The Black Sword would slay yourselves, then."

The Lord of Destruction waved an arm; his mail rustled and scintillated, but did not creak or jingle. "Think you we would place the means to slay us, *us*, into the dirt-grubbing hands of those stupid villagers below?"

"Or," my lord of Dread said, "into the hands of a *warrior* such as yourself?"

"I but hazarded a comment, Lords," Jarik said. *Warrior! Man of weapons! I am a warrior!* After a time of silence he said, "There is a question I would ask."

Annihilation said, "Ask, Jarik, ally of the Lords of Iron."

Sitting up straighter, feeling taller, Jarik took breath. "What—what becomes of the youths my lord gods bring here from time to time over the years from Blackiron?" —*Where stupid villagers net fish, and grub dirt, and are protected but not respected or loved.*

"We can make answer, Jarik," Annihilation said, "but me must then make you forget what we have said."

Jarik considered that. "Then will I not ask again?"

There was the tiniest sound of a girlish snicker, though no heads turned in their direction. The Lord of Annihilation, whose name was Nerseshehir, nodded.

"Jarik our ally, you are shrewd and aye, blessed with great curiosity."

"Or accursed with it," Dread rumbled, for his voice was deepest.

"But you see," Annihilation continued, "the villagers must not know."

Jarik considered; shrugged. "My lord gods have brought me here by some means magickal; god-Power. Can yourselves not then take me elsewhere, send me elsewhere, by the same means? Away from Blackiron, I mean?"

"You agree to that?"

"Aye. And I am not likely to return, am I? Not to Blackiron, where stupid villagers grub in the soil! Once I have my vengeance on Kirrensark, I shall sally up the mountain of Cloudpeak, and I shall slay the Lady of the Snowmist. For my self, for yourselves lord gods, and for—for all humankind. If I try to return then to the village of Blackiron—stop me!"

"A challenge?" Dread said.

"No no Lord God, Lord of Dread! An invitation, an assurance! For I shall have no desire to return to Blackiron!"

"It is many and many you would have to slay to replace Kirrensark as chief of his wark, Jarik of the Black Sword," Destruction said, and there was amusement in his voice thick as the scent of middenheap borne on a summer breeze.

Jarik tightened his jaw.

"Agreed," the Lord of Dread said, and Jarik knew who held most Power.

Jarik nodded, scanned the three masks, and sat back. He had emptied his goblet, which was of gold or something like though he had sought to disguise his excitement and instant lust for it. None had made offer to refill it. He waited, forcing himself not so much as to glance at the surrounding woman-flesh. He thought of those women though, and the lust that rose was different from that he felt at sight and touch of the goblet of fine smooth rounded gold.

"We made promise," Annihilation said, "that Jarik

168

would be back among the warkmen by sunrise of the morrow."

Jarik had forgotten. Jarik's mind was elsewhere. Indeed, Jarik's mind was trying to be in several places at once. Jarik was much impressed with Jarik.

Dread moved, for the first time since he had sat. Jarik, who had already decided that Dread was senior among the Iron Lords, thought also that he was the eldest—and more, that he was old. As he made that movement, a brief deprecatory gesture, that Lord of Iron said, "We will return him to the wark, then. Now."

Jarik, jerkily, lunged forward. His face was full of surprise and showed anguish as well.

"Long enough," the Lord of Dread went on, "for them to set eyes on you, and for you to betake yourself from among them."

"Forever," Destruction said.

"Forever," Dread rumbled, with a nod.

Jarik *felt* his steady gaze, and wondered at the face of Dread, as he did at the faces of the others, and at the color of the palpably piercing eyes of the Lord of Dread. Black, he mused, like his armor—yet he had a vision even then of the golden, glaring eyes of an eagle, ferocious and staring and full of confidence and competence: a consummate bird of prey.

Jarik nodded equably and again sat expectantly waiting for them to move.

They did; he watched as the Lords of Iron drew on their great gauntlets of gleaming black metal. Not iron, Jarik thought. Not iron at all. Metal. The godmetal. Like the superb Sword at his hip, its sheath thrust forward so that he might sit in this chair of incredible comfort. That led him to another thought: the Sword, the Black Sword of the Iron Lords, wanted another sheath. He must make a better one, or find one, or—

Perhaps Kirrensark has a fine sword-sheath!

It was a cheering thought. While he dwelled on it,

169

the Lords of Dread and of Annihilation drew on their gauntlets, and Destruction but one. They stood, and instantly Jarik did. Again he refrained with an effort of will from looking about at the silent women. *Unnaturally silent*, he mused, and vowed to give thought to that, at another time. Not now. Now, the Lord of Destruction was holding out his un-gauntleted hand.

Jarik took it. "How—"

And it happened again, the tingling and the roar and the rushing, and the nausea followed by a little stagger, and he was once more in the village of Blackiron.

Chapter Fifteen:
Jarik of the Black Sword

The Iron Lords returned Jarik to Blackiron not only before dawn, but before dusk. The sun was an orange ball on the edge of the world, flattened a little at the bottom, as though squatting there. Soon it would begin that daily slide into the sea . . . or off the edge . . . or into the maw of the Dragon of Night-Dark . . . or into the jewel-casket of the Gemstone Lady who ruled the night . . . or whichever of those postulates was really the fate of the sun each day—if any of them.

Many voices rose around Jarik and the three Iron Lords. They subsided to buzzing murmurs. Then here and there they rose once more to shouts, as those villagers who saw them called others. It was a day for the long-telling of winter nights: the day the Lords of Iron came thrice to Harnstarl. There might well be 1 o more Jariks in peaceful Harnstarl; impatient youths who would question the accounts of the mystifying and fabulous events that had taken place here this day, and scoff at them. And perhaps the world was not done with producing Jariks, even in quiet, protected fishing villages. And perhaps it had just begun.

Harnstarl gathered about the returned visitors.

Jarik glanced at the Iron Lords, who were of about his height, tall—though Dread seemed a bit shorter. Too, with the curving shoulderplates of beaten metal rather than scale or chain, and the gleaming cuirasses that were of two pieces, back and front, who could say how burly were these gods on the earth? Then there were the helmets with the masks depending before. Who could say how much of that height was helm, and how much wearer?

His questioning glance brought a gesture from the Lord of Destruction. Jarik took it to mean that he was to speak. He sought words, and he aged a bit. All about them gathered the women and children and the men of Blackiron, and Jarik realized that he would not miss them. Torsy was gone and there was a hole in him of that, though he had not had time to grieve. Alye was gone—though she had hardly been Torsy. What he had felt for Alye was not love, but the desire of a young man whose stones, as men were wont to say, were full of seed and the love-itch.

The youth stood tall, tall among the Iron Lords and taller than any of Blackiron including even Blica, whose hoe-handle was of special length. At the same time, Jarik was almost sharply in contrast to the somberly armoured and masked gods on the earth. Wheat-yellow was his hair, and drawn back to be caught by a leather thong just below his nape. This day his ears were bared, and his forehead, which was higher than low and handsomely broad. The color of his skin had obviously been provided by the sun, for he was of the pink people, not the tan. Of medium sky-blue his eyes, and well-curved his lips while he stood among those whose mouths were but straight ugly slits in metal masks. His nose was straight, with only a slight bump just at the point at which it sprang from between his eyes. Strong was his chin, and good, and his beard was but a downy dusting on it and his cheeks. His mustache was yet a pale, pale wisp. Strong and thick-wristed arms emerged from his loose-sleeved tunic of peasant's russet, and sturdy were the legs that emerged from below its hem.

And the sword of god-metal was slung at his hip; the Black Sword of the Iron Lords.

At the gesture of the Lord of Destruction, whose true name was known to Jarik, Jarik spoke. Seeking words, he aged a bit, and looked upon the people of

173

Blackiron. All unbidden the thought stole into his mind; *stupid grubbers in the soil of the earth.* And not a man of weapons among them.

"The Iron Lords," he began "the Gods on the Earth and your protectors, made promise that I would be seen again in Harnstarl ere Shralla began her journey of morrow. See me now. And know that my sister Torsy is slain by the Hawkers. You who have ever called me Outlander know that there is nothing to keep me here. And too know that I am now an ally and agent of the Iron Lords." (With that statement he seemed to gain a bit, in height and thrust of chest.) "I will not be back in Blackiron. I leave on the business of the Iron Lords. Now."

Obviously taken by surprise though a god, Destruction at last quietly interrupted the silence. "Jarik? There is no more?"

"Lord, I have said it."

"Possessions?"

"Oh." Jarik considered; in his excitement and elation, he had forgot his possessions. He felt nothing for Blackiron. He had thought only of leaving it. He had become accepted, and not by mere mortals. He was important.

He had no coin; such was not used in Blackiron, where it was not necessary. On him was the lifestone given him by his second father—or third. In his pouch nestled the two pearls he had from those men who had attacked Torsy on the beach, seemingly now so long and long ago. He was not a trusting youth to leave valued articles lying about, and in that pouch too were a ring and a great long tooth given him by Turibark. As he bore now the Black Sword and a fine dagger off one of the three he'd slain in the wood, he had no desire for his own blades, though they were several. He was breaking with Blackiron; he felt it a break with all the past, even those things that had been his, spoils of combats won. *That was in my youth,* he thought.

In the hut he had called his were some turnips and leeks and a shoulder and two hams of hog, some crockery and two good spoons; a few stones and a necklace and a bracer whose lace was broken; a cloak and a worn tunic he wore in the field. He did not now need the old bearskin cloak, and did not care to think of winter. A few things of Torsy's. The pearl from her neck, that of a fresh-water mussel, had been torn off by one of her killers, and Jarik had forgotten it in his hacking of them and had not sought it among their butchered remains and belongings.

No, he thought. There were no possessions he wanted, not even the old boar spear that was a link to the past. Let all that, like Harnstarl and Ishparshule-wark and Oceanside and Torsy, be in his past, and dead and forgot.

Steed Blackwelder came forward, and all could see what he carried; a one-sleeved leathern coat, flashing with thousands of small rings of iron that were little thicker than wire. The tip of a little finger could have been fitted into any of those rings, but no finger would go far. They had been sewn laboriously, so as to overlap. The coat was of the length of a tunic, that is to fall about to mid-thigh, and the skirt bare of rings, as was just under half of the back.

"Your armour-coat, Jarik."

Jarik looked at Steed, and at the mailcoat.

"It is not finished. You won't wait, or return for it?"

Jarik shook his head.

"Then please take it, Jarish, though unfinished."

After long moments of hesitation, Jarik put forth his hands to take the coat—which was very heavy so that his arms partway dropped under its weight before he arrested their fall. He held it out, and looked at it, and at Steed.

"Please take the swords in my—in the hut I called mine, Steesh my friend."

"Our bargain is complete," Steed said, with his pride on him.

"Take those swords as a gift then, Steesh. Do with them whatever you please; the iron could be reshaped into hooks, or spear-heads for fish or beast-traps."

The two looked at each other, and Steed nodded. He stepped back, away from the youth who stood tall amid the gods on the earth. Jarik looked to Streka Eaglenose, who was foremost among the men of the village.

"All that Torsy and I possessed is in the house we shared, or upon her, and upon me now. The dagger and bracer are to be Sunda Fourfinger's, who fought well today and slew a Hawker who was behind me. All else is for the families of those who were slain, food and goods."

Streka nodded, looking impressed and awed. Jarik felt passing big, and magnanimous, and heroic. *Ally and agent of the Lords of Iron!* What need had he for such paltry possessions as had been his and Torsy's—half and more of which had been accumulated in payment for the services of Oak and his knowledge that Torsy had remembered?

Someone was weeping. Though Jarik knew not if it were for him and his magnanimity or for one of the dead, he felt the bigger. He strove to stand taller still, which was hardly necessary or possible. He turned to the Lord of Destruction.

"Lord God—"

"Jarik—" Streka began, and someone else called his name as well, but Destruction had again taken his hand, and this time when they alit within the keep of the Iron Lords Jarik hardly stumbled. And Harnstarl was part of the dead past. Jarik relieved himself of the weighty burden of that which had formerly been the most exciting thing on the earth: his own mailcoat of good iron links sewn to leather first boiled.

"You gave over to the villagers all your food, all else that you own, Jarik?" Annihilation said, seating himself. He motioned Jarik to the chair of red and red-blue. "It was well received, and very big of you. But—you have no desire for anything that you own?"

"What I possess of value I wear," Jarik said, and his hand touched the smoothly-finished, finger-fluted hilt of the Black Sword. He sat, and laid a hand on his coat of leather sewn with overlapping links of iron.

"You have no food, Jarik . . . of the Black Sword," Dread pointed out, and Jarik thought that again there was amusement in that god's voice.

"If the Lord Gods on whose business I go forth provide none," Jarik said, "I am most capable of finding and killing my own." He thought then of the great boar-spear of Hendrik, that had been for so long so important; a symbol. Well and well; he would not change his mind and go back now!

His declamation had brought a chuckle from behind the mask of the Lord of Destruction. Jarik kept his face very straight and composed. He spoke quickly.

"Again I ask, Lord Gods: What becomes of the youths yourselves fetch from Harnstarl?"

"They are brought here," Annihilation said.

Jarik said nothing; he waited.

"They become Iron Lords," Destruction said.

Jarik pondered that. Fish-netting, dirt-grubbing wark boy into Lord of Iron! He asked, "How is this done, Lord of Destruction?"

"We are not seated as we were before," Destruction pointed out.

"I know, my lord; now I know yourself by voice."

"Wise, you said!" the lord of Dread said, not to Jarik. "Too wise, peradventure. We send away him with the best potential of all in Blackiron!"

"Or him we should slay out of hand," Annihilation said thoughtfully.

Jarik was still, though his heart thumped. He wondered how swiftly he could thrust himself from the chair with his legs and left hand, while drawing the Black Sword with his right. Across his belly and into

Annihilation there on the initial backswing; then in to Dread's neck with all his might. By that time Destruction might well have done death on him—but it was Destruction whose sword now occupied the niche atop Blackiron Stone, so that it stood black and shining over the village it comforted.

The Lord of Dread chuckled, drawing Jarik's wary glance.

"Look at our ally, brothers! Even now the words of the god Lord of Annihilation have set his brain to working as to the manner in which he might attack us!" He waved a gauntleted hand. "Put it from your mind whose wheels can fair hear turning, Jarik, our ally Jarik. It could not be done. Nor will you be slain here. You have said that you are our ally and agent. It is so."

Jarik swallowed and strove very hard to look both relaxed and innocent of guileful thoughts.

"To your question," the Lord of Destruction said. Still Jarik only sought to appear relaxed; he remained alert lest he be tricked and set upon. "Seek not to know overmuch, Strodeson Jarik who is Oak. We will not answer all. Nor do you wish to know all, believe us! We will tell you this. Sixteen years agone we brought here a youth from Blackiron, one Lyd, Hawkbeak's son."

Jarik nodded. He knew this.

The Lord of Destruction also nodded; he gestured at Annihilation.

"I am he," that god said. "Rather, this is the body of Lyd son of Hawkbeak that I wear. I am Nershehir, Lord of Annihilation, Iron Lord, god on the earth. . . and I am Lyd."

"Then yourselves are not gods? Are yourselves not immortal?"

"We are immortal, Jarik. We have lived for centuries. Longer. The body ages, even among gods. Our minds never tire."

Jarik thought that strange, for he knew of the revis-
178

itation of childhood that came upon those few who gained many years. He commented only guardedly: "Truly I see naught of the senility of the old about yourself, Lord of Dread; Lord of Destruction. Nor about any of yourselves."

"No," Destruction said. "We enter new bodies before that time. Our minds do not deteriorate."

Morelike, Jarik reflected, *you first seize the minds of those whose bodies you occupy. For if you can do the one, why not the other?* But he voiced none of this thought.

"All our memories flow into a youth of the village," Destruction went on, affirming that opined truth either deliberately or by error in oversight.

"Such as Hawkbeakson Lyd," Annihilation said.

"Such as Lyd," Destruction said nodding. "Thus we live on, Jarik. We are the Iron Lords, gods on the earth; we live forever, Jarik. I was born Eskeshehir; I remain Eskeshehir."

Straightforwardly Jarik spoke: "I would not care to have been Lyd. I do not care to be an Iron Lord."

Again amusement rode the voice of old Dread: surely soon another lad of Harnstarl would be required and the Lord of Dread would have a new body and voice. He swept a gloved hand through the air in a gesture that included the whole of the keep of the Lords of Iron.

"With all this? All this? Are you certain, Jarik-Oak?"

Jarik let them see him looking about. He allowed himself time to study anew each woman and girl, each handsome chair and couch, every carpet and handsome hanging. He thought on the excellence of the wine and the cleanness of the air tinged with neither heat nor cold, damp nor dryness, and he bethought himself of the cushioned chair beneath his buttocks and the way in which the Iron Lords were received in Blackiron. And he thought on how they had slain three men of the attackers; so swiftly, and dramatically, and coolly. And he shook his head.

"I am sure, Lord of Dread. I do not care to be an Iron Lord. I would be Jarik."

"And Oak?"

"If that must be."

"Only a short time ago you petitioned us to take from you your name, and its memories, and leave you in Harnstarl as Oak, humble healer."

"That was a short time ago," Jarik said, thinking with small amusement that from what he'd been told, Oak was less humble than he. Now Jarik's words, voice, and manner stated clearly that there was an end to that.

"Very well," the Lord of Dread said. "You will not be an Iron Lord." And he leaned back, and seemed to grow a bit smaller and a bit less visible.

"Now you are an ally of the Iron Lords," Destruction said. "Soon you will be the most favored of men in the world."

Jarik was so impressed he was nigh whelmed and might have fallen had he stood. Nevertheless he pressed, to be certain: "But not an Iron Lord."

"But not an Iron Lord, Jarik."

"It is good, Lords! I have no desire to be the . . . the ewer into which your memories flow, Lord of Dread . . . or Annihilation, or Destruction. I have no desire to be an Iron Lord."

Iron heads turned. "What have you desire for, Jarik? Any of these?"

Again Jarik sent his glance winging out over their servants. "Oh aye, all of them!"

Within iron cages blacker than the raven's glossy wing, laughter rang like clanging swords.

"That we promise you, Jarik, and more."

This was Destruction who spoke. At first it had been Annihilation who said the most. Now it was Destruction, perhaps because he had been longer an Iron Lord. But no no; they were always and ever Iron

180

Lords; it was only the bodies within the metal carapaces that changed.

"Once you have accomplished your mission and
ours, we will return you here, Jarik our ally. You may
remain so long as you wish. None will refuse you.
None of our servants will refuse any wish or desire
that is yours. You will be Jarik, ally of the Lords of
Iron, whom by your slaying the Lady of the Snowmist you will have freed to protect all the people of
the earth."

Jarik grew more bold. "Will I not want for better
armor than this coat Steed Blackwelder made but did
not finish? —to face the Hawker chieftain and more
importantly the Lady of the Snowmist, a god on the
earth?"

"Aye," the Lord of Dread said, and Jarik knew he
repressed a chuckle.

"And a better buckler," Jarik pressed.

"Of course," Dread said, closer still to laughter.

Jarik blinked, smiled. He looked around him, and
his stomach rumbled. He was important, an ally of
the Iron Lords who were Gods on the Earth, and he
was hungry. "It is late, past Shralla's Ride. I would
eat, and visit with her," he said, pointing. "And on the
morrow I will go forth in mail, with the Black Sword,
on our mutual business."

"Done," Destruction said, and the Lord of Dread
laughed aloud, and the weavers wove.

Chapter Sixteen:
Kirrensark

Beyond the narrow valley and broad, raised plain below him rose a great double-peaked mountain, all greys and copper and ocher. Each turned white toward its peak, and the warrior knew he was looking on snow that melted only in unusually hot summers. The summit of the leftward peak vanished into a hovering misty cloud like softly shadowed snow, gilded by the sun.

Between him and that twice-spired mountain lay the plain sprawling high above the sea; a small forest, sprawling farmland, and the outbuildings of a large settlement. His heartbeat quickened. He knew that from his hillside, just below the hill's summit, he looked upon the wark of Kirrensark long-haft, servant of the Lady of the Snowmist.

He gazed down upon it. He wore a good iron helm over a leather cap, and the helmet was lined with sponge from the sea. His mailcoat was of signally good iron chain, better than he'd ever seen or deemed could be made, decorated with links of bronze that flashed red-gold against their field of blued iron. A broad bronze-buckled belt supported two daggers and two pouches, for he wore his sword on his back. The baldric's iron buckle gleamed on his chest; the broad strap disappeared over his broad, left shoulder. From the sheath thus slung on his back thrust up his sword's hilt. The pommel was undecorative, of blue-black iron, as was its quillons or guard. The hilt showed red; it was wound and wound, very tightly, with the finest soft leather, which had been well-chewed by old women and dyed. Nothing more showed of the sheathed sword.

His mailcoat was half-sleeved and he wore a bronze-plated bracer or wrist-band of hard red leather that covered his sword-arm from wristbones almost to elbow. On the left he carried a good targe or round shield, worn on arm straps. Red-faced, the shield was of linden edged and plated with hemispheres of black iron.

On the shield's face was emblazoned the black silhouette of a sword that seemed to pierce the pointed, hexagonal boss that stood forth from the shield's center to the length of a man's forefinger.

Long wheaten hair spilled out below his helm, which was unadorned and slightly pointed so as to deflect blows, rather than convey their force to his skull as a round helmet tended to do. The helm's neckpiece was hinged, and its noseguard was not. Though it fitted low on his forehead and the noseguard was broad, excellent vision was afforded by two arches; the wearer's eyebrows were obscured and his eyes shadowed.

For this was obviously a man of weapons, a warrior and well accoutred.

The hill on which he stood might have been called a grassed mountain. It stood well higher than the wark, which was laid out on a bluff rising from the sea to the west, his left. Behind him, the southward side of his hill plunged down into a gorge as if chopped out by the ax of a giant, or a million men. Beyond the gorge rose the dark, dark mass of Dragonmount, this northern face of which had never seen the sun save at its setting and bore snow well down its jagged flank, even into summer. Beetling salients kept those northward slopes in a perpetual gloom that defied Shralla's light.

Nevertheless, the beardless man thought, a sentinel should be posted on this hill. Thus he thought, for he was a man of weapons, a warrior: *acatir*, and gloriously aware of it.

He stood on a hill that plunged grassily down into a broad valley, and the hill on the far side of that was wooded, running up to the wark-lands. There were ranged cropland and dwellings, outbuildings, and animal enclosures, all nestled beneath their roofs of sod or tied bundles of thatch; grass grew on those roofs. There too abode cows and oxen, sheep and pigs and many folk, dogs and a very few horses.

Below, between him and the wark, figuratively at his feet and unknown to any of the wark above them, were four men.

Just at the edge of a tree-line marking a stream they were, in the gloom of the trees on the slope so that all was as if shaded in indigo. All were armed and at the wielding of those weapons; three were attacking one. He wielded a long-hafted ax against their sword and two axes, and his ax-head was large. A large, strong man, with a full beard onto his chest, and it as much grey as darkish blond. He stood still as well he could, using the oddly long-handled half-moon of his blade in great sweeps, only defending himself. Nor did any of the wark see, or by their actions, hear or know of this unequal combat.

The means of gaining acceptance in Kirrensark-wark lay at hand, at the stranger's feet. The three assailants were armored and the lone man not. Wark-men had no need of such warlike attire on their own territory; attackers did. They were the invaders then, surely. They must have come upon the single man of the wark of Kirrensark as they crept up the stream's bank, hoping to sneak up through the trees in a raid. A maiden-raid, mayhap.

A very proud young man now and with his confidence soaring, the warrior on the hillside hardly took time to remove and rebuckle his baldric at his hips, shortening it by looping the strap over itself several times.

Then he descended the hill in a silent charge.

The defender, he saw as he neared the combatants, was good at his defending. He'd not yet been struck—though he also had inflicted no wound. Big he was, and big again, with his huge beard of grey and blond. No youth, the fifth man thought as he slid the last eight or ten feet down the hillside.

At last peripheral vision and sound caught the attention of intent men, and two saw him. Nor, as the newcomer charged, did they know whether they had an ally or an opponent.

The big, big-bearded man did not bother to conjecture. While two of his besetters took note of the newcomer, their intended victim lowered his ax-swing, lengthened it by a stride, and chopped off a sword-arm just below the elbow. The man screamed and blood flew while the third attacker just missed slaying the grey-beard.

The newcomer was charging in now, red-shielded and wielding a sword with a long, strangely refulgent blade of jet black. He must be faced. Not by the wounded man; he sank to his knees, clutching the gushing stump of his arm and staring at it with great round eyes.

"I'll take him!" one of the remaining two called.

A moment later sword struck shield, chopped half a man's breadth into its upper rim—and its point split that man's cheek from eye to mouth. He grunted even as he swung his own blow. His ax was turned on the newcomer's scarlet shield and the shield's owner hurled himself forward. His body forced back the buckler on which it was wedged until some two inches of black swordpoint slid into a face already wounded. That man staggered back, mouth and cheek pouring blood, and still he flailed another stroke of his ax for some men did not notice wounds until they'd got their deaths. The ax rang off the boss of the red shield and hot sparks flew. The red targe's owner yanked his sword free. Rather than pounce away, he struck again,

185

low. His edge ate well into his opponent's thigh. The man fell sidewise and the black sword whipped up and down to smash collarbone and lower neck.

The third attacker took note. He was trying more desperately to get past the greybeard's arc-rushing ax; that big fighter was far past forty and perhaps even fifty, but much strength remained in his right arm. His assailant caught movement from the edge of his eyes and snapped a look. He saw both his comrades down. One was sprawled and twitching; dead or seconds from it.

Very rapidly the last of the trio backed three paces—and then he turned and ran, eastward and away from the wark.

The man with the black sword started to follow.

"No no," he with the full beard called out, and he was winded. "Let him go—he is after all my cousin's son."

"Cousin's son!"

"Aye," the man of Kirrensark-wark said sadly.

His rescuer shook his head. Then he pointed to the man whose hand had been cut off; he had sunk low and could only just maintain his grip on the bleeding stump.

"This one is yours."

Greybeard said, "Get up and return to your wark."

His ax-victim looked up at him with eyes full of anguish. "I—I'll never make it," he gasped. "How did you—"He broke off. His face was very pale.

"You'll not make it up the hill to the wark either, then."

There was a long silence. "Slay me, then. Give me the gift of death."

"I will not."

The wounded man turned his dulling gaze up to the newcomer. "You then. I'd not . . . bleed to death, in pain. . . . And I can't get to my . . . feet. I've lost too much . . . blood already."

"I will give him the death he desires," the new-

186

comer said, and both others saw that he was youthful.

The man with the big grey-and-blond beard moved his mouth, turned away. "It is not at my desire. Nor will I forbid."

"Wa—wait. I would know who gives me. . . my my death."

"My name is Jarik." And the Black Sword chopped. It was necessary that it chop twice, to sever the man's head from his neck.

The big man with the ax heard the two chunking strokes without turning. He did now, without looking down at the corpse. "Methinks I owe you this life, Black-sword. You have no further name? I know of no name 'Ch—Chairik'?"

"I am Stro—" Jarik paused. He decided on the instant to seize on the sobriquet this man had given him. He resolved no longer to identify himself as the son of any man. "I am Jarik; Jarik Blacksword."

"I note that almost you used another name, Jarik Blacksword to whom I am indebted."

"My father's name is. . . dishonored, and I will not use it. I am Jarik Blacksword."

The other nodded. As he slipped off his shield Jarik was astonished to see that it was fixed with a special set of straps; the fellow's left arm was without a hand. A much stouter man than the one just given death, then—though this one had not had the additional horror of knowing he had lost his sword-arm. Or rather ax-hand.

"Why did you come so to my aid, Jarik Blacksword? Know you me?"

Jarik shook his head jerkily, forcing his gaze from the stump. "No. I saw three attacking one, and knew that you must be of the wark on the hill, for you are not girded for combat. As they were, I assumed they were would-be raiders who'd come upon you by accident." He shrugged. "I'd not see murder done so on any man."

"You are an unusual man as well as stranger then,

187

Jarik Blacksword. As unusual as your weapon. Of an eagle's eye and good brain too, for you have the way of it. Though those three came not a-raiding, but with intent to slay me."

"Good, then. No man likes assassins. A watch should be kept posted up there." Jarik jerked his head to indicate the hill he'd just quitted. "Vision is good."

"We have not been attacked or raided in long years, Jarik Blacksword. A watch would merely become bored—and if attack or raid did come, he'd only be the first to die."

Jarik considered that, and saw its logic. He knew then that he was not yet ready to rule a wark or even command its defenses. He nodded. "I make apology for. . . forwardness," he said.

"You owe no apology and must commit a terrible crime indeed to owe me one, Jarik Blacksword. You have surely saved my life, for I could not have held off those three young bravos much longer. You saw that I was winded, and they not." And the man grounded his ax so that its long handle rested against his leg, and he showed Jarik his open hand and beside it the stump of another that would have been open.

Hurriedly Jarik stooped and cleaned his sword on a dead man's leggings—although the blood had nearly all run, like oil, off the impossibly sleek-smooth black blade. Rising, he sheathed the weapon and returned the gesture of respectful peace, showing the other man his hands.

"I am your brother, warrior."

"I am your brother, warrior." And then Jarik went on: "Because of the dishonor on my father's name, I left my wark forever. Nor will I tell you its name—but it is many days' journey from here." *Unless,* he mused, *one is magicked across the distance by the gods on the earth.* He gazed with an open face on the one-armed warrior, who was a very big man with his very big beard of stone-and-straw.

188

"You will come up the hill with me, Jarik Blacksword, to board and hearth. Perhaps you will think to join this wark. My savior would be more than welcome."

"Might a grateful stranger ask whom he has helped?"

"It is my wark," said the old, one-armed man with the beard full of grey. "My name is Kirrensark Longhaft."

Jarik stared at the other man, who was old enough to be his father, and more, and Jarik's legs went weak. His body felt all hot and prickly, with too a feeling of weariness on it. Kirrensark after all these years! Jarik's face held as much anguish as had the wounded man to whom he'd given the gift of swift death.

O, ye gods! Oh Jarik, poor fool Jarik, ever acting so swiftly and with courage—and wrongly! I could have stood on that hill and let them slay him. Oh no, I had to interfere, to charge down and be the hero. All I had to do was stand still, and watch, and contain this impetuous self that is poor miserable Jarik, ridiculous Jarik who works against himself! I could have joined those three, and see him dead, and be honored in their wark. Instead I have enemies there, with one who knows me. He will talk of me. . . and now. . . Seeker of vengeance across all these years! I have saved him. I have saved Kirrensark the killer! And how can I do death on an old man with but one hand?

He could not.

And thus did the weavers weave it so that Jarik saved the life of him who had shattered his life, had led the murderers of Oceanside. And Jarik went up with him to his wark, and into his house as honored guest, and Jarik was far from happy. On two occasions now he had sought to be the great hero, and twice had he failed even while he succeeded.

Shralla of the sky rode on down the sky, and she cared not. The Iron Lords cared not, who had told him some things that were true and some that were not while seeing in him a tool; a young and impetuous opportunist—and superb fighter—in aching need of acceptance, and importance, and purpose. And the weavers wove on, and they cared not either.

Chapter Seventeen:
Jarik of Kirrensark-wark

The houses of Kirrensark-wark were not wholly un-
familiar to Jarik. Those of Ishparshule-wark were
similar, as the warks and their people were similar.

Very steep roofs of sod or tied bundles of thatch and
occasional birch-barks slanted down over low walls of
mud-daub on wicker. Carven gables rose to cross in
wedge-shapes above every entry, projecting above the
ridgepole to end in the head of a wolf or a bear or
the fabled hippogryf. Animal enclosures crowded
close, with partitions of timber and occasionally stone
forming stalls in the barns. Both barns and houses
sprouted live grass, so that to a giant a wark proper
might resemble an area of particularly roiling turf.

Down amid the houses and in their shadows, heavy
timbers formed boardwalks to rise above snow and
that which followed it and was worse: slush and mud.
These streets were wide enough for three people to
walk abreast, or for two to meet one without having
to step off or one behind the other.

Kirrensark's house was large and the gable-ends
were carved into large white birds that were not
seafowls.

Jarik had never before been in a house with three
rooms. Most were of one room; some had two. The
benches that ranged the walls of the main chamber
were for sitting at mealtime or mending or aleing of
an evening and, with eiderdown or fur covers, for
sleeping at night. A long hearth of stone stretched
down the center of the main room. It provided
warmth, and light, and cookfire. The table was near,

with the usual single high seat for the master; the rest of the family and guests ate seated on the benches. The table was thick, long planks stretched atop a center X-frame and one at either end, all of square-sawed legs. While the high seat was customarily at table's center, Jarik saw that Kirrensark's was at its end, facing the entry.

Meat and a few drying vegetables hung from beams. Like the people of Ishparshule-wark, these ate mutton, beef, pork, and occasionally the meat of seals and pilot whales. And, less often, seabirds. Meat and milk, butter and cheese and bread; these nourished. Things that grew green from the ground were merely for seasoning and garnish—aside, of course, from the oats and barley that were so tenderly and assiduously nourished by all during Lokusta's growing season of five—or four, in some years—months.

Braces of iron-strengthened wood supported two thick iron rods over the long hearth. Most knew to keep water in at least one of them all winter; its evaporation helped combat sore and bloody noses and the dry-eye. Water was easily come by in winter; it was piled high outside, white and solid.

When Jarik entered Kirrensark's house with its master, snow was months away and meat simmered aromatically in leek- and spelt-laced grease to which a little water had been added; a very little. On the table waited two knives and three wooden bowls and wooden spoons, with mugs for ale or barley-water. A man used his own dagger for eating, but was proud to have knives for wife and children, when he could.

The greatroom was dim. While Jarik saw no less than three lamps made of soapstone, two fantastically carved. None was lit. The hearth-fire provided a flickering, yellowish, grease-hazed light. To all this, of course, was Jarik Blacksword accustomed.

In that large house of Kirrensark, long ago commander of those who had brought destruction and horror and annihilation to Oceanside, Jarik met Kirrensark's wife with her grey braids to her waist, and their daughter Iklatne. Her barley-straw braids would have fallen past her sturdy waist, though presently they were wrapped about her neck as a sort of boa.

Lirushye was fat though not obese. Her daughter was but a little younger than Jarik, a big sturdy girl with large hands, mighty breasts, and a lovely mouth under an unfortunate nose. She was neither wholly unattractive nor beautiful, and not slim either. Jarik wondered why she was unwed. Iklatne was tall, even among her tall people, with deepset eyes that were much in shadow—and much on Jarik. He saw that she had been down at the sea today; her stockings were stretched to dry on the usual stone at hearth's end, a slab the size of Jarik's torso.

Both women wore blue and grey with sleeves ending at mid-forearm, and he knew their aprons had been white, or nearly. The brows and lashes of both were, weirdly to Jarik, blue. Aye, the eyebrows. So were those of most of the women of Kirrensark-wark: blue. The heartily-introduced guest was too polite or perhaps proud to comment or ask about this oddness.

Eventually he learned that the color derived from the same wood plant whose water-steeped leaves also provided dye for clothing. Here in Kirrensark-wark he discovered, too, how the reddish-blue hue—archil—was made. A certain plant and a specific lichen were imbued in old urine and its effluvia that so assaulted the eyes and nostrils. (There were disagreements as to the urine of what animal or human or sex made the best dye.) The shade was not, however, so beautiful as those purples of the Iron Lords; this of Kirrensark-wark was dull and murky looking.

Kirrensark told his story, while his wife's eyes shed tears and Iklatne's remained huge, directing their gaze mostly on her father's savior. Jarik, who had no concept of the effects of age and sureness-of-manhood on false pride, thought that Kirrensark was lacking in pride.

Fat Lirushye hugged her husband, who'd come so close to death. He patted her back, looked uncomfortable, and promised not to go again alone into the woods, much less through them down to the stream. And Jarik anguished.

That monster Kiddensahk of old had a wife who loved him, and had fathered sons, and a daughter who had married and had died, at fifteen, in childbirth. Iklatne remained, and her no beauty—though, as Jarik naturally took closer note and his eyes accustomed themselves to the interior grease-hazed gloom, she was sensuous enough. And Jarik had saved Kirrensark for them.

Having hugged her husband to his embarrassment, Lirushye let go at last. She turned her moist cheeks and tear-sparkling eyes towerd Jarik. Next moment he was worse than embarrassed, for she hugged him.

"There, woman, cease and leave off. He's a youth'd rather be hugging a younger lass, and a hero as well."

Releasing Jarik at her husband's words, Lirushye stepped back a pace and held him with a hand on each of his arms. "I hug and welcome you not as you're a well-favored youth or a hero, Jarik, but as you are he who saved my foolish husband who should not fare alone abroad."

"Woman."

Aye, she'd overstepped a bit, and Lirushye returned her attentions to the evening's meal. She muttered that this night she should have cakes and a big fine leg of mutton or rib-roast standing, not this stew. Iklatne brought the guest warmed water for the washing of his hands, and she did not avert her gaze from his. She also made their hands touch, and their arms.

"It is a hard thing to be a daughter and not a wife, so that I may not embrace my father's savior!"

"Iklatnish!" Lirushye said sharply, while Kirrensark chuckled.

Jarik was glad to bow his back and splash water on

his face, which had grown warm. Then he removed his weapons and armor—placing a dagger on the table for the eating with—and laid them aside; as he'd taken no blow, the mail would not need to be checked for broken or weakened links. He knew he must have care to cleanse it of blood—none his—but that would keep for later. This had been a most busy day indeed, from the keep of the Iron Lords through a battle to Kirrensark's very home!

And me a guest in it, rather than a conquering avenger, he thought with a return of anguish.

All three of his hosts wore necklaces set with the amber that they called sea-gift: *tennik.* It was found, in chunks, not infrequently on the beach below the wark, washed up as if a gift from the ocean. The ears of mother and daughter had been pierced and from them swung amber wheels large as Jarik's thumbnail and five times as thick. The First Man of Kirrensark-wark wore a large ring consisting of a gold band with its amber setting caged in two thin arches of gold. Amber appeared elsewhere in the house. Jarik was to learn that it was almost common in this wark, to which the sea was kind. Jarik particularly admired a sheathed dagger slung from a peg on one wall. Its hilt was of beautiful red bronze and its pommel was a perfectly domed piece of amber the size of a sheep's eyeball.

"Several times have your eyes strayed to that wall," Kirrensark said as they ate; Jarik had refused the high chair as if scandalized.

"Several more times than they've strayed to me," Iklatne said.

"Iklatnish!" Lirushye said sharply, but Kirrensark chuckled.

"I admire the dagger there," Jarik said. "As I've told you, where I lived the whole wark had not so much amber as you three."

"We have other earrings too," Iklatne said. "The

195

centers of these wheels form drops. I'll wear those the morrow."

"It was our youngest son's," Lirushye said. "The dagger."

"Our third son," Kirrensark said. "The fourth, but one died at birth. Kirrenar was our last born and last to die."

Jarik was silent. He'd told his host he was sorry Kirrensark had fathered four sons and had none for his sunset years or to be First Man when he was gone, but Jarik was not sorry.

"It has hung there unused these seven years," Lirushye said in a voice that was as if elsewhere. Her eyes had gone away, too.

"Kirrenar loved that dagger," Kirrensark said. "The morrow it will have a new owner. I will make you a gift of that dagger, Jarik."

Jarik finished chewing and swallowed; hardly necessary before speaking, but it gave him a minute for thinking. He took up his ale-mug.

"I will not accept it."

"Of course you will."

Jarik looked at him. "I will not. No."

Kirrensark blinked. "But—why not? It is a gift. It is a good blade, and a handsome grip and pommel. It is unused. I give it to you."

"I will accept no gift of your hands, Kirrensark Long-haft," Jarik told him, looking full and steadily into the big man's eyes. They blinked again. (Kirrensark squinted a bit.)

"But. . . Jarik," Lirushye began.

"I have my *life* as a gift of *your* hands, Jarik!"

"I will have none of yours," Jarik said, and they ate for a time in silence, with Kirrensark looking more surprised than pained.

Then it was time for the aleing, and Kirrensark sent Iklatne to fetch other men. Lirushye decided to go and spend the night with the Widow Senyish. Iklatne announced that she would remain and fetch and pour for the men. Lirushye objected; this would be no place for a girl. They argued briefly, and Kirrensark spoke. Then Lirushye went to spend the night with Widow Senyish and Iklatne stayed to fetch and pour—and listen, of course.

Jarik met a half-score men, all of whom were told of his deed. He was hero, and enjoyed it while wishing that he were not. Again, and again he was told how welcome he was in Kirrensark-wark. That did no happiness on him either, though he pretended.

They drank. If they asked Jarik a question a bit overmuch to this or that point, Kirrensark interrupted. The wark-men thus learned nothing of Jarik other than what he had told their First Man and that he had never married; that yes, he had slain aforenow, in defense of self or wark. He did tell them that he'd had a sister, and what had befallen her. That story he combined with her assault on the beach outside the serpents' cave, and freely answered their questions about that combat—though he disguised the fact that it had taken place at seaside.

Jarik was as careful with his imbibing as with his talking.

Iklatne brushed close when she came to fill—or offer to fill—his mug. The other men had brought theirs; Jarik was loaned one, for the First Man was a man of property.

They left eventually, straggling. One had to be borne by two others hardly suited to the task; neither walked well. Kirrensark continued to drink, and talk, and he thought that Jarik drank with him. Jarik heard of the deaths of Kirrensark's three sons. Two had died of arms, the other, after an accident, of the flesh-rot that sometimes followed wounds. Now Kirrensark's cousin Ahl sought to have him slain, and Kirrensark waxed sad and maudlin, in his cups.

At last he sagged into helpless sleep, drunk. Jarik aided Iklatne in getting her father onto a bench, and she showed Jarik to one of the house's other two rooms; here he would sleep.

Iklatne left him there, but she returned.

Next day Jarik walked out with his host whose life he had saved, and he met many people who bestowed warm greetings on their First Man's savior. They fared beyond the buildings and then the outbuildings, with Jarik dressed and accoutred as a warrior. None other in the wark was attired so. They walked well abroad, inland along the plain.

"I lay with my host's daughter last night," Jarik said.

"I know."

After a time of silence, while Jarik dealt with his astonishment at those simple words and what they implied, he added, "Under his own roof."

"I know."

After another time of silence, Jarik asked. "You know? That is all?"

"It is all, Jarik."

"I come invited into your home, and will accept no gift of you, but lie with your daughter under your own roof, and you have only to say 'I know'?"

"Yes. You seem to seek to goad me, Jarik. Why?"

Jarik was silent. They had halted, on a green plain bounded by mountains and roofed by a sky bluer than blue. A small white cloud seemed to chase a much larger one like a pup herding sheep before him.

"I am no longer young, Jarik. I am no longer sure I should be called warrior. I am not a young man, and without sons, and resigned. I will not challenge you or be goaded into the clanging of iron, Jarik—though for some reason you push me."

Kirrensark paused then, and gazed levelly, openly at Jarik, but Jarik remained silent. "Others," Kirrensark said, "have lain with my daughter Iklatne. None was the weapon-man you are, Jarik Blacksword, and none had saved my life."

Jarik showed interest in a flock of sheep at the mountain's foot, and in their shepherd, who was a woman and young.

"Jarik: Go before the Lady Mage with my daughter Iklatne, and be my son, Jarik Blacksword."

Jarik's jaw worked, and he spoke deliberately to be cruel. "I and others have lain with your daughter, Kirrensark Long-haft. I will not wed her."

"You *do* seek to provoke me! Why?"

Jarik turned to the First Man at last, and under the blue sky his blue eyes were like ice. "I came here to slay you, Kirrensark Long-haft."

"You—but you saved my life!" Kirrensark seemed all but physically staggered by Jarik's statement.

Jarik nodded. "I did not know who you were."

"Ah! Now I understand your look when I gave you my name ... and had you known?"

Jarik met the older man's eyes full on. "I would not have come to aid you."

Kirrensark paled a bit, stared, looked away. "I do not know you; never heard of you. Yet you came to slay me. Will you tell me why?"

Jarik told him.

At last Kirrensark Long-haft said, "It was not I that slew your foster mother that long ago day in ... Oceanside, Jarik."

"I know. But you were in command. You led them. Who was the man?"

Kirrensark stood with his stare fixed on ugly Dragonmount. "Deep sorrow is on me, Jarik Blacksword. I understand why you came here to do death on me."

"And—"

"And nevertheless I will not tell you the name of the man who slew your foster mother of Akkharia."

"Not to save your life, Kirrensark?"

"I am not young, Jarik Blacksword," Kirrensark said again, and Jarik noted that the Long-haft would not say that he was "old." "I have one hand left me, and few years. In winter the fingers in the hand I no long-

199

er have ache with the cold. My toes grow cold very rapidly now and my joints pop and ache when it is wet. My children are dead, all but Iklatne, though my wife has borne me six. I have only illnesses and the joint-ache and the ebb-tide of my life to look forward to, now. Or more likely. . . death from the men of my cousin, who would make this Ahl-wark. No, I will not tell you the name of the man who slew your foster mother of Akkharia, Jarik Blacksword." While he spoke, Kirrensark appeared to age ten years beyond the man Jarik had met last night. "Not even to save my life. It is yours, this life of mine. Yesterday you saved it, and made me a present of it."

He turned to face Jarik then, and again linked their gazes. "Today—take it."

Jarik stared at the man who was not young, and as hopeless as he—no, more hopeless, for Jarik had a short ugly past and a future that might be anything. Kirrensark knew both his past and his future.

"I will accept no gift of your hands, and I will not stay and go before the Lady Mage with your daughter Iklatne, old man. I would not be your son, or the husband of a daughter of yours. And had I yesterday to live again, I would not prevent your death, but joy in it."

Kirrensark nodded, and the First Man's face showed little pain. "My life is yours now, Jarik Blacksword. I give you some small thanks for it."

Kirrensark turned then, and headed back to the wark. Jarik stood looking after him, his eyes glassing a bit as he thought on what it might be to be old and without hope and pride. Well beyond Kirrensark he saw Iklatne at the door of her father's house. Watching. Waiting. *Clever maid*, he thought. *You failed. Again?*

It was then that the strange pearl-white mist came flowing down from Cloudpeak and across the plain, like the thinnest of milk. It came to Kirrensark and passed over him, so that he turned to watch it flow toward Jarik. Ten paces from him it came to pause, and swirled, and coalesced. . . and in that midst She appeared.

Jarik had seen her aforenow. Somehow, he had seen her one day when he was but eight; the same day he had first seen Kirrensark. But Kirrensark had been real that day, while she had been a dream, or a vision. Today Jarik was sure that he really looked upon her.

The Lady of the Snowmist.

Chapter Eighteen:
In Snowmist Keep

She was most excellent of female form, in body-molding armor like fabric or the skin of a fabulous serpent. All in white and grey and silver she was, a vision passing beautiful and almost blinding in the sun. As part of her helm she wore a frosty, sparkling silver mask; it was like snow in the morning after a night of freezing rain, all sparkly and fulgurant. No eyeslits pierced the mask, though high-arched "brows" of dark grey provided an aspect of regal hauteur. The "mouth" was shaped, rather than slitted like those in the masks of the Iron Lords. It was, somehow, a lovely female mouth.

The mask was attached to a shaped, close-fitting helm of silver that formed a dome. It was winged and the wings were white. The hilt of her sheathed sword was polished silver and its pommel a strange stone that was colorless and yet faceted so as to glint with various hues at her slightest movement. On each of her wrists, over the silver-grey armor, a silver bracer flashed. The pearl-grey gloves that sheathed her hands were seemingly dusted with silver shavings.

She stood before Jarik and gazed upon him—or so he must assume, for nothing of eye or flesh showed of the god. Silver sword confronted black.

"My Lady of the Snowmist!" Kirrensark said low, and with both awe and some pleasure. He had turned back, and was behind her.

She did not turn her head the merest fraction toward him.

"I would have you come with me." Her voice was ... silver. Liquid silver floating down a mountain stream.

"I am ready," Jarik told her at once.

She put forth a gloved hand. Jarik took it without pausing to see if his hand were soiled.

"Ja—"

He never heard Kirrensark finish pronouncing his name. Came the instant of disorientation he expected, the brief mild nausea, the rushing sensation as of flying, the slight stumble on arrival.

Jarik looked about at the keep of the Lady of the Snowmist.

Jarik would have liked this domain of the Iron Lords' enemy to be a place foreboding, all somber and dread-filled with a pervasive unease. It was not, and he could not pretend that it was.

The colors of chairs and couches and drapes, pillows and cushions and walls, were in general less dark than those in the Iron Lord's keep. Here, within the mountain, the huge room was not barn-like. The ceiling was indeed twenty feet above the floor. But . . .

From it, all of it, emanated a soft light that was pearly with the merest tinge of blue. Columns rose from floor to ceiling, and they were like unto trees, complete even to bark and high-set branches. Shrubs and flowers seemed to grow from a carpet that was grass-green and deep-piled as a bear's fur in autumn—or a good stand of uncropped grass. The walls were muraled, every one, from wall and floor to ceiling: trees, shrubs, a sprawling meadow where deer grazed, a distant mountain in blues and pinks, and white on top. Apparently Milady Snowmist loved the countryside and had found this means of bringing it inside the cold mountain with her. And the doing of it, all of it, was miraculous to Jarik; impossible and magical.

The room was large, oh aye. It was nevertheless not so stupefyingly so as that sprawling plain that was the main chamber of Dread, and Destruction, and Annihilation.

A welcome similarity lay in the occupants of this incredible great room. All were female and attractive. The colors of their garb were those of spring and of summer. Sleeveless were the clinging dresses, with straps over the shoulders each no broader than a finger. The gowns fell to the floor, save on those who were manifestly girls. Their gowns were tunics. Every woman and every girl wore a set of silver bracers on her wrists, and most wore necklaces. He did not even know what to call some of the colorful stones, which must have been sufficient to buy a kingdom.

He saw too a child, a girl-child of no more than nine or ten. Her hair was nigh white and her eyes were his, and already beauty had touched her as with the brushing of a soft, soft feather.

"You seem not overly startled, Jarik. You know where we are?"

She knows my name. "We—we must be within Cloudpeak itself, Lady," Jarik said, and had no need of forcing awe into his tone, though he'd been inside a mountain before, very recently indeed. "I am more than startled. I am . . . awed."

"You speak remarkably well, for one such as you," she said, and went on before he had time to puzzle over that. "You will bathe, and be given less warlike garb, and we will talk."

She made the merest gesture. Two lovely women in their twenties—he supposed—came at once. They conducted him to a room that was far more luxurious than could have been dreamed of by any wark-dweller, and yet that was somehow not soft.

"Is it here those others come, whom the Lady of the Snowmist Chooses from the warks?" he asked.

"You must ask her. None has come here in armor aforenow, warrior! How is it removed?"

"With help!" Jarik smiled, trying not to stare at her so-womanly form within the soft and clingy dress of gentlest yellow. He unbuckled his weapons belt. "Or thus."

Tugging up the skirts of his mailcoat, he bent forward as he pulled the heavy iron links higher, and then bent far over, and wriggled. Too heavy for any man to lift and doff as a shirt, the mass of small chain circles slipped downward. It came clinking and rustling down his back and over his head and down his shoulders and arms, to lie in a gleaming, warlike puddle on the carpet—which was precisely of the green of sheepgrass in June.

When he straightened and gave his head a jerk to straighten mussed hair, it was to find the two women smiling at his head-down, rump-up pose, and his necessary wiggle to start the chain moving. He affected not to notice. There was comfort in the fact that the servants of a god on the earth did not know everything! Having just seen, for the first time, a man remove his armor in the only possible way unless he was aided, they were amused.

Jarik removed his vest of quilted padding. He was handed a goblet that was apparently of silver, beaten and wrought and etched. It contained ale—no! A most marvelous yellowish-white wine. More awaited in a handsomely decorated earthenware amphora of orange and red and vermillion and amber.

Sipping, he watched them draw a curtain—to reveal a sunken place in the floor by the far wall. The long oval depression was faced with pale blue god-metal, or something like, all refulgent and sleek. While Jarik stared at her backside and went throat-dry despite the wine, one of the women bent over the depression. She did something—and Jarik started. From the bill of the wrought eider's head on its arching neck, water gushed from the very wall!

The tub filled rapidly. The two looked at Jarik. Trying very hard to be sophisticated, he sipped his wine and gazed back—occasionally letting his glance flick to the water gushing noisily into the sunken tub against the wall.

"It will soon be full, and is neither hot nor cold. We are to bathe you."

Jarik breathed while he drank. He coughed, and burped and was embarrassed to shed the automatic tears of what his people called gulping a wind-demon.

"Bathe . . . me?" He tried to be unobtrusive in the clearing of tears from his upper cheeks.

They nodded. The grey-eyed one said, "Shall we help you to undress?"

"I. . . I. . . am not accustomed to being bathed, or undressed. I had rather do both myself." Why did her voice seem so . . . dull?

"We will wait, then," the bluer-eyed one said, and he realized that they did not care—and that her voice was just as dull. "*She* will be waiting." And she tarried, looking serenely upon him, while the other one went and stopped the water's flowing.

You *are* a fool, he told himself, Jarik Blacksword! More foolish than the gigglebirds, who build their nests amid the barley! Yet he knew that he could not handle the situation they suggested. Stripped, by those twice-comely women? Naked? *Bathed* by them? Never. Body and mind could never assimilate such. He'd only embarrass himself.

He entered the tub, and washed himself comfortably in water of good temperature. Tinkering, toying with the irresistible, he started the water's flow and would have embarrassed himself had he not been alone. He looked around. He bathed. When he had done, he emerged to drip on the thick moss-colored rug beside the tub—which he had discovered was not of metal, but some smooth, slick substance that was not earthenware nor yet glass.

They came in and dried him then and Jarik embarrassed himself. Silently he cursed his body.

The silent two arrayed him in an incredibly soft, flowing robe the color of the stone called samarine. He sipped more of the marvelous almost-white wine and was asked if he hungered. No. He had eaten a normal, indeed standard breakfast of porridge, butter-milk (which Jarik abominated) and leg of ewe, and had done nothing to stimulate hunger in the three or so hours since. Jarik did not eat unless he hungered, and for the past couple of years he had not known hunger unless he had exerted himself, or considerable time had passed. Eating was no sport or occasion among his people, but the daily necessity. And so he said nay to the servants of the Lady of the Snowmist, and they nodded complacently and one of them went away.

Jarik was Jarik; he took up his weapons-belt and buckled on dagger and the sheathed Black Sword, with its hilt now disguised in red leather wrapping. For he was a warrior.

"Where do you come from?" Jarik asked the bluer-eyed one, her who had started the flow of water into the tub. She was very fair. Her unusually wavy hair and deeply dimpled chin fascinated him.

Her hand drifted through the air in a vague ges-ture. "It is unimportant; I dwell here. Where do you come from?"

She does not care to tell, Jarik thought. *Well, nei-ther do I!* "Outside," he said, and smiled, and asked her name. Metanira, she told him.

"Metanearye?"

"Metaneerah."

He said it after her, that strange name, and she smiled so that dryness assailed his throat while his stomach curveted within him and he was glad he had last night breached Kirrensark's hospitality. They looked at each other. Thus they were when the other returned to say that the Lady of the Snowmist would speak with him now. Jarik accompanied her of the grey eyes while Metanira turned into a branching corridor.

She awaited him in a room of whites and yellows of citrelain and lovestone and sundane and the blues of perisine and samarine, and she wore silver and white. Standing to the far side of a table, she was hooded and masked in a pearly pale grey. The mask-face looked sterner, and just as regal. The table was of neither metal nor wood—and it was blue!—and supported a soapstone lamp oddly carven as a demon, and a ewer and two goblets. They looked to be of gold. His guide poured, and departed with no sound other than the rustle of her long gown. It clung marvelously and Jarik was at pains not to look.

He stood before the Lady of the Snowmist, and was sworn to kill her. She gazed at him—he supposed. This mask, too, had no eyeslits.

"Why. . . am I here, Lady?"

"Drink your wine, Jarik. It is excellent. Relax, Jarik."

He went to the table. He discovered that it was made of neither bone nor soapstone. He took up a goblet. He was sure that it was indeed gold: that fact and its weight staggered his mind. Jarik, who had seen no barons and no kings, was now in the presence of a god—again.

"Lady. . . your pardon. . . your mask has no holes for eyes. Are you—are you looking at me?"

"I assure you that I am, Jarik."

Jarik thought, *The Iron Lords do not use the first person singular;* and he said, "You see me though the mask has no eyeholes. And you know who I am."

"Yes, Jarik; two yesses."

An interesting way to put it, he thought. How little sophistication he had! He proved it, with the goblet somewhere betwixt table and lips: "The god on the earth urges me to drink. Is the cup drugged?"

And he saw that she was shaken! The god! "Aye, it is. Whence came you by your sword, Jarik called Black-sword?"

He set the goblet down with firmness. "I stole it. It is a good sword."

"Aye, Jarik, a good sword. A good sword, aye," she

said, with a subtle edge to her voice. "It neither bends nor nicks nor will it break, nor rust or even lose its edge. You know all this, Jarik, about your good sword?"

Jarik shook his head. His heart thumped. "I am glad to know it all! I stole well!"

The eyeless mask briefly blurred with her head-shake. "A thief lies, Jarik; he does not say 'I stole.' You lie now, Jarik, by saying that you stole the weapon. Therefore you did not. Shall I ask again?"

Jarik considered for a long while. The Lady of the Snowmist waited, so that the silence grew too great to be left unfilled. Jarik decided. He told her of living in Blackiron, of the Hawker attack, of his taking the Black Sword and beating off that attack, killing seven or more of the assaulters. When he paused, Lady Snowmist prompted.

"The Hawkers were made fearful by my attack, and the wark-men were encouraged. We drove off those raiders who survived."

The mask shook. "It will not do. Still you lie, Jarik. Had you taken the sword thus, during an attack, something else would have happened. Tell me of it."

Jarik stared at the floor, as if contemplating, indecisive. His heartbeat quickened as he paced alongside the table. He reached its end, paused there. Leaning one hand on its smooth top, he looked at her as if in pain.

"*They* came," he said, as if fearfully.

"They?"

He took a step, and the weavers wove. He gestured. "The—the Iron Lords." He took another step toward her, as if nervous. "They—they came, Lady. They—" Then he lengthened his pace, and as he rushed her he drew the Black Sword. The Iron Lords would be surprised to have been served so swiftly!

She vanished. The room seemed to grow larger. Then a man was in it. No woman was; Snowmist had disappeared utterly.

The man stared at Jarik from beneath dark brows just above which his helmet rested. Brows and mustache were like none Jarik had ever seen; their color was dark brown! The man was burlier than he though no taller, and similarly armored save that he wore bronze greaves up his thick legs. And Jarik was no longer armored at all, but dressed only in the robe of medium blue! The man bore an ax, a war-ax and huge, with two blades that nearly formed a circle at the end of the short haft.

He came for Jarik, swinging up the ax. It flashed in the room's lighting, which was pale blue and emanated from the whole ceiling.

Jarik had no buckler. Nor did he try to parry that heavy ax-swing with his Sword. He did not know what might break such a blade as this, and he did not care to find out. He yanked himself back, bending far backward at the knees. The ax rushed across between them, humming its deadly song, the breadth of a thumb from Jarik's chest. Immediately he flung himself forward and, as the man's mighty swing of the big heavy ax carried his arm well to his left, Jarik's right, the Black Sword sheared nearly through his wrist.

Without making a sound, the man dropped his weapon. It struck heavily. Jarik's backstroke drove his edge well into the man's neck. Blood spurted and the man vanished. So did his dropped ax, and the blood.

The demon-thing with the awful jaws, talon-ending arms, and hooved feet came from the very wall. Shaggy hair nearly covered it and the hair was red. Its hooves thud-clacked as it came for Jarik. The talons were as long as his dagger, which he drew to arm his shield-less left hand.

The corner of Jarik's eyes and a corner of his mind told him it was strange that the soapstone lamp, carved into the likeness of this same demon, was alight. Its oil sent up a flickering flame, blue and white and orange.

Jarik struck. His Sword chopped into a red-furred arm and was held fast; the thing came on. Its flesh seemed to have closed on the blade like a trap set for game in the forest. Long claws barely missed his face when Jarik twisted desperately away. His wrist was wrenched; the Sword would not come free. Without thinking, he stabbed the demon-thing's other arm with his dagger. He was beyond thinking; he was fighting. The dagger, too, stuck fast. Nor was the thing stopped. A hoof struck Jarik's shin, and he missed leggings and buskins then; the blow *hurt*.

Still sword and dagger would not come free. Jarik's grips on their hilts bound him to his fell opponent. Its jaws came for him, armed with teeth long as his little fingers.

Still Jarik did not think; he was fighting; he was the machine-that-fights. Had he been thinking rather than *morbrin*, he'd not have done what he did: no thinking warrior released grip on both his weapons! A wild crouching dodge, a partial wheel, and his hand half-scooped, half-pushed the lamp off the table. Without ever closing his fingers on it, he flung the flaming, soapstone likeness of the demon into its awful face. Burning oil splashed and red fur crackled, sizzling. The impossible attacker staggered back ablaze—and faded away until it was no longer there. Both Jarik's blades fell through empty air to the floor. He bent for them...

... and smiled down at Metanira, who lay naked and smiling in his bed here in his chamber in Snowmist Keep. She put up her round soft arms to him, and her lips curved into a lazy sort of smile, and Jarik sank down onto her. A while later she began to laugh, and he saw the teeth, the awful teeth, and Jarik kicked his naked body off the bed. While he sprawled on the floor, it rose up on the bed, slavering. It seemed to grin at him. As it came off the bed for him, Jarik kicked up into a shaggy sporran of red-brown fur he hoped covered its genitals. The demon-thing

211

bent far over, braced on his leg. As it fell toward him Jarik rolled desperately aside—and then back.

On the furry back of the dreadful demon-thing that had been Metanira, Jarik twisted its head with all his strength. His muscles stood up in bulges on arms and chest and back, and his jaw clenched so hard his gums hurt. He heard the crack of a breaking neck. In elation, panting, he rose up and dragged the thing up and hurled it overboard.

The sea lapped and gurgled along the sleek sides of the hawk-prowed ship and an armored Jarik looked about at his shipmates. They were one-handed Kirrensark Long-haft and several others. Two Jarik recognized as from Kirrensark-wark, and knew that all were. All but one. . . . His head rang and he blinked, squeezing his eyes shut. Also aboard was a strange tall woman, no stripling, and her clad in strange armor and with a very long mass of *blue* hair drawn all around to the left shoulder so that it hung down her chest. A warrior woman, and with that weird mass of hair, and a quiver of arrows on her back!

She and Kirrensark and all the others were looking skyward.

Jarik looked up. The sky was pleasant enough, blue strewn with clouds like tufts of fleece. Jarik hardly saw the sky, though: he had seen the great blue-black bird aforenow. It was somehow mailed, impossibly but surely. There had been two, that day in Ocean-side when It Happened. This one, alone, swooped toward the ship, attacking, wings moveless, blue-black in the sunlight.

Men were crying out and waving swords and axes. Using a most unusual doubly curved bow, the warrior-woman loosed an arrow at the bird. It *glanced off*, and Jarik heard the ring, thought he saw a spark. She was young and comely, this warrior woman, with a scabbed cut on her forehead, a new cut. The bird continued its diving attack, racing down like a hurled

212

black stone. Another arrow missed. She screamed and all the men of the ship were yelling.

The bird of black metal struck Jarik then, in the throat, and it was like the impact of a spear thrown by a powerful man. Terrible metal claws tore into his throat. Yelling, Jarik heard his voice burble liquidly, redly. The talons tore his throat out. Blood bubbling forth so that he could not even cry out, Jarik knew terrible pain, and he died.

Chapter Nineteen:
The Lady of the Snowmist

Jarik awoke, and the horror of death was still on him so that his heart pounded.

He found that he could not move. So disoriented was he that much time was required for him to ascertain that he was naked, lying face up on a table—to which he was bound. He was looking directly at the Lady of the Snowmist, who sat in a fine carven chair above him. The chair was suspended in air by no means that he could see. This time her mask was a featureless white, and it was eerie and fearsome.

Yet he knew that she was staring down at him, naked and bound.

"You are not dead."

"I was slain. My throat—"

"You hear yourself talking? Your throat is untouched. You experienced what might happen, if you follow one course of action. Now be quiet, and listen!" Her tone was stern, and the liquid silver in her voice had hardened and cooled so that it rang metallically. "You have met my brothers. Destruction, and Annihilation, and Dread—didn't they choose lovely names! They sent you here to slay me. Me! Your reward was the Black Sword—which like your armor was not forged in your world—and a vengeance you have not even taken. Poor Jarik! You are but a rusty hoe in the hands of a stout farmer! A tool, Jarik. Had you succeeded in killing me, you'd not have lived out this day! The Iron Lords could not suffer you to live. Nor are you the sort of tool they would merely hang up in place of honor on the shed wall. You would be less than an ant beneath their world-stamping feet!"

Helpless, once again totally miserable, Jarik stared impotently up at her. *Lies*, he thought, with desperation. *Lies, lies! Surely—*

"O fool, foolish brave know-naught pathetic warrior without parents or cause for your striving! Abandoned. . . adopted. . . and then you saw them slain, they who adopted and raised you. . . adopted again . . . exiled. . . one friend you had, one only, she who had been your sister and who was not—and now her slain, too. And now. . . And now, Jarik. So brave, such a superb fighter. Jarik Blacksword, is it? Two men in one, a confused troubled troublous treacherous brain, result of a child and boy crushed again and again with more than he could bear. The Man Who is Two Men! Man? Not yet! Jarik of the Black Sword . . . and Oak of the InSight, Oak the Scry-healer; Jarik-Oak of the Iron Lords!"

So overwhelming was all this that he did not dissemble. "How—how can you know?"

"I have seen into your mind—minds. You have no secrets from me, Jarik-Oak."

"Why—why did you bid that I be abandoned by my parents?"

"Call me Lady, you! And I did no such thing!" A god, with indignation in her voice. To be believed?

"Then. . . you have seen into my mind. *Who am I,* Lady?"

"You do not know. It is not in your mind. I do not know, Jarik-Oak. You are a Mystery on the earth. A very, very central pawn. Neither do the Iron Lords your *masters* know, poor Jarik—and they have some fear of you."

"Fear?" The Iron Lords?! He blustered; why had she sent Kirrensark and his Hawkers against his people in Oceanside?

"I did not. I did not, Jarik. I do not do such. Nor has Kirrensark always been . . . of my people. The Iron Lords must have sent him, those years and years ago . . . just as *they* or their allies sent other Lok-

215

ustans, Hawkers as you call them, against their own protectorate of Blackiron, to impress those people with their Power."

"The people of Blackiron already believed in them, venerated them! They had no need of such proofs! That is horrible!"

"It is indeed," the white mask said, without eyes or mouth. "I believe the Iron Lords must have known that you were in Blackiron."

"Believe?"

The god on the earth heaved a sigh that was surely a trifle elaborate. "It is time you learned, Jarik, that we do not know everything. They do not, and I do not, and the Fog Lords do not, nor any of the other gods on the earth."

Jarik stared up at her. *Too much. I have learned too much, all in this tiny space of so few, few days! And yet—what have I learned? What is true? What is not true? Who lies to me—or do they all? A hoe in a strong hand—a rusty hoe. A tool. No, no!*

"Metanira."

Jarik turned his head. At the god's call, which was not loud, Metanira came, of the blue blue eyes and the thatch-straw hair and the broad exciting backside. She wore different garb; she wore a black tunic, sleeved, and no leggings so that Jarik saw her calves were not large. She was barefoot, and wore an anklet of bronze, slim and tight.

"Take his sword and place it beneath me."

Jarik saw now that all this while his Sword had lain beside him, on the table to which he was bound. Metanira took it, and he could not catch her eyes. She took it several paces away, and while he strained to look between his toes she stooped to place it on the floor beneath the suspended, floating but motionless chair of her godly mistress.

The Black Sword returned to Jarik's side; his left side. It lay down beside him, like a most faithful dog, black and loyal.

Astonished was a word of insufficient force to describe Jarik's reaction. "Why? How?"

"It is yours," The Lady of the Snowmist told him, the Lady Sharahshihar. "You took it up, and used it. It will not leave you. It is yours."

With a sudden rush of nervousness Jarik thought, *Or I am its.* But he did not speak.

"Release him, Metanira. You see, you are indeed Jarik Blacksword... the man with the silver bracers!"

And Jarik was free of the table. He sat on its top and lifted his hands to look with wonder and trepidation on his wrists. Each was encased in a bracer or long bracelet of silver. Their length was such as to cover most of his forearms; seven inches perhaps, though neither was heavy, or thick. He turned his hands at the wrists, inspecting, testing. Mobility was unimpaired. The bracers were without seam. They were not uncomfortable. Indeed, they would brace his wrists, which was why farmers and woodsmen and warriors wore bracers, of leather or bronze. No seams! No faintest mark betrayed the method of their fastening around his forearms, of how they might be removed. With his hands still held so before him, both arms crooked up from the elbows, he looked up at the god in the floating chair.

"Take up your sword and attack me, Jarik. You sought to do death on me—do it!"

And though he saw nothing done to cause it, the chair descended. Jarik stared, while his right hand went across his waist to close on the red-wound hilt of the Black Sword. The chair reached the floor and settled gently. The Lady of the Snowmist sat and gazed upon him without visible eyes, and he thought that this must be the way a queen sat enthroned in such places as farmers' sons never saw.

He had a mission; a purpose; he had an agreement with the Iron Lords his allies. Naked, Jarik hurled himself off the table and pounced with sword extended to spit this god on the earth.

The pain did not begin and build; it was immediately egregious and unbearable. Jarik cried out and shuddered in agony, his body going spastic.

Terrible cold emanated from the silver bracers. It seized his hands as though he had plunged them through ice into a mountain pool in winter. Cold assaulted his arms, leaped like a physical force into his body. His teeth chattered. Pain and cold overwhelmed him and he knew that he could never bear such cold, and live.

Then the sky was full of fire and dominated by an enormous ball of pink and white that loomed over him and those around him like a falling moon. A ragged corona of fire surrounded it, and flames leaped too around him. Marvelous buildings lofted and eerily pallid people cringed and fled like ants in a disturbed hill. Their mouths gaped in screams that rose together into an awful crescendoing cacophany of shrillness.

He had heard that one scream of many before, that night he had traveled with the Guide. Jarik had heard this awful sound then, the death-cry of an entire world. For so he knew it was, though he knew not how he knew. Prodigious winds blew and buildings seemed to elongate ere they toppled to become killing rubble sprouting flames. He and the others about him—gods, he was sure—felt a dread lightness and the heat and final, utter horror. That ball in the sky—no longer a ball now, but larger, nearer, three-quarters of a ball that owned the sky, that *was* the sky—was another *world*, and it was crashing into—

Monstrous pain and agony whelmed his brain and for a brief moment he could not even bemoan the death of a world, for his own individual agony was too great to think of aught else. It was paramount; it was all there was. It was death.

Jarik awoke. He was covered with sweat, and chilly and panting. All his life he would be poisonously haunted by what he had endured. Though it was no more than a vision, all his life he would know the horror and unassuagable sorrow for a destroyed world. Lying on the floor almost at her feet, he looked up at the Lady of the Snowmist, and he fought to control his shivering. Sweat made a slurping noise under him when he moved.

"The bracers protect me from you, Jarik. And they bind you to my bidding."

He fought the abysmal umbrage in his brain, and was able to stare defiantly—which brought another attack of all-encompassing pain, and the cold—and then the same unutterably horrible experience as before. Again the impossible magnitude of a collision of worlds, when he had known there was but one, and—

Again he awoke. When he looked up at her this time, Jarik knew that she was indeed a god on the earth, and that he could bear no more. His stricken eyes mutely screamed the eclipse of his spirit. She had proven her point and her power. He was hers to control. He dared not even attempt to assuage his demeaned spirit by scowling or looking defiant; that would be as stupid as fighting those who sought to lead one when one was already in chains. And he was chained, chained to her.

This time he saw that she had changed clothing. How long had the horrible vision, the ghastly experience, lasted? And after; how long had he lain "dead"? Time enough for her to have ensheathed her tall womanly form in snowy white, like the tightest of snug leggings, all over, from toes to chin to fingertips. Over that she wore a sleeveless round-necked tunic of shimmering silver. And she was unmasked!

No—no, he saw that it was a mask she wore. It was a face of great beauty and regal serenity, and as much like (pale, so pale) flesh as flesh itself. And surely that she wore no helm did not show him her hair, the true hair of a god on the earth—for how could that silvery wavy flowing waterfall of hair be real? The Lady of the Snowmist, in white and silver.

"I have a task for you, Jarik."

Jarik said nothing. A task. Yes. Of course she

would. The Iron Lords had a task for him, too. He had tried to perform it. He would try to carry out hers, too; he would try his best, and not by choice.

"Get up, Jarik, and sit on the edge of the table."

He did, discovering that he had been dressed. He wore again the robe of medium blue seemingly taken from the gemstone called samarine. He seated himself on the edge of the table that was not wood or bone or horn or metal. He looked at the floor between himself and the god on the earth, while he listened.

"A task, Jarik. Attend. Akkharia where you first lived is far from here. It is a large island, as islands go. Well off its western coast lies another island, smaller. On that isle is a temple, raised to Osyr."

Osyr. Do I have some knowledge of Osyr? Do I? I am not sure. Gods O ye gods—am I ever to be cursed with these visions of past and future and other places and futures-that-might-be? Osyr . . .

"Your mind wanders. Attend me, Jarik. In the temple is a statue raised to Osyr. In one hand is a rod, a wand. It is white and the statue is black. You will fare there, to the Isle of Osyr, and fetch that rod, Jarik. You will bring it to me. Do you understand?"

He nodded, looked at her. "Lady—"

"The bracers will link you to me, wherever you are. You are subject to me, Jarik. You *will* go, and fetch the rod I must have. You cannot escape. The bracers will *know*, Jarik. Return to me with the White Rod of Osyr and I will remove the bracers from your arms. You must do this, Jarik. You must essay until you succeed, or die. And while I had rather have the rod . . . consider. What care, Jarik, have I whether you live or die? You came to slay me. You leave me but two choices; to slay you or control you."

"And if I succeed—"

"I will remove the bracers, Jarik."

He knew that was all the assurance he would receive. She was a god. She told him what she would do. If she were lying, what could he do about it? The mission, the rod, and her promise were the only hope he had. He tried to tell himself that it was purpose, that he was important, and his brain refused to believe. No. His purpose was her purpose. He was important only to her, whose slave he was.

Dismay was on him cold as the hand of the Dark Brother.

Miserably he said, "I have the words of the Iron Lords that yourself is evil, and that was yourself sent Kirrensark to my home in Oceansi—in Akkharia, and that you knew of me then, and bade that I be abandoned. And that if I did slay yourself I would be freeing their bonds, the bonds yourself put on the Iron Lords; they will be free then to protect others than the people of Blackiron. Such as those who were my people, in Oceanside of Akkharia. And I have their word too that I shall be most favored of the Iron Lords."

"Aye."

Dismay and disquietude and an unequivocal feeling of impotence spread through Jarik, for that was all she said. Suddenly he hoped that there would be many warriors on the Isle of Osyr, for he wanted to slay and slay. Silence lengthened and was thick as fog in the lowland after days of rain. She let her single word lie there between them so that he knew she need not make answer to him, not to *him*.

And then she answered, having let him understand that it was because she chose to do. "I will tell you this, and it will aid you. When the Bands of Snowmist on your wrists grow cold, you are in danger."

He regarded the silver bracers, seamless and jointless. The Bands of Snowmist. The bonds of Lady Snowmist!

And she said, "Such word you have from the Iron Lords, Jarik who bears a god-sword. And you have *my* word that you will do as I bid you now or suffer unendurable cold and pain and the horror of colliding worlds; and that once you have accomplished what I bid and return to me with the White Rod of Osyr, you shall be free of the Bands of Snowmist. And those are my promises to you, Jarik of the Black Sword."

He waited, contemplated. He did not want to say, "That is... all?" But he did.

"That is all, Jarik."

Jarik sat on the table's edge and pondered, considered. Then he slid from the table, in the blue robe, and again he drew the Sword—tentatively. The bracers began to grow chill at once and they grew increasingly colder as sword cleared sheath and rose in the air. Starting to shiver, Jarik lowered the black blade. The cold subsided. And Jarik knew that he was enslaved.

Jarik of the Black Sword? No; Jarik of the silver bracers—the locked, enslaving Bands of Snowmist. Jarik ally and agent of the Iron Lords? No; Jarik, slave of the Lady of the Snowmist.

Those great gods on the earth, he reflected, had used him, flung him about, victimized him with their lies, used him as a rusty hoe in the hands of a stout farmer. Truth? He had no idea of it. He had no idea as to which story was true, the Iron Lords' or Milady Snowmist's. He had no idea which . . . faction, was lying; what was "good" and what was not good; evil or "bad."

He was Jarik Blacksword, still an orphan, no longer a boy, slayer of men, and he possessed the finest of weapons and armor. And he was not free, and was more miserable than before.

Then I knew what I did not know; now I do not even know what I know.

He looked up at the face that was not a face, and he looked away from its eyes (which were like samarines). "And how... am I to reach this island so far from here, Lady?"

"Why in a ship, Jarik, of course."

Chapter Twenty:
The gods decide, and the weavers weave

And so certain assurances were made to Kirrensark One-hand who had been Kirrensark Long-haft, and Ahl his cousin, assurances concerning the interest in their affairs of the Lady of the Snowmist, and each made promises to her and the other. And so Jarik set forth to sea at the behest of her he was to have slain: Jarik Blacksword who was Oak the Healer and had been Orrikson Jarik and Strodeson Jarik; agent of the Iron Lords and now unwilling agent of the Lady of the Snowmist. With the Black Sword by his side, the silvery bracers on his arms to bring obedience or unbearable torment. It was on a hated hawk-prowed ship of Lokusta he sailed, and it was commanded by the man on whom he had vowed vengeance, the man responsible for the deaths of his foster father and mother and his youth: Kirrensark One-hand the Hawker.

And Kirrensark's wife and daughter watched them fare forth, and they wept, but not for Jarik.

And so Jarik was allied with his enemies, and yet indeed knew not which were enemies and which were not. And he wondered if he were cursed, in that he had been found and adopted so long ago, rather than died as a result of abandonment by the parents whose names even the gods did not know.

This was
the first
of the chronicles
of
Jarik of the Black Sword
in
War Among the Gods on the Earth